'You said you would ha[...] the boat. Changed your m[...] Horace Higginbottom; n[...] Lottie was held so tight [...] against Adam's shins, though she longed to stop his hateful words.

'Thou hast no need to fear me,' he continued, 'but others might not be so kindly with thee. When you invite a man to kiss you, keep that in mind.'

Numbly she raised her face to Adam's. He didn't understand. She didn't ask other men to kiss her. She had only asked him so that she might be free of him. 'I'm giving you good advice, Lottie,' he went on. 'Don't let yourself be swept away by a handsome face. Go slow and careful. Be sure of your feelings.'

Why was he warning her? Lottie opened her mouth to ask that question. The words were never uttered. Adam's lips closed on hers . . .

Barbara Cooper was born in Montreal, Canada, the second of five children. She was educated there and earned an Arts Degree from the University of Montreal. She met her first husband working at the Canadian Atomic Energy Project at Chalk River. They made their home in Oxfordshire and later in Lancashire. When he died she turned her hand to part time work to have time to bring up her three children. Now married again, she writes romantic fiction. Her first longer historical romance, BEYOND PARADISE, was published earlier this year.

FORTUNE'S KISS

Barbara Cooper

MILLS & BOON LIMITED
15–16 BROOK'S MEWS
LONDON W1A 1DR

First published in Great Britain 1986
by Mills & Boon Limited

© Barbara Cooper 1986

Australian copyright 1986
Philippine copyright 1986
This edition 1986

ISBN 0 263 75468 5

Set in 10 on 11 pt Linotron Times
04–0786–74,300

Photoset by Rowland Phototypesetting Limited
Bury St Edmunds, Suffolk
Made and printed in Great Britain by
Cox & Wyman Limited, Reading

CHAPTER ONE

'I SENT THE money for Kate.' Adam's eyes were hard with anger as he surveyed Charlotte Earnshaw. 'Not for anyone else!'

Lottie gulped and trembled. She was weak with hunger, sick with apprehension. Why had she ever thought he'd accept her in her sister's place?

'She's not coming,' Lottie faltered. Her heavy case dropped from her nerveless fingers on to the floor of the big circular hall of Castle Garden Immigration Center in New York. She still clutched the awkward bundle of her swansdown pillow to her chest as though somehow it would protect her from Adam Hardcastle's scorn, from this strange new place.

'Where is she?' Adam demanded. His eyes swept the crowd milling about them, searching for her.

'She's married.' Lottie's stiff lips moved of their own volition.

Adam drew back. 'Married? She promised to marry me. That's why I sent the money for her fare.'

He looked so shocked and stunned that Lottie almost forgot her own desperation and loneliness. She reached out a hand to touch him. 'Eh, lad, it was good of you.'

He snatched her hand away from him. 'I don't want your sympathy. I want my Kate.'

Lottie bit her lip. She tried to balance herself as a man and woman screamed greetings over her head to some relative, and the girl behind her moved forward crying, and colliding with the empty food-basket dangling from Lottie's arm.

It struck against her side and she gasped for breath. Adam righted her as she swayed against him. He took the wicker basket from her.

'By rights I should put you straight back on the ship!' he exploded. 'But they wouldn't take you. You've cleared Immigration and Customs now. I'm landed with you.' His expression was grim.

Lottie looked at his face and looked away. This was worse, far worse, than she had expected. She heard people crying and laughing all around her, but she saw none of them.

In her mind's eye she saw that day in March when Kate had opened Adam's letter and the dollar bills had fallen out in a great cascade to lie scattered on the carpet before them. Her sister had laughed and picked them up and stuffed them in a bundle towards her, saying, 'You shall go in my place, dear Lottie. You shall have a new life away from brother Jeremiah and his Lizzie, away from fat old Horace Higginbottom and his shop. It's your chance—fortune's kiss at last.'

It seemed an eternity since that day and the hope which had lived in her ever since. Yet it was only May 1850, barely three months later.

'Didn't you . . . Didn't you get Kate's letter?' Lottie found the courage to ask in spite of the hostility in Adam's blue eyes.

'What letter?' he demanded. 'I had no letter.'

Lottie had not believed that her spirits could sink any lower, but they did. If that wasn't just like Kate—forgetting to send the letter they had concocted between them! Lottie would never have come if she'd known Adam didn't want her. *'A lass from Lancashire,'* he had written in the letter that accompanied the money. *'A lass from Lancashire to marry me!'* She had held on to those words right across the Atlantic. How many times had she repeated them to herself on that fearful trip in the steerage hold! Now she said nothing.

Adam reached into the jacket pocket of his good-quality worsted suit, and drew out a piece of paper which he dangled before her. 'Read this.'

'What is it?' she whispered, not touching it. She couldn't help noticing how wavy his hair was, and how clean. He looked so well and fine.

He waved the paper at her. 'Never mind. I'll read it to you.' He unfolded it. 'Your bride sailing on April 22nd on *Black Swan* out of Hull.' He held it out.

This time Lottie took it, staring at the words. How could Kate have done this to her?

'That was cruel, lass.' Adam Hardcastle looked her up and down. 'Did you think I wouldn't notice?'

Lottie quailed before that glance. She was conscious that the old black work-dress that she wore was frayed and dirty, her straight brown hair was lank and lustreless. Although she'd never been pretty like Kate, she'd never been ashamed of her appearance as she was now. She'd not been able to wash or change before the *Black Swan* docked: the hold didn't run to luxuries like that. She had simply put on her good, deep red bonnet and matching fur-trimmed waisted wrap, three-quarter length, loose sleeved and clean, but very wrinkled because it had been rolled into a ball to keep it safe in her pillowcase. What a sight she must look! She stared down at her white cotton gloves. She'd wanted so much to look her best, and had been sure that spotless gloves would excuse all the shortcomings. Adam hadn't even seen them.

A single tear brimmed from one eye and slid down her cheek. She didn't have the power to brush it away. Why, oh why had she come? Another tear followed it, and she wasn't able to stop it.

'Dry your tears,' Adam instructed her sharply. 'I can't stand a woman crying.'

She sniffled and drew the backs of her white gloves across her cheeks, trying to stem the flow. They soon became streaked with dirt and wet. Where had the old Charlotte Earnshaw gone? The Charlotte Earnshaw who had brought up a younger sister and brother— the Charlotte Earnshaw who'd had the courage to leave Rochdale and come to America, following a dream?'

'Go away!' she told him. 'I don't need you to watch me crying. It's naught to do with you. It's all so strange and frightening. I want to go home.'

To her astonishment, Adam smiled at her. 'Poor Lottie! If the truth were told, that's how most immigrants feel. But home's a world away, and what's to do with you now? Eh, lass, you've made a pickle of it.'

Perhaps it was the broad Lancashire tongue, the breath of home, that stopped Lottie's tears; perhaps just the rough kindness of his tone. She gulped, and wiped her cheeks dry. 'I'm sorry. If you'll just tell me where I may find a room? I have some money still.' 'Your money,' she might have added, and was grateful when he didn't point that out.

'What then?' he asked. 'What do you mean to do?'

'Get a job and earn my way. Never fear, I'll pay you back what I owe. Everyone knows wages are high in New York.'

This time Adam laughed. 'Not so high as you might think. Your best plan is to come with me. The boarding-house where I stay is clean and the woman decent. You'll look better for a wash and a meal.'

It seemed to Lottie that his nose wrinkled in distaste as his gaze assessed her. She seethed. Did he expect her to emerge immaculate from the dark hold of the *Black*

Swan? She couldn't help being as she was. A gentleman wouldn't have mentioned it.

'No!' she exclaimed, hating him.

'Nay, lass,' he told her. 'You've no choice. I've no designs on you, but I'll not let Kate's sister fend for herself in a foreign . . .'

Lottie didn't let him finish. 'You needn't trouble about me. If you'll just point out some quiet lodging near by, I'll find my own way.'

For answer, he picked up her case. 'I don't intend to argue. Just follow me with that dirty laundry you're hugging to yourself.'

She followed, protesting, 'It's not dirty laundry! It's a pillow, a swansdown pillow and of first quality. The clerks at Higginbottom's gave it me when I left.'

'For your bottom drawer, I suppose,' he said over his shoulder. 'What a thing to bring across the Atlantic! They have pillows here.'

That made her bridle. The pillow might be a joke to him, but it was important to her. She caught up to him. 'I can manage for myself, you know.'

Adam stopped and faced her. 'My little swansdown bride, you wouldn't manage ten minutes in this town on your own; the wolves outside would swarm round you.' He pointed to the doors of the building just before them.

'What wolves?' she faltered.

'They're of the species that infests ports. They wait out there to pounce on young green girls fresh off the boats.'

'I'm twenty-four!' She tried to regain some dignity. 'I'm neither young nor green.'

'As old as that!' He gave her a searching glance and began to move towards the doors. 'You don't look it.'

Lottie moved after him. When she saw the men and women waiting outside, she took a firm hold on Adam's jacket. She found she was very glad of his presence when one or two of the bolder ones tried to speak to her. He pushed them aside and swept on.

'Where are we going?' she panted, as they crossed a cobbled road at a headlong pace.

'To get you a cup of tea and something to eat.' His stride didn't slacken. 'You're starved skinny.'

Lottie followed him into a narrow street of high buildings and squalid-looking shops. At the corner of a dingy road, he halted before a small eating-house.

'It isn't fancy,' he told her as she peered in at the windows and saw wooden chairs and oilcloth-lined tables, 'but it's clean and cheap.'

They went in, and Lottie put her pillow on one chair and sank gratefully into another as Adam gave their order.

'Soup for one, and bread and butter and tea,' he directed the woman who came to serve them. 'And make sure the soup is hot and strong.'

Bread and butter were brought immediately, and she helped herself to a slice. It was weeks since she had tasted fresh bread. She felt its texture, and smelled its intoxicating flavour.

'It's for eating, lass, not for looking at!' Adam exclaimed, and pushed the butter nearer.

'Ay, of course.' Lottie's cheeks were hot. She took a bite of the bread and then another, and then the soup was brought. Dipping her spoon, she began to eat greedily.

'Not so fast,' Adam said. 'If you eat like that, your stomach will rebel. How long since you've had a real meal?' He poured a cup of tea for himself and one for her.

Lottie tried to think. All she wanted to concentrate on was the delicious hot soup. There were chunks of meat in it, and potatoes and onions and carrots—a feast! She finished it before she answered, and then licked her lips and wondered if she might ask for more. 'I took things in my basket—apples, raisins, cheese, pickled eggs and onions, oranges, oatcakes, lemons, biscuits, salted meat and nuts.' She paused and buttered another slice of bread. 'Arthur said I must take two bottles of gin—so I did.'

Adam nodded. 'You were well provisioned. Who's Arthur?' He shot the question at her.

'Kate's husband.' When she replied, she saw the spasm of pain that crossed Adam's face.

'When did she marry him?'

'Four weeks ago.'

'Then she knew in March, when I sent the money, that she had no intention of coming.'

Lottie found she couldn't face those accusing blue eyes across the table. She stirred her tea vigorously. 'She wanted me to come.'

'Why was that? Did she think I was so desperate for a wife that I'd accept her sister?'

As she tried to raise the cup to her lips, her hand shook. She mustn't let him see how much she minded the disparaging words and the wounding tone in which they were uttered. 'That's not the way it was,' she protested. Some of the tea splashed on the oilcloth as she put down the cup.

'No? Then tell me how it was. Did you laugh together and agree that one girl was much like another in any family?'

This time Lottie couldn't look away: his eyes held hers.

'You're nothing like her at all,' he continued.

'I know I'm not.' Lottie's voice was a croak in her own ears. She saw that the group at the table next but one were looking at her, but she didn't care what they thought. 'She's blonde and pretty and always laughing. I'm dark and plain, but I'd make you a good wife all the same.' She might as well state her case; he couldn't think any worse of her than he did already. 'I'm a good worker,' she added, as if that might tip the balance in her favour.

Adam's smile was grim. 'Do you suppose that's what I'm looking for in a wife?'

Lottie flushed under blue eyes that raked her from head to foot, and said nothing.

'A good worker,' Adam's tone was soft. 'That sounds more like your brother Jeremiah's style than mine! Tell me: do you think this Arthur looked at Kate and decided she was a good worker?'

'He loved her—whatever she was.'

'So did I,' he sighed. 'She chose another. Perhaps if I had been there, the outcome would have been different.'

There was nothing that Lottie could say to that. Perhaps if he had been there . . . but he hadn't. He'd been away three years—too long to expect a girl like Katie to wait. Besides, she'd been only fifteen when Adam had left. Kate hadn't known her own mind then.

'Come, drink up your tea,' Adam instructed. 'Have the last slice of bread.'

Lottie shook her head. Her appetite had suddenly deserted her, but she sipped her tea. She had proposed to this man, this stranger whom Adam had become! No, that wasn't fair, he'd always been a stranger to her —he'd been engaged to Kate, and neither of them had seen him for three years. She had proposed to him! Not in so many words, but the thought was there between them. She dared not ask again.

'I'm sorry, Lottie,' he said. 'It wouldn't work, you know. Did you really think it would?' He stared into space.

Lottie looked down at her lap. She'd hoped it would, but if she were honest with herself, in her heart of hearts she'd never really believed that Adam would calmly accept her instead of lovely Kate. What man would? And Adam had always been the kind of man whom all the girls had liked. No, she had known he wouldn't want her. Well, she wasn't going to break down and cry—not again! She tried to smile. She imagined that she should somehow feel closer to Adam. They'd both been dis-appointed today—it might have brought them together. She hated him, she told herself. He was rude, he was insulting! She vowed she'd never marry him, not even if he went on his knees and begged her to accept him. She'd had a lucky escape. Why, then, was there such a lump in her throat that she eyed the remaining bread with disgust?

'What—What do you mean to do?' she stammered painfully, as the silence between them threatened to go on indefinitely.

Adam started, as though suddenly awakened from a dream. 'I'll take you with me to Mrs O'Rourke—she's my landlady. There are empty rooms. The winter-overs have moved out to the country at the top of the island. She'll be glad enough to have you, though she may prove a bit expensive for you.'

'The winter-overs?' Lottie questioned, glad to talk of anything save marriage and why she'd come. 'What are they?'

Adam's expression lightened. 'People flock into the boarding-houses in the centre of town when it's winter, because they don't want to fight the ice and snow getting to work. But once the spring comes, they want a breath of fresh air and to get away from the worst of the heat. They go to the farms and the open places beyond 14th Street.'

'Oh,' said Lottie, not altogether understanding. 'Is Mrs O'Rourke's where you were going to bring Katie— if she'd come?' she asked baldly.

'We would have lived there after we were married. For a while, at least.'

'But she'll know you expected to bring a bride.'

'Yes. I'll tell her you've come instead.'

'Won't you . . . Won't you feel embarrassed?'

She thought at first that he wasn't going to answer. 'Yes, I'll feel embarrassed,' he agreed at last. 'They all know about Kate.'

'Wouldn't it be easier if I went somewhere else?' she suggested diffidently.

'Easier for who? You or me?'

'Both, I suppose.'

'That's honest at least.' Adam shrugged. 'I don't think it makes much difference. Situations have to be faced. You might as well do it right away as hedge round it. Running away doesn't help—or is that what you've done in coming here? Who were you running away from, or what?'

'I wasn't!' she denied hotly, and wanted to say that she was running *to* something—a dream of happiness—not *away*.

'Come on, Lottie,' his voice was coaxing. 'Kate got married. Did Tom leave with her?'

'No, he didn't. He ran away and joined the army. Jeremiah drove him to it. All Tom ever wanted was to work with animals, but Jeremiah found him a job in the mills. I swear he did it to spite the lad. Tom went to the cavalry.'

'Jeremiah always loved to rule the roost, didn't he?'

Adam poured her another cup of tea, and signalled for a pot of hot water.

Belatedly she tried to spring to her older brother's defence. 'He held the family together when we were orphaned.'

'You held the family together,' he corrected her. 'Jeremiah only supplied a wage—but then, so did you.'

She was surprised. She hadn't expected Adam to remember her at all. Not that it made any difference. He didn't love her, and wasn't going to marry her.

'Jeremiah wanted the house—was that it? He wants to get married, I suppose. Found a good worker, has he?' Adam wouldn't let the subject go.

For the first time, Lottie smiled. Let him think that was the reason she had come! In a way, it was. She couldn't abide Lizzie, and living in the same house would have been unbearable.

'Lizzie Hopkins,' she supplied.

'Daughter of Cyril Hopkins who kept the grocery shop on the next corner to you?'

'Ay.'

'A sharp-tongued girl! You didn't want to share a kitchen with her? I suppose . . . I suppose you had no offers of your own?'

'What makes you suppose that?' she asked tartly, and could have bitten off her tongue when he smiled at her.

'Who, then? Who offered for you?'

She had gone too far not to give him an answer now. 'Horace Higginbottom.'

Adam whistled. 'You've surprised me. You mean the draper—the one with the big shop? He's married, surely?'

'A widower this twelvemonth.'

'You worked for him, didn't you? That's where you've got this idea of a good worker being the open sesame to marriage. I suppose he would have saved your wages if you'd agreed.'

'Ay.'

'And used you in his bed. Poor Charlotte! You didn't fancy him?'

'I hated him.'

'I suppose I should be flattered to be the lesser evil,' Adam laughed. It was a proper laugh, and made the others in the eating-house look at him. 'But then I was a thousand miles or more away. Distance lends enchantment . . .'

'Ay.' Once again, Lottie agreed.

'You'll have to learn to say "yes" instead of "ay" if you're to get on here. How long did the *Black Swan* take to cross?'

Lottie blinked at the abrupt change of subject. 'Three weeks.' Three awful weeks, she might have added.

'Why, Lottie? You could have been here in a week on a fast clipper. I sent enough money for that.'

'I tried to get a clipper, but they were all booked for months ahead.'

'You could have waited.'

'Once I had decided to come, I didn't want to wait.'

'Impatient to get here, were you?' Adam's good humour seemed to be restored. 'Didn't want to disappoint the bridegroom languishing in New York?'

'You needn't make fun of me!' She took a hasty drink of tea, and found it scalding.

'No, that was unkind. But take heart! When you've fattened out a little and cleaned up, you'll find someone. I remember you were always quite presentable, not pretty like Kate, certainly, but attractive enough in your own way.'

Lottie spluttered over her tea. It was one thing for her to say that Kate was pretty, quite another for Adam to tell her she was plain and scrawny and dirty, even if it was the truth.

'I expect you'll get a job,' he went on. 'You'll need lighter clothes, of course. Summers here are very hot. I might be able to put you in the way of some bargains.'

'But you're in men's tailoring, surely?' She was suddenly finding Adam easier to talk to.

'Not any more,' he was quick to say. 'I've branched out on my own, but we can talk about that some other time. You'll want to have a wash.'

'Ay,' Lottie answered sharply. Why did he keep harping on that? She no longer felt quite so angry, only very tired. She yawned, and tried to hide it behind her hand.

'Sleepy? You'll be glad to be in a proper bed tonight.'

A vision of white sheets and comfort formed in her mind, and she nodded. 'Last night,' she confided, 'we were on the deck all night. The *Black Swan* berthed out in the bay and there were lights everywhere—coloured lamps on the ferry boats crossing from one side to the other, gas lamps illuminating the whole town on this side. It was lovely—like a fairytale—with all the lights reflected back in the water. It was wonderful, and so warm. I never dreamed New York would look the way it did. At first, everyone was so excited. They were all talking and laughing, making plans. After a while they went very quiet and drew together as though they were frightened of what lay ahead. Some said their goodbyes then—goodbyes to friends they'd made on the ship, friends they'd probably never see again, for they were going on to different places. It was very lonesome.'

'Ay.' This time it was Adam who used the word. 'Did you have friends who said goodbye?'

Lottie sighed. 'I didn't know how fond I'd grown of them until that moment. Angelina and I hugged each other, and she cried just a little. But I might see her again, as she and her brother are in New York.'

'Good! You must keep in touch with them.' Adam got to his feet and went to the counter to pay.

Keep in touch with them? How would she face them? Paolo had stolen her candlestick, her link with home and Kate. She tried to tell herself that it must have been someone else, but she knew it was Paolo who had been minding her case. He knew the candlestick was there. Why hadn't he asked her for it? She owed him so much that she couldn't have refused. To steal it was unforgivable, an act of treachery. It killed any trust there had been between them, and betrayed their friendship. Absently, she took up the last slice of bread and pushed it into the pillowcase. No sense in wasting good food.

'Ready?' asked Adam, lifting up her case and waiting for her to pick up her pillow and her wicker basket. He didn't seem to notice that the bread had disappeared.

Lottie followed him to the door, not caring where they were going. They walked in silence to what appeared to be a main street, and there he hailed a stagecoach.

'Is it so far?' she asked.

'Far enough.'

The stagecoach, pulled by two horses, came to a stop beside them, and he helped her in, for she was encumbered with the pillow, and the step was high. He led her to a bench seat, and reached up to a hole in the ceiling to pay the driver who sat above their heads.

'It costs ten cents; five for each of us.' Adam showed her American coins. 'You must get used to them; that's why I'm showing them to you.'

It was a kindly thought, she reflected, but she didn't want to think about strange money as well as everything else for the moment. She looked about the carriage. It was clean, but as rough as an old-fashioned country wagon. The seats were wooden, and the other passengers looked no more comfortable on them than she did.

A glance out of the window showed her that they were passing through shabby and dirty streets with tall dark buildings.

'Tenements,' Adam's voice sounded in her ear. 'Dank holes where whole families are packed into one room with scarcely any light. No heat in winter, no breath of air in summer. I spent my first winter here in one.'

Lottie swung to face him. 'In one of those?'

'Ay, and I was lucky to be there! Like you, I found friends: friends who helped me, who stood by me—true friends.'

She sighed. If only Paolo had been a true friend like the ones Adam spoke of. 'I thought New York was rich and fine . . .'

'And you had only to set foot here to find a fortune!' he finished for her. 'There are fortunes to be made, so perhaps you'll be lucky. After all, you've told me you're a worker. You'll need to be!'

This statement made her feel even more deflated. If Adam had had such a hard time, how could she hope to achieve much on her own? Yet, she mused, he was well dressed now. His suit was of a good cut. He had money in his pocket, and enough to send for a bride from Lancashire . . . No use thinking of that, she told herself firmly, and looked out again.

'We're on Broadway.' He nudged her with his elbow, and she strained for a glimpse of this fabled street.

This was more as she had imagined New York. The street must be sixty feet wide, and shops and houses and hotels jostled each other. Some buildings were of marble, some of stone, and some of iron. Trees lined both sides of the street: poplar trees—she recognised them at once. She marvelled at the number of people walking, or standing staring at the shop displays. Traffic was heavy too, and the stage slowed almost to a walk because of the carts and smart carriages and other stages.

'Is there something special on today?' she wanted to know.

Adam only laughed. 'It's Saturday afternoon, lass.'

Lottie couldn't stop looking. She knelt on the seat, and pressed her face to the glass.

When the stage turned off Broadway, Adam said they were in Fifth Avenue, and it was time to alight. They got down, and walked along several small streets. She was too bemused even to register their names or direction, but did notice that one of them was wood paved, and that the lane it led into was only dirt and gravel. She raised the hem of her coat so that it would not trail in the dust.

'This is Jones Street,' Adam announced, 'and Mrs O'Rourke's house is just along a bit further.'

Lottie clutched her pillow tighter. There would be strangers to face here, strangers who knew Adam and would wonder at her presence. Her steps slowed. The houses in the lane, though large, were not pretentious. Some looked as if they might have belonged to farms originally, for they had long verandas and white picket fences.

He halted before one of them and unlatched the gate. 'We've arrived! I'll ask Mrs O'Rourke if you can have a bath right away.'

If Lottie had had any energy or fight left in her, she might have objected to him mentioning her sorry state yet again. As it was, she meekly murmured, 'Ay, Adam, ta very much,' and was grateful that he was in charge.

Mrs O'Rourke, a round fat woman with dark hair under a spotless white cap, met them at the front door, and exclaimed, 'Is this your bride, then? Sure and I thought she was a lovely fair-haired buxom sort of girl, from the way you told it.' She gave Lottie a very undecided sort of look.

'So Kate is,' Adam's voice was expressionless. 'This is Charlotte Earnshaw in her place. Her sister.'

Mrs O'Rourke looked towards Lottie again. 'And do you mean to marry her?'

'No,' he replied. 'But she'll need a room, and a bath right away.'

Lottie felt like shrivelling up at the next glance from the little landlady. Adam drew the woman to one side, and she was sure that some money changed hands before Mrs O'Rourke once more turned to her and announced that she could have the attic room, and a hip-bath shortly. Mary, the maid, would take her case upstairs.

As Lottie went up the stairs, following Mary, Adam watched them. Mrs O'Rourke had disappeared into the back of the house, and for that he was grateful. He didn't want her sympathy. He didn't want her questions, either.

Slipping out of the front door, he went round the side of the house to his little shed. A feeling that he might be caught and stopped came to him as he quickly undid the lock and checked to see that no one was looking from one of the windows of the house. He entered the shed. He just wanted to be alone. With a sigh, he sat down on the tall stool facing his work-table. He didn't look at the cloth waiting there, or even think about it.

This was to have been the day when Kate arrived. He'd planned it all, looked forward to it. And now . . . What did he feel? He wasn't sure. Had it just been an impossible dream? It had been so long ago that she had promised to be his wife and wait for him to send for her.

She hadn't come. Lottie had come instead. Lottie —bedraggled, pale, hungry. Even in his anger and disappointment he had pitied her. He hadn't been able to leave her to her own devices. Why had she come? Simply because her brother wanted to marry, and Horace Higginbottom wasn't to her taste? That was what she had said, and yet her eyes had told a different story. They had been wary, wounded. There was something she was holding back from him.

He supposed she might tell him what it was in her own good time, if he allowed her to do so. No, better keep her at a distance. Certainly help her to stand on her own feet, but that would be enough. He had no duty to her. It might have been a mistake to bring her here, to Mrs O'Rourke—and the girls. But the girls would be kind to her if he asked them. Rosemary, especially, might be prevailed upon to take her under her wing and help her to find a job. That would be the best plan. No sense in letting himself become too involved. At least he'd made it plain that he didn't mean to marry her, and she seemed to have accepted that.

Poor Lottie! Three weeks on the *Black Swan*. She hadn't complained, and hadn't told him anything about it except for seeing the lights of New York last night. She must have been desperate indeed to have come and faced the terrors of a ship's dark hold, emigrant class. But, of course, she hadn't known on setting out just how bad it could be. She knew it now. He'd seen that in her face. He'd realised it again when she snatched up the bread from the table. She'd known hunger.

Why was he thinking of her, he asked himself. He should be thinking of himself and of his loss. It wasn't so much an aching pain, this absence of Kate—rather a terrible sense of emptiness. He'd struggled so hard to succeed, and what had it been for?

There was no use in brooding; there were arrangements to be undone. The minister would have to be told, the wedding cancelled. Ada would be expecting Kate to stay with her. He must let her know that she hadn't come, and wouldn't be needing a place to stay before the ceremony. It had been kind of her to offer hospitality for the week leading up to it, but now there would be no wedding. He must tell her.

He made no move to get to his feet. Ada would suppose that the ship had berthed late, or that Customs and Immigration had taken forever. She knew how it was.

Ay, but it had been grand all the same to hear the pawky tongue of Lancashire again in Lottie! It had brought home nearer to think of Lizzie Hopkins's father's shop. The sweets he'd bought there as a lad! And fancy—Horace Higginbottom wanting to marry Lottie Earnshaw! Eh, she'd be able to tell him of friends and neighbours long forgot. He'd only to ask her.

What nonsense, to be homesick at twenty-eight for a Rochdale that he'd left three years ago to make his fortune in America. Ay, but he felt comfortable with her in a way he hadn't felt comfortable with anyone in a long time. She was a breath of home. No one ever forgot that tie, or would ever want to. It was too much a part of him.

Adam picked up a piece of the cloth lying on the work-table. He wouldn't work today. He'd go to Ada. She'd exclaim, and cry that he'd been wronged, but she'd lift his spirits and make him feel better.

He threw down the cloth, and left the shed.

CHAPTER TWO

LOTTIE, WHO had scarcely had a wash in over three weeks, luxuriated in her hip-bath.

Mary had carried cans of water up to the room and taken away the clothes Lottie had worn for so long.

'I don't want to see them again, ever!' Lottie told her.

'Good,' exclaimed Mary, wrapping them in a bundle, 'Mrs O'Rourke said they must be burned. Sure you mustn't be minding, for she knows what it's like to wallow in the Atlantic in a vile black hold. Didn't she arrive in the same way—and she with a house of her own and a nose that turns up at ship's smells?'

At first, Lottie was rather put out about the edict of her clothes being burned, but as the little maid went on, she lost her anger and began to smile.

'Soft beds there are in every room in this house, and two fine water-closets—one on each floor—you just have to run down one flight of stairs to the nearest. Isn't that a splendid thing?'

Lottie agreed that it was as she rubbed every inch of herself with the bar of fine perfumed soap that she had brought from home and never been able to use on the voyage. She washed her hair, too, and sang as she poured rinsing-water with a jug.

'There's a fine-tooth comb for your hair,' Mary produced it from a pocket. 'Don't be taking on now, it's kindly meant! Mrs O'Rourke can't abide creepy-crawlies in the head, and I'll hang out your coat on the line and beat it like a carpet, just in case. Mr Hardcastle said I was to help you every way I could. He gave me twenty-five cents. He must think a lot of you, sure he must.'

Lottie opened her mouth and closed it again without saying anything. She was too embarrassed to comment. To think that Adam had paid this child, for that was all Mary was, to rid her of vermin. But the hold had been filthy . . . she had been filthy. She almost cried with mortification.

When at last she left the bath and Mary had taken it away, exclaiming at the blackness of the water, she towelled herself dry and used the comb. She was glad there were no signs of any nits. Paolo had been very wise to make her wear that shawl over her head all the time.

What a pleasure it was to be clean and fresh, with her hair floating long and free about her! It was hot in the little attic room, and she took a loose cotton nightdress from her case. That had never been worn on the trip across the Atlantic. She unpacked her few possessions. The two dresses were creased, but they were clean. Perhaps some of the wrinkles would fall out.

Hair almost dry now, the tiredness she had been fighting all day overtook her, and she lay on the bed. It was strange to lie on such softness, between sheets, after all those nights on the floor of the hold where it had been noisy and dank and dark. She was at last by herself, and she missed the lulling motion of sail and sea.

She thought of Adam, and of Kate and home. Kate was in the distance waving to her as she had that last day at Hull. But Adam was as she had first seen him on the day he brought a reluctant Tom home to her.

'I've saved him from the Constable!' he'd told her. 'I caught him pinching apples. What are you going to do with him? Tell his Da?'

That had been impossible, of course, because Da was dead.

Tom had blubbered, and Lottie had known it meant another beating for him from Jeremiah, and he was only a little lad. She tried to explain it to Adam without excusing Tom from blame, and she must have succeeded, for he had looked at her and at Tom and said she needn't tell Jeremiah.

'There isn't a lad alive, I reckon, who hasn't scrumped apples,' he'd declared, but he'd made Tom promise that it wouldn't happen again.

Adam had been younger then, thinner and slighter, but when he'd smiled at her, she'd thought him handsome. He was a tailor, he'd said, just finishing his apprenticeship with George Harrison, Gents' Furnishers.

They'd stayed talking on the stoop for quite a while in the autumn sunshine and she'd wondered if she'd see him again. Of course, when she did, he came calling on Kate, not on her. But even when he called on Kate, he always had time for her sister. While he waited, they'd chatted; he with a smile and an easy remark about the weather or the doings of the day. He was pleasant.

It was the Christmas party at Adam's house which had changed all that. He had insisted that Lottie and Tom must come, as well as Kate. His family had made them very welcome. There had been neighbours, too, and it had been very jolly with crabapple wine, and the rugs rolled away for dancing. A sprig of mistletoe hung over one of the doors. Kate had been caught there several times, and even Tom had a turn with Adam's young sister.

Lottie had managed to avoid its vicinity when any of the men had been near, but towards midnight Adam had danced with her and they had hovered near the doorway. The others called out, and a laughing Adam said she must pay the forfeit. She liked Adam—of course she did—and made no real protest when he put his arms about her. All she expected was a brotherly peck. After all, he was Kate's friend.

As his lips touched hers, he drew her closer still. It was as though she had been seared by lightning. Every sense in her body awoke at his kiss . . . A hot flame of longing had engulfed her. Her legs trembled, her lips opened under his and she tasted the hard masculinity of his mouth, the sweetness of his body pressed close to hers. In the soft glow of gas-lamp from the wall holders, Lottie had entered a different world—a world where a man demanded and a woman gave.

She returned his kiss as though this was what she had been waiting for all her life. What the others made of it, she never knew. People had been kissing under the mistletoe all the evening, but Kate had looked at her rather strangely and been very quiet. When they drew apart, Adam had kept his arm about her waist for a moment and his face had worn an expression of what —puzzlement, amusement?—she wasn't sure. Then Kate had called to him, and he had gone.

Lottie had been shaken to the very core. She supposed it was because it was her first real kiss, if you could call it that. Adam, she told herself, had kissed before. It probably meant nothing at all to him. It couldn't have. He never referred to it, but Lottie couldn't get it out of her mind.

In a way, that kiss had spoiled her life. She wasn't the beauty that Kate was, but she had had her chances. Always it had been that kiss of Adam's that had stopped her from taking them. Had she imagined it? she asked herself quite often. Imagined a kiss that set her alight? It had never happened again, except perhaps the night —two nights ago—when Paolo had kissed her on the deck of the *Black Swan* after she had danced and laughed at the moon.

Was there a madness in her that she enjoyed only kissing unattainable men? She must be very careful. But if Adam could be induced to kiss her now, might she not find she had been cured of him and thus be free of that impossible dream she'd cherished? She could make a new life for herself here, and find a true man to love.

If only she could ask him to make the test. Her pride rebelled at that. He had beckoned to her sister to cross the Atlantic and come to him. Lottie had come instead, and had been repulsed for her pains.

No, it was unthinkable. Adam was the last man in the world to beg for kisses. He was beneath contempt. He had refused her, sent a fine-tooth comb for lice, and bribed Mrs O'Rourke to take her in. What a poor thing she must seem to him! In her tortured dreams she held out her arms to him, and always he turned away.

Lottie woke to a knock on her door and the sight of moonlight shining through the window on the bare boards of the floor.

'Come in,' she called, gathering the sheet round her.

Mary, the little maid, entered with a tray. 'Are you hungry? I wanted to wake you earlier on, but Mr Hardcastle said to let you sleep through supper. He went out to see his friends, he told me. I know it was Miss Ada that he meant. He often goes to her. I saw them out once—ever so striking she is, with black hair and lovely clothes . . . a picture. She's Eyetalian. He speaks the lingo, too—I heard him. Certain sure she likes him, looked at him as if to eat him—like our black puss with fish.' Mary set the tray on the bed.

Lottie sat up, propping her pillow behind her. There were sandwiches on the tray, a mug of cocoa, some cherries and a slice of cake. She was starving! It made no difference to her if Adam had a girl friend. But Kate might have felt very different about it if she had been foolish enough to come!

She bit into a ham sandwich and took a long drink of cocoa. 'Ta ever so, Mary. What time is it? You should be in bed.'

'I'm on my way there now.' She winked at Lottie and made no move to leave. 'Promise you'll not let on to Mrs O'Rourke! She's very strict about food in the rooms, but Mr Hardcastle wouldn't have you hungry. When I came across the sea, I'd no fine man to meet me and make things easy. Aren't you the lucky one, though?'

Lottie nearly choked on her second sandwich, beef this time. She wouldn't have called herself lucky with Adam. He didn't want her. He'd gone to Ada, hadn't he?

She held out the plate to Mary. 'Sit down and help yourself. I don't suppose your Mrs O'Rourke is fattening you up!'

Mary giggled and sat down. 'They're yours, really.' She snatched a thick sandwich. 'Sure, Mr Hardcastle's been hungry in his time. He had a fever when he landed, and was set upon by thieves. They took all he had—Mrs O'Rourke told me so—left him for dead. Them Eyetalians took him in, thanks be to God. That's why he helps folks like you, passing on the kindness. If I could get hold of that sister of yours, I'd give her such a shaking, disappointing a good man like Mr Hardcastle! I don't know how she could. Sure, she must have a heart of stone.'

Mary refused any more food and sidled out of the room, taking the cocoa cup and the plate with her.

Lottie was left, eating cake and cherries. There wouldn't be any crumbs for Mrs O'Rourke to pounce

upon, she reflected as she settled down to sleep
again.

The next morning, Lottie came down to breakfast in her
wine wool dress and with her hair in two long braids
which she crossed, coronet-fashion, on top of her head.
She knew the style gave her a certain amount of dignity
—a dignity which she felt she would need in meeting the
other inhabitants of the boarding-house. When she entered the dining-room, she found she was the only one
there. Mary came to serve her, bringing porridge, bacon
and egg and thick slices of bread, and a pot of hot
tea.

As she was finishing, Adam came in, resplendent in
grey striped trousers and a navy frac, a short-tailed
jacket cut away at waist and front. She felt unaccountably tongue-tied to find herself alone with him, but at
least, she consoled herself, she looked a good deal
smarter than the day before.

'Does no one else eat breakfast?' she asked hesitantly,
as he tucked into bacon and egg.

'The girls often don't bother.' He helped himself to
tea. 'They'd rather sleep than eat. Sunday's their only
day off, of course. I'm an early riser.'

'So am I.'

'Sleep well?'

'Yes, thank you. And thank you for the sandwiches
Mary brought.' Lottie belatedly remembered them. She
wondered why Adam didn't say something about her
improved appearance.

'That's all right.' Adam waved his hand in dismissal.

She was uncertain whether she should leave or stay.
She didn't know what was expected of her, and toyed
with her tea cup.

'I'd forgotten it was Sunday,' she said, after silence

had fallen between them. 'Could you tell me where the nearest church is, and how I may get there?'

'I'll do better than that,' he offered. 'If you can be ready in ten minutes, I'll take you.'

When she protested that it would be too much trouble for him, 'Nonsense,' he told her firmly. 'You can't be expected to know your way about yet. Come with me today; next week you can do as you like. Go and get your titfer, woman, and stop making such a fuss over nothing!'

Thus it was that Lottie found herself walking beside Adam through a different maze of small streets as he escorted her to church that Sunday morning. They turned a corner suddenly, and were in Broadway. Lottie recognised it with a thrill of pleasure. The people walking along it were proceeding more slowly, and looked more dressed up than the day before. Some were in carriages.

'It's a bit of a walk,' Adam said, 'but you're looking a lot stronger this morning.'

'And cleaner,' Lottie added, not giving him the chance to say it.

'Ay, altogether more presentable.' He nodded with no more than a cursory glance at her.

She felt like hitting him. But the sun was shining, and she was enjoying being on solid land with a good breakfast inside her. That was just his way, she told herself. He wasn't a man to give needless compliments to a woman, to try to flatter her, so she turned her attention from him to the streets and the buildings. Impressive houses sat beside shops, tall buildings beside squat ones. People leaned out of third- and fourth-floor windows to catch a glimpse of the street or of the sun. Children played down small alleys. There were chickens there too, and dogs; even several cats sunning themselves on railings or ledges. It was a town of ordinary folk today.

'Mary said Mrs O'Rourke was also immigrant, and that she owns her house now.' Lottie felt she must make some attempt at conversation.

'Married well,' was Adam's comment.

She thought he meant to stop there, but he continued, 'She lived in shanty town—just shacks the Irish put up on waste ground in the centre of the island. They say the city's going to claim the land now and make a park. But I'm not so sure. Some of it's swampy, and it's far out, too.'

That seemed to dispose of that subject. Lottie searched for another. She wondered why Adam was so silent this morning; he'd had enough to say yesterday. Was he regretting already his offer to accompany her to church and the fact that he had taken on the responsibility of her presence at Mrs O'Rourke's? Well, he needn't think she was going to be a burden to him. Tomorrow she'd get herself a job, and he could forget all about her.

It was a relief when they reached the church and went in with the others. Lottie sank into a seat and gave grateful thanks for a safe arrival in this new world. Everything wasn't as she had planned and hoped, but she was here and in good health—and Adam was beside her. She didn't know why that should be a comfort when she intended to be independent of him so shortly, but it was.

The sermon was on laying up treasure for the next world, and was delivered in a very stirring style. She couldn't help eyeing the well-fed and well-clothed congregation, and reflecting that they hadn't been slow to lay up treasure in this world. Nearly all the men had top hats and wore frock coats. Many of the women had the very wide skirts that proclaimed the presence of the new steel crinoline.

Lottie chided herself for hypocrisy. Wasn't she planning to follow their example? She sighed, and noticed the ladies' bonnets. Of straw, they were decorated with ribbons and flowers. She felt her fur-trimmed hat, though smart enough, was somehow wrong and out of season. So were her coat and dress. These ladies had light summery dresses in pastel shades with much finer wraps or cloaks. With difficulty, she forced her mind from the subject of clothes.

It was a subject which was borne in on her on the way home again, for Adam insisted that she look in the shop windows and note the styles. Why he was doing that? Was it just to make her feel dowdy, or could his tailor's eye not resist fashions? She remembered he had said yesterday that he could put her in the way of a bargain.

'You'll need some lighter things.' He drew her towards another window. 'Something like that blueish green thing over there—the colour would suit you, and it's cotton—and cool.'

In her woollen coat and dress, Lottie was sweltering. She'd never known heat like this in May. She gazed at the dress with yearning.

'It's ten dollars and eighty-three cents!' She was scandalised. 'That's more than two pounds for a dress. Who can afford that?'

'You can pay a lot more than that for a frock,' he told her. 'Come and have a peep in this window. There isn't anything there under twenty-five dollars.'

She looked, and saw that he was right. This must be a very expensive place to live! She began to wonder what she would have to pay for her room, but couldn't quite bring herself to ask.

'Would I be able to work in a shop like this?' she asked.

'Why not, if they've an opening? You worked for Higginbottom's.'

'What do you think they'd pay?' Lottie tore her gaze from the fashions and faced Adam.

'They'd try to start you at five dollars a week. Of course, a good saleswoman might get to ten, after she'd proved herself. Kate always said you could sell anybody anything! Are you that good?'

'Ay—I mean yes,' Lottie replied baldly. She could sell anything—except herself to Adam.

'No false modesty about you!' he observed.

'You asked me a question. I answered it.'

'They mightn't be taking on help,' Adam pointed out. 'You might have to start somewhere lower. You mightn't be able to afford Mrs O'Rourke's rates then.'

'How much . . . How much does she charge?'

'Five dollars a week for that little attic room you're in.'

'Oh!' Her spirits sank a little. 'Well, I shall just have to find somewhere cheaper in that case.'

'Ay, cut your cloth to suit. It seems a pity.' He seemed lost in thought. 'We'll talk about it again, later. Now it's time to think about getting back to lunch.'

They began to walk again, but he seemed in no particular hurry, adapting his pace to hers.

'I expect you'll make friends with the girls in the house,' he said. 'And what about the friends you made on the boat—people who meant to stay in New York? Have you made plans for meeting them again?'

'No, not exactly,' Lottie admitted. 'But they do have your address. They weren't sure where they'd be staying.'

'They'll probably get in touch with you, then.' Adam took her arm as they crossed a road.

'Ye-es,' she said, not quite sure that she wanted to hear from Paolo.

Perhaps he sensed her reservation, for he shot her a quick glance. 'Don't you want to see them again?'

'I don't know. They were very good to me. I don't know what I would have done without them.'

'Well, why do you hesitate? Were they not quite the sort of people you would have mixed with at home? You must remember, Lottie, it's not the same here as it is in Rochdale. People don't stay in the same narrow classes. It's much freer. And, of course, there are people from all nationalities. You may have to change some of your ideas: shake yourself loose from stern Lancashire morality and customs.'

'Ay,' she retorted, colouring to the roots of her hair. 'You think I'm narrow-minded and a snob!'

'I didn't say that!' Adam protested. 'It seems to me that you're not very sure of these friends of yours. Tell me about them. It may help you to talk. Who are they, first of all? English girls like yourself?'

Lottie made up her mind suddenly. It wouldn't matter if she talked to him. 'I'll tell you about them. I didn't mean to snap your head off.' She was a little ashamed of her reaction. He wasn't necessarily judging her and comparing her with Kate; he was perhaps just trying to show a polite interest. 'They weren't English. They were Italian.'

'Ah!' he exclaimed. 'There's a coincidence! I have very dear Italian friends.'

She didn't remark that she had heard as much from Mary, nor did she ask if his Italian friends had ever stolen from him.

'Only one of them was a girl,' she went on. 'Angelina is her name. Her brother is Paolo, Paolo Tardi.'

'Younger brother, I suppose? Travelling with their

parents, or coming to join them?'

'No, travelling on their own to join another brother here. Paolo is twenty-six, and Angelina seventeen. But they both spoke quite good English—Paolo better than Angelina. Paolo said another brother was coming as well.'

'From a good family, then'—Adam's voice was easy—'an educated family?'

'An ordinary family. They're entertainers.'

'What sort of entertainers?'

'Jugglers, dancers, singers,' Lottie smiled, remembering.

'I wouldn't have thought you'd have much in common with them!' Was there only surprise in Adam's voice? 'I've never heard that you had any talent for any of those things.'

'No, that's what Paolo said, too. He tried to teach me juggling; made me sing, and wished he hadn't. But I can dance.'

'There couldn't have been much chance of dancing in the hold.'

'Of course not.' An imp of mischief had worked loose in Lottie. Adam had declared she must lose some of the stern morality of home. Somewhere in the hold she must have done. 'I danced one night on the deck.'

'With this Paolo?'

'No, by myself. Paolo played the flute, and I danced.'

'Before a crowd of people?'

'Oh, there weren't many on the deck—only those who had the price to bribe their way there, to be in the open air at night. They were all asleep save me and Paolo.'

Adam's steps had slowed to a halt. 'What time of night did this dancing take place?'

She shrugged, and thought to place the time. 'Perhaps midnight—or thereabouts. I remember the moon was shining, and the sea was silver. For the first time in all that journey I didn't want to be anywhere but on the *Black Swan*, dancing.'

'You astonish me!' He was standing still, looking down at her, his blue eyes showing no sympathy. 'What were you thinking of to do such a thing?'

Lottie frowned. 'I wasn't thinking of anything—I just did it. It was good to be alive.' For a moment she almost recovered that moment of sorcery under the stars.

Adam shook her and spoiled the reverie. 'What happened then?'

She removed herself from his grasp. 'There's no need to be shocked! You're the one who said customs and morality were different here—they were different on the *Black Swan*, too. If you must know, Paolo applauded, and said if I'd begun early enough I could have made a dancer.'

'Ay, and then?'

'What do you mean—and then?'

'What happened then? You know perfectly well what I mean! You allowed yourself to be alone on deck at midnight with this man. Anything might have happened.'

Lottie longed to say that something had happened, that Paolo had kissed her—as he had and drawn away. She wanted Adam to know that another man had found her attractive, even if he didn't. She bit her tongue. Why should she tell him anything? He had no right to know.

'We went and lay down on the deck in our places, and went to sleep,' she said in a matter-of-fact way. Neither did she add that her place had been on one side of Paolo with Angelina on the other.

He began walking again, and Lottie had to hurry to catch up with him. 'I thought you'd make the crossing with some family or married couple. That's what I asked

Kate to do.' Adam shot the words at her. 'I wouldn't have wanted her to make friends with a juggler . . . a foreign juggler.'

'I'm not Kate!' she retorted, incensed that he should bring up her sister's name.

'You needn't remind me of that!' was his swift rejoinder. 'I know it all too well. I'd like to meet this Paolo and judge him for myself.'

She wondered why Adam wanted to meet Paolo. It had nothing to do with him how Paolo had behaved towards her. She had thought to tell Adam of the candlestick, but nothing would induce her to do so now. He obviously thought him a knave or a rogue. And if Paolo was, she wasn't going to expose him to Adam's scorn. Paolo had been kind to her, had given her protection and friendship when she had sorely needed both.

Adam couldn't have said why he was so put out by Lottie's revelations. He well knew what the hold of an immigrant ship could be like. But as far as he could judge, she had emerged unscathed from her experience —a little dirty, perhaps, but that was only to be expected. No, what had shocked him was her lowering of her standard of conduct. To dance before a man in silvery moonlight and remain untouched suggested a total innocence and lack of experience . . . or an accomplished liar. Neither explanation quite fitted in with his memory of Lottie as a girl. She'd been the mainstay of the family. As to dancing—where had she learned to dance? He remembered suddenly that she could dance, that he had danced with her one Christmas night and she had fitted nicely into his arms, her steps matching his. The feel of her had not been the soft roundness of his Kate, but it had been satisfactory in its own way. He had enjoyed his dance well enough. Had this Paolo held her in his arms? There was no reason why that thought should disturb him, but if he ever met this fellow, he'd have a few words to say to him!

Nay, he counselled himself, it was naught to do with him. Lottie could clearly take care of herself. Yet there was more to the story than she had told. He was certain of that. Why did she seem unwilling to tell him more, to tell him anything at all? It was only when he had pressed her to do so that she had confided that much.

He glanced at her as she strove to match her steps to his long stride. In that wool frock and coat she looked hot and tired. Marks of perspiration showed on her face, round her forehead, on her upper lip. He slowed down.

'Here, take off that heavy coat,' he told her. 'You're not dressed for the day, or used to it. I'll carry it for you.'

She protested at first, but looked grateful when he insisted and helped her out of it.

'What will people think, to see me coatless in the street?' she asked.

'I wouldn't have thought that would bother you!'

Lottie gave him a look of distaste.

That barb had gone home anyway. For a girl who had supposedly come to marry him, she wasn't all that compliant, nay, nor soft and pleasing to his ways.

She reminded him of someone—something—ay, that kitten that he'd rescued from a baiting. She'd spat at him too, not been able to believe he meant her no harm. She'd scratched him and bitten him, and then accepted him and purred every time she saw him.

Adam began to laugh and wouldn't tell Lottie why. Perhaps she just needed gentling like the cat, only he wasn't sure that he wanted to be the man to do it. He swung her coat to his other hand and took her arm, still laughing.

CHAPTER THREE

LOTTIE HAD just enough time to change to a lighter dress, a yellow and white sprigged lawn, the only light one she had. She washed her face and tidied her hair before going down to lunch.

Adam was already at the table, and so were two other guests. He introduced them to her at once.

'Dorothea Spencer and Rosemary Pike.' He pointed to each in turn. 'This is Charlotte Earnshaw, who's come to make her fortune.'

Two very different pairs of feminine eyes surveyed Lottie as she slipped into a vacant seat. Dorothea's were large and blue and set off her pretty blondness. Rosemary's were dark, as was her hair. She was very striking in pale green with a black collar and bow. Lottie judged her to be in her thirties, and took to her at once as she gave her a cheerful smile.

'I'm pleased to meet you. Your sister didn't come, Adam says. That's a pity.'

'Ay,' said Lottie, forgetting she'd been told to say 'Yes'.

'Did you come in her place,' Dorothea asked, 'to explain to Adam how it was?' Her gaze was frankly critical, and dismissed Lottie as no competition. She was sitting beside him and put her hand on his arm. 'I am sorry, Adam,' she sympathised, 'you must have been very disappointed—and angry. But never fear'—she gave a little laugh—'there are plenty of pretty girls here in New York who won't be slow to offer consolation.'

Lottie's cheeks burned. She tried to devote herself to

her soup which Mary had just placed before her. It was so hot that she burned her tongue.

'Never mind,' said Rosemary kindly. 'You mustn't rush at Mrs O'Rourke's meals. They're meant to be taken slowly and enjoyed. I'm sure you'll like it here, once you've got used to different ways.'

'Ay,' Lottie agreed, wondering just how long she'd be able to afford to stay here.

'Did you enjoy your first sight of New York?' Rosemary asked. 'Was it as you expected?' She raised a spoonful of soup to her mouth.

Lottie felt very shy as they all waited for her answer, but she wasn't going to say 'Ay' again. She didn't speak as they did, in what she described to herself as a fast drawl, but at least she had a tongue and she would use it.

'When we saw Staten Island—the sailors said it was called that—we were all surprised to see it rising a hundred feet above the water. People said there were pretty suburban villas and villages on the low shores of Long Island in the distance. Of course they were too far to see properly. I think we all felt a little frightened, and a little unwelcome, when we saw the guns and the fortifications along the shores.'

'Aren't there guns on the English coasts?' Dorothea asked, looking as though she were surprised that Lottie could censure anything American.

'Ay, I reckon there are,' Lottie admitted. 'But I've never faced them coming in from the sea.'

Rosemary laughed. 'Did it seem very strange to you?'

'Let lass eat her dinner,' Adam said, smiling at Rosemary, 'before you ask her questions!'

Lottie half-expected Rosemary to be angry, but she seemed in excellent humour. 'I am awful, Adam,' she agreed. 'It's the reporter in me that can't resist finding out how other folk find us. I shall get your Lottie in a corner after, and write down what she says.'

'You mean you work for a newspaper? Do girls here really have jobs like that?'

'Our Rosemary's one on her own,' Adam said. 'You should read the things she writes about!'

'A celebrity,' Dorothea added, as Lottie tucked into her soup. 'The principal at my school reads her articles aloud to the big boys and girls. He says they should know their heritage, and how the frontiers of America were won.'

Lottie had no idea what they were talking about. She guessed Dorothea must be a teacher—she looked like a teacher, now that she came to think of it, and acted like one. Very sure of herself, she was. And she smiled a lot at Adam. She was a lot younger than Rosemary, too —no more than twenty-four, surely.

'Rosemary is a real American,' Dorothea went on, eating daintily all the while. 'She's from pioneer stock. She's just finished a series of articles on the life they lived. I remember especially the one she wrote about her mother making clothes for the family—pants for the boys out of buffalo hides, jackets out of raccoon fur and bearskins. Do you know she made all the girls buckskin petticoats and matching moccasins?'

This certainly suggested to Lottie a life of hard work and privation. 'Where did she get the furs and the skins?' she asked, turning to the older girl.

'My father trapped those and brought them home for food and clothing,' Rosemary told her. 'We were a family of nine: six girls and three boys. She was a worker, was my mother, and all six of us girls learned to make bread and cheese, can fruit, preserve buffalo tongue and bear bacon and jerked venison. We pickled cabbage and candied nuts and made our own soap—and that's hot, hard, work.'

Lottie was entranced. She'd heard about settlers in the Americas, but of course she'd never met one at first hand. Her eyes were round. 'Was it . . . Was it a good life?' she asked hesitantly.

'It was the only one I knew till I was thirteen or so.' Rosemary shrugged.

'What happened then to change it?' Lottie's curiosity was aroused, her soup allowed to grow cold.

'A series of things, really. Two of my sisters got married, one of my brothers went homesteading further west, and my mother's sister here in New York asked me to come for a visit. At first I didn't want to, but Mum was determined I should. She said there was a better life for me. I didn't have to be like her—old from the age of thirty. I never thought of her being old, but then I began to look at her and see the lines in her face and her rough hands, and to realise the amount of work she got through.' Rosemary allowed Mary to take her plate away and to replace it with another piled high with roast lamb, boiled potatoes, carrots and cabbage.

'I never went back.' Rosemary cut a piece of meat. 'My auntie saw to my education, and then, later, my uncle had a friend with a newspaper. He gave me a chance when Uncle Matt died, and I worked myself up till I became a feature-writer.'

They all devoted themselves to the main course for a few minutes. Lottie reflected that it was encouraging that a girl could attain such heights of success here. Since Rosemary didn't object to talking about it, she wanted to know more.

'Did you never miss your family unbearably and want to return?' she asked hesitantly.

'Of course I missed them, but I gradually came to learn—as you probably will'—Rosemary gave Lottie a smile—'that there isn't any going back. There's only going on. My sisters and brothers were facing changes in their lives, too. It couldn't ever be the same again . . .' She stopped, her fork swirling a piece of potato in the hot, thick gravy. 'Perhaps that's why I've written about pioneer life. I remember the good times and want to share them. To live them over again, if you like. But I wouldn't want to go back to the kind of life my mother lived. My most vivid memory of her is working all the time—at the loom weaving broadcloth after all the other chores were done, or mending and patching by the light of a candle and the wood fire that was never allowed to go out.'

'She sounds a grand woman,' Lottie observed, for Rosemary's mother had come alive in her mind.

'She was that!'

'People love to hear about her,' Dorothea pointed out, 'and about the pioneer life. I never knew it myself. My family are third generation. They have a big farm in upstate New York, and they've seen to it that all of us had a good education. One of my brothers is a doctor, another is a minister.'

'Ay,' said Adam, having cleaned his plate and sitting back. 'You're one of the lucky ones. Lottie and I have still to find our way and our fortunes.' He smiled as though the prospect wasn't daunting at all.

Lottie was grateful for his enthusiasm and for being included. She was also grateful to Rosemary, because doubts had begun to creep into her thoughts about her future.

At the end of the meal, after strawberries and cream, and a pot of tea had been brought in, Lottie was so far in sympathy with Rosemary that she was quite willing to go out on the veranda with her to be interviewed about her journey to America.

Her protests about people not being interested in

her were swept aside, and Dorothea and Adam begged to be allowed to listen as well. They promised to say nothing. All four settled into comfortable wooden chairs, Rosemary having slipped upstairs to fetch a pad and pencil to make notes.

She began by asking Lottie what ship she had sailed in, and from what port. The information was supplied haltingly. Now that her every word was being taken down, Lottie felt a little uncomfortable. Besides, Adam and Dorothea were listening.

'I wonder if you'd mind telling me what it was like on the ship,' Rosemary put her pencil behind her ear. 'Just tell it in your own words as though you were talking to me.'

'It wasn't comfortable . . . Are you sure you really want to know?'

'Tell me.' Rosemary was very calm. 'I've heard stories before, but they were second-hand or after people had been here for a while and forgotten some of it. It'll be all fresh with you, and I think it's time someone did something about the immigrant ships and their conditions. Perhaps, if it's in the paper . . .'

'You mean my name will be in your paper?' She took fright at the idea.

'My name's in the paper every day,' Rosemary remarked gently. 'I haven't come to any harm from it.'

Thus encouraged, Lottie began to speak. 'We were all packed together in the hold.'

'Men and women?'

'Ay, and children too, crammed in, frightened, excited, wet from the rain. The smell was stomach-turning even that first day—and it got worse when the sea was rough. Babies were crying, men shouting, women greeting to be leaving home. It smelt'—Lottie paused, recalling it—'What can I say it smelt like?' Her nose wrinkled.

'It smelt of despair. I'd thought folk would be full of hope and smiling, but they weren't. It was like they suddenly realised what they were doing and wanted to turn back. It was too late for that.'

'Were you with friends?' Rosemary was willing her to go on.

'I was on my own. I had my basket of provisions on my arm, and my case in one hand and my swansdown pillow in the other. Someone pushed me—a German man, I think, a great big chap—and I sprawled on the floor. I managed to get to my feet again and a small dark girl helped me with my belongings. She led me over to a space where a tarpaulin had been spread. She said I could share it with her brother and herself. That's how I met Angelina and Paolo Tardi. They'd been on the ship since Hamburg. They were entertainers coming to join their brothers here.'

Rosemary took down the details. She wanted to know what provisions Lottie had had in her basket, whether the Tardis spoke English, and if she had trusted them from the first.

'I took to Angelina right away,' Lottie admitted. 'She were right friendly, and pretty too in her Italian way. She had big brown eyes and a grand smile. Paolo, I wasn't so sure of.' She might have added that she still wasn't sure of Paolo, but she went on evenly, 'Paolo's a real looker, flashing eyes and teeth ever so white and strong, waving black hair.'

Adam interrupted this catalogue of Paolo's attractions. 'Were there rats in the hold, Lottie?'

'Ay!' She shuddered. 'I hated them. I cried that first night when one ran near us, and Paolo . . .' She paused, not wanting to tell them.

'What did Paolo do?' asked Rosemary. 'Kill the rat?'

'Nay, he slapped me.'

'Slapped you?' Dorothea's blue eyes were round and shocked. 'How dared he?'

'He slapped me because I was crying and laughing both, I was that upset. I can't abide rats. I told him so, and he said I'd have to learn. They were a fact of life in the hold. I hated him and wanted to move away, but Angelina begged me to stay. She was right sweet, was Angelina. It was her who made me change earlier on from my good wool dress to my old serge work one. She made Paolo help her to hold up a blanket and not look or let anyone else.'

'Why? Why did she want you to change?' Dorothea seemed to have forgotten completely her promise to say nothing.

It was Adam who answered her. 'She didn't want to attract attention to herself, of course. I would have thought, Lottie, you'd have had enough sense to consider that in the first place!'

'How was I to know,' Lottie demanded angrily, 'that men were such beasts! That women were attacked night or day—that they were fair targets of men's needs—and that no one would go to their aid.'

Lottie and Adam glared at each other. It was Rosemary who claimed the attention of both by asking, 'Did you see such attacks?'

'Ay, there was one that first night. The German man pushed himself on top of an Irish girl. I was glad I was with Paolo and Angelina then. It was that same German who'd knocked me down. Later on, when we'd been at sea for some days, he went for Angelina. He had her down on the floor of the hold and I hit him with a candlestick—a silver one I'd brought from home. I'd taken to carrying it with me—just in case, like.'

Dorothea gasped. Rosemary wrote furiously.

Adam asked, 'Where was this Paolo, then, that you had to save his sister?'

Lottie sprang to the defence of her friend. 'He couldn't be there every moment of the day! You know how it was: there was one hot soup served to each one who stood in line with his wooden bowl at lunch-time. We took it in turns to go, because someone had to stay with our possessions. Angelina was the one that day. It was just luck that I got back in time. I put my soup bowl down by the door and flew over to them. And do you know, when we'd calmed down and made sure the German wasn't dead, my soup was gone? The bowl was empty!'

'Did you go hungry that day?' asked Dorothea.

'Ay—and most days,' Lottie answered sharply, her eyes on Adam. She couldn't read the expression of his eyes, but she knew they were on her. 'Some had brought scarcely any food and were famished from the start. We had to watch the food we had with us. My basket never left my arm even when I slept, and the rats came closer in the nights. I was glad Arthur had made me take the gin with me.'

'Did you drink all of it?' Dorothea sounded more shocked by this revelation than by the attack on Angelina.

'Not all at once,' Lottie tried to explain. 'But every night before sleeping.'

Her listeners looked at her in fascination. 'Weren't you afraid of its effect on you?' Dorothea whispered. 'It might ruin you for life.'

'Happen it might,' Lottie retorted, 'but it didn't. It was a blessing. Paolo had some wine. We shared what we had between us. Some nights we'd have a little wine, some a measure of gin. We drank it as secret as we could by the light of the one lantern left burning in the hold when most had settled. Sometimes we had English cheese with it, sometimes a bite of garlic sausage.'

Dorothea shuddered' delicately. 'How could you endure it? I'm sure I never could have.'

'You'd be surprised what you can endure when you have to!' Rosemary looked up from her notes briefly. 'But people shouldn't have to endure this sort of thing. That's what we're hoping to change. People shouldn't be treated worse than animals.'

'Ay,' Adam agreed. 'If you can improve conditions at all, Lottie will have done something by speaking out.' He smiled at the girl. 'Thou art a brave lass then, and must have wanted to come right badly.'

Lottie realised that Adam must be moved to drop back into the personal 'thou', because for the most part he seemed to have adopted the American way of speaking.

'Yes, I did,' she replied shortly.

He looked at her strangely, puzzled. Even Dorothea didn't ask the question that Lottie could guess was hovering on her lips about why she had come.

'Did the food you had brought last out the voyage?' Rosemary wanted to know.

'Not really.' Lottie bit her lip. 'There were storms, and the *Black Swan* took three weeks to get here. I gave some food to the Irish girl, because the German man had taken hers and the people she had been with would have nothing to do with her. Paolo said I shouldn't, because I'd go hungry myself; but I noticed he gave her a handful of raisins and a boiled egg when he thought I didn't see him. And he sometimes let her sit close when he was doing his juggling and making the children laugh.'

'Were you always kept in the hold?' Rosemary questioned. 'Weren't people sick in the storms?'

'Some were sick all the time. One man died, and so

did a child. After that, we were allowed up on deck for an hour every day. The sluices were in a terrible state.'

Dorothea didn't question the statement about the sluices. Perhaps she didn't understand about them. 'Were you seasick?' she asked.

'Like to die!' Lottie told her. 'If it hadn't been for Paolo and Angelina, I might have done just that. It was the last four days. I couldn't keep anything on my stomach—not the greasy soup, not the mouldy biscuits I had left. I couldn't even think about the one shrivelled little orange in the basket. I turned my head to the wall and gave up. But Paolo wouldn't let me. He carried me up on deck and bribed I don't know how many sailors to let me stay there, hidden away like, under a pile of sails. The fresh air cured me—that and a sip of gin and the little orange, and an apple that Paolo bought from someone.'

'But when you went back to the hold . . .' Adam began.

'I never went back to the hold,' she said. 'They let me stay on deck that night and the night after till the ship berthed and the Customs men came on board the next morning. Paolo and Angelina stayed with me. I don't know what it cost or how he paid for it, but he said Italians always knew where to place a bribe.'

The others exclaimed at that, but Lottie was suddenly overcome by remembering the debt she owed Paolo. Why had she allowed herself to feel so betrayed when she realised that he had taken the silver candlestick? It was a small price to pay for her life. But that was it—she would have given it to him gladly, even though it was her link with home, with Kate. For Kate had the other one of the pair, and had said that neither of them should ever be parted as long as the silver candlesticks endured.

Lottie shook her head and felt the others looking at her. 'Did you say something?'

'I just asked if you still had the candlestick—the one you hit the German with—and if you meant to carry it about with you?' Dorothea repeated.

Lottie felt the blush that stained her cheek. 'Why?' She tried to speak calmly. 'Why do you want to know?'

'I'd just like to see it—that's all.'

'I don't have it any more.' Her reply was very sharp, and she felt Adam's eyes on her. 'I—I gave it away.' She wasn't going to admit the truth that Paolo had taken it. 'I gave it to Angelina—she wanted it.'

'As a keepsake? A pretty grisly keepsake—I wonder she took it.' Dorothea appeared to have forgotten that she had wanted to view that trophy.

Rosemary was frowning. She must have sensed that something was wrong, but it was Adam who spoke.

'Was it one of that pair of silver candlesticks that sat on your mantle in Rochdale? A handsome pair, I always thought.' He smiled at Lottie, and she noticed that Rosemary, satisfied, had shut her notebook.

'Ay. Kate still has the other. Jeremiah didn't want to give them up, but she gave him such a bother that he gave way.'

'Thank you very much, Lottie,' Rosemary smiled. 'This will write up splendidly. If you'll come upstairs with me, there's something I'd like you to have for your help.'

Lottie protested that she didn't want anything,·but Rosemary was so winning and so insistent that she went with her.

Adam was left alone to his thoughts, though Dorothea was eager to comment on what Lottie had gone through.

'She should have come on a clipper,' he stated. 'It would have taken only a week. She would have been saved all that.'

'Yes, of course,' Dorothea agreed. 'She was very foolish to travel on her own. Why did she?'

It was one thing for Adam to question Lottie's reasons, but quite another for Dorothea to do so, however well intentioned.

'Probably couldn't find anyone to come with,' he explained, 'and didn't want to wait. Besides, she's always been an independent sort of girl—had to be, I suppose—there were the younger ones in the family to look out for.

'Very brave of her!' Dorothea was all admiration. 'I didn't like to ask her her reasons. One doesn't want to pry. They must have been very pressing to bring her here to find her own way.'

'Ay.' He wished he knew what they were, Adam thought. And he wished he knew why the mention of the candlestick and its whereabouts upset her so much. It was plain to him that it did, although the others mightn't have noticed.

'Did she really come just to make her fortune?' Dorothea might not want to pry, but she clearly wanted to find out.

'Why else?' Adam shrugged. 'She saw it as an opportunity to better herself—as I did three years ago.'

'But it's different for a man.' Dorothea pouted. 'He has to think about making his own way. A girl looks towards marriage.'

She smiled at him, and it would have been very easy for Adam to admit that Lottie had had that in mind, but he didn't. He wasn't sure whether it was loyalty that prevented him, or the knowledge that Lottie would have been hurt to have thought she was discussed. Dorothea meant no harm, of course. She was a pleasant sort of girl—and very pretty.

'Oh, Adam!' she sighed. 'You must have felt very upset when Kate wasn't there. I want you to know that I really admire you for taking it so well and for bringing Lottie back here with you. It takes a really generous man to behave like that. But you mustn't let her be a drag on you. You must protect yourself a little.'

He smiled back. It was rather nice to be appreciated. Dorothea obviously was quite sincere.

'I shall see that she finds her feet. Of course, if you girls are friendly towards her, that will help a lot.'

'Naturally,' Dorothea agreed. 'For my part, I'll be delighted to help you. I'm sure Rosemary will, too. She's probably telling her now about people she knows who might help her to find work.' She put her hand on Adam's arm. 'Why don't we take a little walk round the garden and talk about how we might both help her?'

Dorothea was mistaken in supposing that Rosemary was discussing jobs with Lottie. She had led the way upstairs to the very large bedroom which was hers and waved her to a comfortable chintz-covered chair.

'We couldn't talk properly with the other two there, could we?' Rosemary draped herself elegantly on a padded bench in the window, and offered her guest a chocolate. 'I have no intention of telling my readers the real reason you came to New York,' she announced with a little laugh. 'I want to put your mind at rest on that.'

Lottie nearly choked on her candy. 'The real reason?' she stammered. 'What's that?'

'Adam.' Rosemary's reply was succinct.

Lottie didn't meet her gaze, but looked instead at the handsome rose and black quilt on the bed and at the rose rag-rug that lay on the floor. She sighed.

'How did you know?' she asked softly. 'Is it so apparent to everyone?'

'No,' Rosemary replied, offering the chocolates again. 'I don't imagine it even occurred to Dorothea. If it's any consolation to you, she's written you off as no competition at all.' She gave a sudden grin. 'But I think there's more to you than meets the eye. A girl who has the wit and audacity to save her friend from attack might accomplish something for herself.'

'Oh! That were naught. It was lucky I were there.'

'And now you're here.' Rosemary winked at her. 'What are you planning to do?'

'Get a job.' Lottie frowned. She might have added that she intended that Adam should kiss her, but hesitated. Though Rosemary was speaking plainly, she wasn't quite sure that she could trust her with this secret.

'I didn't mean that.' Rosemary's smile was charming. 'Dorothea is a very pretty girl, don't you think?'

'Ay.'

'And clever.' Rosemary held out the box of sweets again. 'Men are sometimes caught on the rebound.'

'Ay. Are they—Are they friends?' She bit into a caramel, and chewed at it.

Rosemary shrugged. 'Are a man and a woman ever friends? In my experience, one or the other isn't satisfied with that state of affairs. In this case, I'd say Dorothea would see her chance of enlarging on friendship.'

Lottie finished the sweet and licked her lips. 'Why are you telling me all this?'

Rosemary looked at her reflectively. 'You remind me of myself at your age. I hope you won't take this the wrong way, but you're just as I was—not sure of myself in a strange new world. You're not feeling your best, or looking your best. You're not handsome. You haven't pretty clothes, but given time and a little assistance, you can make more of yourself.'

Lottie considered this in silence. She wasn't exactly offended by the other girl's remarks; there was truth in them. She just didn't know what to say.

'When I started to work for the newspaper, I felt as out of place as you do now. I felt myself just as gauche and unattractive.'

'Did you?' Lottie leaned forward. 'But you're handsome, and you dress so fashionably.'

'Exactly,' Rosemary agreed, laughing. 'I notice you said handsome—not pretty. That's part of the illusion! You could make people believe the same of you. You have a good figure, or you will have when you put back a little of the weight you've lost. You have lovely eyes —such a soft brown—and such thick eyelashes. With your hair done in a becoming style, and a clear colour to bring out your fine complexion instead of that insipid white and yellow thing you're wearing, you have possibilities. Will you let me take you in hand?'

Lottie was very tempted to say 'Ay' immediately, but she was a cautious Lancashire lass at heart, and it sounded as though Rosemary's plan would take some brass. 'How much . . .' she asked hesitantly. 'How much would it be likely to cost?'

'How much can you afford?' Rosemary replied quickly. 'Or, put it another way, can you afford not to try? If nothing else, a better presentation will secure you a better job.'

'Maybe.' Lottie saw the practicality of that. 'I have the twenty-five dollars every immigrant has to bring to get into America, but that really belongs to Adam. I'll have to pay him back.'

'He'll wait,' Rosemary suggested. 'Has he asked for it?'

'Not yet, but I promised. Besides, it's only honest.'

'I'm not meaning you to be dishonest. Think it over. Talk to him. Explain that you'll get a better job and pay it back more quickly.' Rosemary was very persuasive.

'Yes, I'll think on it. It's kind of you to want to help me.' Lottie was still undecided.

Rosemary waved that aside and glanced out of the window. 'Come here,' she beckoned.

Lottie rose to her feet and went towards her. She looked out of the window, to see Adam and Dorothea walking arm in arm round the back garden, and that she was looking up at him and smiling.

That did it. 'All right! When do we start?'

'Will the morning suit you?' Rosemary grinned. 'I should be able to pop out for a while then. I'll write out you directions to where we can meet. Just tell Adam you're going to meet me—if he should ask, but you don't need to tell him anything about it. He won't expect you to be going off to work tomorrow, anyway. It'll be our secret. And you might as well take the rest of the chocolates. Cheer up, it's not going to cost a fortune, you know!' Rosemary laughed her doubts away.

Of course she was right, Lottie told herself. She had been determined enough to come to New York. She must be equally determined to get on here. Even if Adam had refused her, there were still opportunities here for the taking. And she was going to take them!

CHAPTER FOUR

DOROTHEA AND ROSEMARY went to church service on Sunday evening, and Adam told Lottie that he wished to see her in the parlour.

She followed him in and sat down on the edge of a straight-backed chair, looking about the room with interest. He sat in a rocking chair, motionless.

The carpet was brightly patterned, and comfortable well-worn easy chairs were grouped before the fireplace. The fire was not lit, since it was so warm. There were lace curtains at the window and heavier drapes of maroon velvet at the sides. It was very quiet. Lottie could hear the clock ticking on the mantelpiece and the beat of her own heart. They seemed to be the only sounds in the whole room, in the whole house. She waited for Adam to speak, but he seemed to have no inclination to do so.

She studied his profile, for he was half turned from her in the embrasure of the windows. He was a good-looking man with even features and very blue eyes. Now a dappled sunbeam from the lace curtains played round his head, making his fair hair glint and glisten in its light.

Lottie cleared her throat. 'You . . . You wanted to speak to me, Adam?'

His blue eyes fastened on her, and she wished she had as much self-confidence as he seemed to have. She supposed this was the time when she should tell him about the money, and ask if he would allow her to repay it over a period of time. She had no intention of being beholden to him for ever, but neither did she want to return it now. She hesitated, and he startled her by speaking very gently.

'I'm sorry you had such a harrowing journey across the ocean, Lottie. I didn't have a pleasant crossing either.' He smiled at her. 'I should have remembered that when I met you at the boat, instead of being so angry that you weren't Kate. Tell me, has she married a good man? Will this Arthur be right for her?'

This was an altogether more approachable Adam. She began to feel a little sympathetic towards him. After all, he had had a great disappointment.

'Arthur suits her well,' she replied. 'He works for the railway, and has just had a promotion to Doncaster. That's what made them decide to get married right away. I went with them to help them settle. They're very happy together.'

Adam nodded. 'So she left Rochdale for him. That tells me something.' He stared into space.

'Ay,' Lottie sighed. 'She was very young, Adam, when you left—fifteen to your twenty-four, too young to know her own mind.'

'Maybe, but I knew mine. Well, that's all over now, but it eases my mind a little to know she's well settled.'

Lottie was torn between admiring his generosity of spirit and wondering why everyone always excused Kate and considered her feelings even when she'd behaved badly. Was it only because Kate was so pretty, rather like Dorothea in her blonde fragile good looks? No one ever had tried to shield Lottie from harm.

Neither was Adam doing so now. He was questioning her. 'Well, Lottie, what do you mean to do? I think we better clear up a few matters first between us. Why, exactly, did you come?' He began to rock the chair gently.

Lottie bit back the impulse to ask him to kiss her so

that she might decide once and for all what she meant to do. She wouldn't ask him to kiss her if he were the last man on earth!

'I mean to get a job and make my own way and pay you back your money,' she answered stiffly.

'We'll leave the money aside and talk about it some other time. I mean to get to the bottom of why you really came. Best to confide in me, Lottie, whatever your secret is. If there's a bairn on the way, it will soon be apparent anyway.' His tone was kindly.

But Lottie wasn't listening to the tone. She heard the words, and coloured up to the roots of her hair. 'There's no bairn on the way! Why should you think that of me?'

Adam shrugged. 'You're flesh and blood like the rest of us, aren't you?'

Ay, she thought. My blood turned to water when you kissed me, my flesh . . . She brushed the thought away, rubbing her cheek with one hand as though that would banish it.

'Answer me, Charlotte!' Adam demanded. 'Are you flesh and blood beneath that prim exterior?' His eyes held hers. 'Or don't you understand what I'm talking about?'

That goaded her beyond endurance. 'I understand right enough, Adam Hardcastle! You needn't sit there judging me and wondering if I have feelings. I do, I do—and no one has ever considered them, either! Not Kate, who had men to choose among; not Jeremiah, who wanted me to stay and be a slave to him and Lizzie and their childer; not Horace Higginbottom, who saw me as a wife-clerk he wouldn't have to pay; and certainly not you, who would have sent me back to Rochdale yesterday if it had been within your power.' She was shaking with emotion.

To her surprise, Adam smiled. 'Well, well! Right

enough, I asked for that. So the worm has turned. You ran away from Rochdale, then?'

Lottie was beginning to feel elated by her own anger. She'd held it in too long, and it felt good to let it free. What did she care what Adam thought of her outburst? He had begun it. She wasn't prepared to stop now.

'I didn't run from Rochdale! I ran to America and a new start—somewhere I could be myself.'

'But why to me, Lottie? That's what I don't understand.'

Lottie might have told him then, but she couldn't quite bring herself to do it and risk a further rebuff.

'You sent the money. The time was right.'

'So I must take the consequences?'

'What consequences? I've told you I mean to stand on my own feet.'

'Yes, you've told me. I'm not so sure you can.'

Lottie glared at him and he glared back.

'You don't know what it's like!'

'It can't be as bad as the *Black Swan*.'

'You didn't know what that was like, either. You wouldn't do as you were told and come by clipper.' Adam seemed to have forgotten that it was Kate who had been instructed to come by clipper.

'It's different from when you came!' Lottie exclaimed. 'You fell among thieves. Mary said so. But even so, you made your way. Now you live in a good place, and you have good clothes and money. Why shouldn't I do the same?'

'It's harder for a girl. Wages aren't as high for women. No, I mean to help you, even if you fight me every inch of the way!'

Adam was hanging on to his temper with difficulty, and Lottie wondered why he was so incensed. She wasn't likely to turn down his help, and would tell him so.

'If you have any ideas about employment, of course I'll listen. I want to do as well as I can for myself.'

'We'll have to think about it carefully. You don't want to rush into anything. Dorothea has a friend in the victualling trade . . .'

That was enough for her. She put her nose in the air. She didn't want favours from Dorothea.

'I've never worked with provisions.'

'I suppose you can learn, if the money's good. You'd do well to keep an open mind.'

This time Lottie managed to hold on to her temper. Adam was trying to help her, but she resolved that she wasn't going to accept his help. She'd find her own job.

'Any road,' he said, 'it's not something you have to decide tonight. Take a day or two to rest. You'll look better for it.'

There he was again, harping on her looks, probably comparing her to Kate and Dorothea! Well, she wasn't Kate, nor ever would be. And after tomorrow he'd see a new Charlotte Earnshaw.

Lottie got to her feet. 'Ay, Adam,' she agreed, feeling she had been dismissed. Suddenly she was very tired, and the only place she wanted to be was in her bed upstairs. She yawned. 'I'll have an early night, I think.' She put her hand on the back of the chair to steady herself. Why should her legs feel so weak?

'Just one thing before you go.' Adam stopped rocking.

'Yes?'

He paused, as if deciding how to put what he wanted to say.

She waited, yawning again.

Adam got up and stood above her. 'If I had agreed to accept you instead of Kate, would you have married me?'

Lottie felt the slow blush that stained her cheek, and cursed at her own frailty. She forced her eyes to meet the blueness of Adam's glance. She wanted to shout 'No, never', but she had been honest all her life and lying came hardly to her.

'I—I don't know,' she faltered. 'I hardly know you. It wouldn't be a very good basis for marriage, would it? I know, in the Bible, Abraham married Leah, the sister of the girl he wanted . . . I've always wondered how she dealt with that . . .'

'Particularly as he waited seven years and claimed her sister too,' Adam added drily.

She found she couldn't tear her glance from him. His eyes were so kind, so understanding. She might have asked him then to kiss her, but she hesitated, and the moment was lost.

'Away to bed,' said Adam. 'Good night, Lottie. Pleasant dreams.' He put his hand on hers.

She snatched her hand away as if she had been burned. Her breathing was uneven, her heart racing.

'Good night, Adam,' she managed to get out before she ran from the room and up the stairs to the haven of her bed. A kiss would have been madness if the touch of his hand awakened such sensations in her.

Adam closed the door of the parlour. So she had come to marry him—he was almost sure of it. Of course she couldn't care for him. She had seen him as the answer, the solution to running away. Now she was coming to a different way of thinking. She was a sensible girl. Why did the thought niggle at him that she didn't want his help now? He'd meant it when he'd said he was going to help her.

A funny little thing she was, with so much dignity —and nothing really to be dignified about. He had to admire her grit. He'd see what he could do. It would have been different if Kate had come. Kate was always easy to talk to. He could have told Kate his plans, his dreams. Together they would have overcome the problems. When a man reached twenty-eight, it was time he was married and thinking of a home and family of his own. Well, he must put thoughts of Kate behind him. She had chosen someone else. The trouble was that Lottie reminded him of Kate in some strange way he couldn't fathom. Not in looks, not in spirit—Kate was pretty and loving and trusted him, or had seemed to. Lottie looked at him askance, not willing to confide in him, probably not liking him at all—the way she'd snatched her hand from his. He meant her no harm. Why should she resent him? And why was he wasting his time pondering on it? He'd best plan his work for the week. There was the warehouse to visit tomorrow and the bank, and perhaps he'd drop in to see the workshop and Ada.

Lottie met Rosemary on Monday morning without any difficulty about finding the way. The map she'd left for her had been very clear. She went into the newspaper office and told the man at the desk her name, and he sent a young lad to fetch Rosemary. Within a few minutes she came down a long flight of stairs, wearing her hat and a little outdoor cloak. She greeted Lottie with a smile, and they left the building together.

'I thought the hairdresser's first,' she said, and led Lottie across Broadway and down a side street. 'I've made an appointment for you.'

Even at this hour of the morning, there were a great many people abroad and all sorts of carriages in the streets.

Once inside the shop, which was spotlessly clean,

Rosemary and Monsieur Charles entered into a quick discussion. Both of them studied the uncomfortable Lottie, commenting on the shape of her face and the lack of any curl at all in her hair.

'I leave her in your hands,' said Rosemary at last. 'I have every confidence in you.'

The hapless Lottie, not quite sure what was going to ensue from this consultation, was left to be ministered to by Monsieur Charles's staff.

A young girl, with the same accent as Mary at the boarding-house, insisted on washing Lottie's hair. It was useless for her to protest that she had done it herself only two days earlier. While it was being dried vigorously and perfumed, another girl put Lottie's fingers into a solution of warm water and scented soap. She then rubbed oil around her nails and tut-tutted about their condition.

When Monsieur Charles approached with his scissors, Lottie was outraged.

'You're not going to cut off my hair!'

'No, no,' he reassured her. 'Just trim it a little. Perhaps a small fringe at the front to make Mademoiselle's face look fuller, to show up her beautiful eyes.'

Lottie closed her beautiful eyes and allowed him to get on with it. She reminded herself that she had asked Rosemary to help her, and Rosemary had gone, promising to come back when she was finished.

Monsieur Charles was quick. Snip-snip went his scissors, and his tongue kept pace with them. Lottie heard about the many wealthy ladies who came to him every week, every two weeks. He was certain she would never regret her decision.

'Mademoiselle isn't married? What an oversight on the part of the male population,' was his verdict. 'It will soon right itself, that!'

Lottie began to smile and then to giggle, and Monsieur Charles complimented her on her dimples —two deep ones either side of her mouth—like little round dots, Kate had always said.

Monsieur Charles fussed about with curling-tongs, and the little girl who had washed Lottie's hair put a concoction of what smelled like strawberries, and tasted of them as well, on her cheeks, saying that it was the very preparation for rough skin.

By the time Rosemary returned, Lottie was so pleased with her reflection in the mirror that she paid Monsieur Charles the five dollars that he asked with scarcely a qualm at such extravagance. It wasn't extravagance, she reasoned firmly with herself, when she looked so much better and felt so much better.

Monsieur Charles had given her the most becoming little fringe, and two kiss-curls on either side of her face. He had swept the rest of her hair into a full, fat chignon at the back of her neck. The whole effect was of feminity, softness. Her eyes did look larger. Even the expression of her face seemed to have changed. She hadn't become a beauty, but there was a piquant look to her. It was the sort of face that one might look at twice. And life had returned to her hair. It was shining. Rosemary exclaimed at it. So did Monsieur Charles and his girls. Lottie was delighted.

Rosemary insisted on treating her to lunch in a very pleasant little eating-house, and she didn't feel out of place even though there were many more men than women customers.

Some of the diners seemed to be known to Rosemary, and they greeted her with a smile or a wave. She told Lottie who they were and what they did—bankers, doctors, lawyers, managers—she appeared to know a good deal about them.

By coffee time, Lottie was feeling quite relaxed, and that was when Rosemary shot a question at her. 'What's Adam hiding?'

Lottie choked. 'Is he hiding something?'

'I'd say so.'

'What sort of thing? Is he in trouble?' She couldn't explain how worrying she found that thought.

'Not money trouble, I'm sure. He seems quite affluent. He must be, to afford Mrs O'Rourke's rent and manage to send money to England for a bride.' Rosemary set down her cup. 'I thought it was because his girl was coming that he was in such a state of excitement.' She frowned, and Lottie waited for more.

'She hasn't come, and he's still worked up, pleased with himself somehow—like the cat with the cream. I know it's none of my business. You don't have to tell me.' Her smile was charming. 'Perhaps he'll tell you about it—or maybe he has already?' She looked enquiringly at Lottie.

'All he's told me is that he means to help me, whether I want him to or not.'

Rosemary laughed at that. 'I can just hear him saying it. Once our Adam sets his mind on a course, he sticks to it. That's a good sign for you. It shows he feels responsible for you.'

'I don't want him to feel responsible for me!'

'Don't be like that. If friendship is what he offers, take it. You can build on that. You're a girl from home. That counts for a lot with Adam.'

Lottie didn't point out that that wasn't the way she wanted to count with Adam—in fact, she wasn't sure that she wanted to count at all.

'We mustn't sit here all afternoon chatting, however pleasant it may be. The next stop is some new clothes for you. How much are you prepared to spend?'

It was difficult to know how to reply. The precious twenty-five dollars which had seemed a fortune on the other side of the Atlantic was fast dwindling away. Ten dollars was gone with her rent for the week and to pay Monsieur Charles. Lottie had ten dollars carefully saved over the years; hers to spend as she liked. When she suggested this sum, Rosemary's eyebrows lifted.

'It's not very much. It'll be a challenge. You'll need more than one dress, of course, but it'll be a start. We'll look!'

And look they did. In and out of big shops and little shops, Rosemary wouldn't let them give up. When Lottie asked if she didn't have to get back to work, she brushed that aside.

Then they found the frock that Rosemary decreed she must try. It was cotton with a shiny finish, a deep tawny colour. 'The colour of your eyes,' was how she described it.

Lottie tried it on. The girl who stared back at her from the mirror was a far more exciting creature than the one who had landed from the *Black Swan*. She drew in her breath.

'It's perfect,' she agreed. 'But it's a plain colour—it will mark!'

'It suits you.' Rosemary was firm. 'You'll just have to be careful. After all, it's cotton, so you'll be able to sponge out any stains and wash it when it needs it.

'It's twelve dollars!' Lottie bit her lip.

Rosemary winked at her, and began to haggle with the saleswoman–owner. They struck a bargain at ten dollars ninety-nine cents, and the woman produced a small straw bonnet for another dollar.

'She'll wear them,' Rosemary decreed. 'Wrap her other dress up.'

'There's someone I want you to see.' Rosemary stilled Lottie's protests as they left the shop. 'You want a job, don't you? I have a friend who's the manager of the best shop in town. We'll just go in and see him.'

By five o'clock a bemused Lottie was back at Mrs O'Rourke's boarding-house. She mounted the stairs to her room in the quiet house, determined that there was something she must do before this astonishing day was over. No one else was around. Now was the very time. She put her parcel down on the bed and took off her new hat, patting her hair into place before the little mirror on the dressing-table. Oh, it did suit her!

She still had that piece of bread she'd taken from the café on Saturday when Adam had fed her. It was hidden in a handkerchief in the top drawer, and she took it out. Of course it was hard and stale, but she didn't need to hoard it any longer. She'd go out and give it to the birds. It was a sin and a shame to waste anything.

Down the stairs she went again, out to the back garden, glad that there was no one to watch her. She broke the bread into tiny pieces and scattered it on a bit of grass by the path, noting that most of the space was planted with vegetables. In the May sunshine, she could see the first green growth of carrots and potatoes and beets and onions. It was very peaceful.

There was a wooden bench near one of the sheds. She'd go and sit on that, and watch the birds at their feast. She sank on to it, glad to be able to think over the events of the day. Suddenly Adam came out of the door of the shed and scowled down at her.

'What are you doing here, then?'

She couldn't understand why he looked so cross. 'Just feeding the birds. Why are you here?'

The birds, of course, had fled at this interruption a few feet away from them.

Adam looked at the crumbs. 'Ay, someone's put down bread.'

'I have.'

He grinned. 'I'll be bound it's that piece of bread you snaffled on Saturday! Didn't think I'd seen you, did you?'

Mortified, Lottie admitted that she hadn't.

'Why are you throwing it away?'

'I shan't need it,' she answered with as much dignity as she could muster.

'Oh, ay! Come into a fortune, have you?'

'No, better than that,' Lottie laughed. 'I have a job.'

Far from being pleased at this news, he frowned at her. 'I thought you were resting up for a few days.'

'I'm rested enough.'

Adam looked at her carefully. 'Ay, you are proper gradely, I'll grant you that. You've cleaned up nicely. Your hair shines in the sun and your eyes look clear. That colour suits you. I've never seen you wear anything like that before. Where's this job, then?'

Lottie was torn between indignation and disappointment at his reaction to her new appearance. At least he'd noticed it—when it had been pointed out to him! But she was too excited about the job to hold back on it.

'At the Mart. Rosemary knows the manager there, and we went to see him.'

'I knew naught of this,' Adam commented sharply.

Lottie might have said that he knew nothing of the rest of the day's happenings either, but she refrained.

'You'll do well there,' he conceded. 'No reason why you shouldn't.'

'No reason at all,' she agreed, more than a little miffed at his lack of enthusiasm. She had supposed he'd be delighted to have her settled and off his hands. 'There's only one thing. They don't want me to start for six weeks. Still, I'll find something from the advertisements in the newspaper to tide me over, like. Rosemary says they run them every day. I'll read through them tonight.'

'No,' he said, 'there's no need to do that. I'll give you work.'

'What sort of work? I'm not a tailor like you.' Lottie was surprised by the quickness of his offer.

'You can sell, can't you?' he demanded. 'You can sell for me—from my workroom.'

'And you'll pay me?'

'Of course I'll pay you! How much are they offering you at the Mart?'

'Nine dollars a week—and commission.'

He whistled. 'You must have impressed them.'

'I think Rosemary did. She told the manager all about interviewing me, and how I'm going to be in tonight's paper, and he was very interested and very kind. He's ever such a nice man.'

'Young?'

'No, middling. About forty, I suppose. Very tall and broad-shouldered, handsome.'

'Liked him, did you?'

'Ay, seemed a fair man, good to work for.'

'I don't know whether I can pay you that much,' Adam shrugged, 'but I can go some way towards matching it. What if I start you at seven?'

Lottie wasn't sure that she wanted to work for him. 'And commission?' she suggested. 'If there was commission, I could start paying you back a dollar or two a week, maybe.'

After a minute, he agreed, 'I suppose that's fair. The more you earn, the more I sell. Done.'

'Should we shake hands on it, or exchange thrupenny bits? Something to show it's an agreement?'

He laughed. 'First there's something I have to explain to you—about the work.'

She turned her eyes from three white butterflies hovering over the cabbage plants. What had Rosemary said about a secret? 'What?' she asked baldly.

Adam, who had seemed so sure of himself up till now, hesitated. 'You must promise not to tell anyone.'

Lottie looked at him, perplexed. 'The Adam I knew back in Rochdale wouldn't have anything to do with something dishonest. All right, I promise. What is it?'

'I meant Kate to be the first one I told.'

She felt a swift stab of pain. It always came back to Kate, just when she was thinking she felt close to Adam.

'She didn't come. You did,' he went on. 'I like to think she would have thrown her arms about my neck and kissed me, and then helped me in every way she could to get started with my invention.'

'Happen she would have,' Lottie agreed, and added grimly, 'if she'd come.' She resented him harping on it. 'Out with it, lad,' she directed, 'if we're not to stand here all evening.'

'Ay, it's an invention. I've invented a sewing-machine!' He looked at her, waiting for her reaction.

'A sewing-machine?' Lottie had never heard of such a thing. 'Does it work? How does it work?'

'Of course it works! You should see the work it gets through in a day. You will see the work it does. I'll show you—there's two, right here in this shed.' He indicated the wooden building behind him.

There was so much suppressed excitement about him that she was impressed. 'Two—is that all there are?' She frowned. 'But if it works so well, why aren't there more? Every woman in the world would be glad to have one. Does it really mean, Adam, that hand-sewing is gone for ever?' Lottie wanted to believe in it, but she couldn't quite.

'Ay, Lottie, if we can get the money for a factory to turn them out. But first it's only on a small scale: two here, four in my workroom, and more promised. That's why I need some selling help. We'll be turning out such quantities of garments, good quality things—I'm doing it already!'

'But that's wonderful!' She began to see the possibilities of his invention. If it was only half as good as he thought . . . 'It will free women. The world will be clothed, and they'll have shorter hours and more leisure.'

Lottie got to her feet, and put her hand on Adam's arm. 'Show me.'

He put his other hand on top of it. 'Presently. Tomorrow I'll teach you how to operate one here. You can start right away, can't you?'

'Yes! Yes, I can.' She thought he must have forgotten that he'd told her to take a few days off. 'I thought I was going to be selling, not operating a machine.'

'So you are, but there's a lot to learn first. I don't suppose you know anything about cutting or costing? You'll have to master those, so that you can answer questions and keep us in profit. Margins are narrow.'

Lottie could understand that, and nodded. 'Will I be in the workroom for a few days, then?'

'No, here in the shed with me. I'm going to teach you myself.'

'Just you and me—in that shed?' She removed her hand from his grasp.

'And the machines,' Adam added. 'You needn't worry about your virtue! You'll be safe with me.'

She bridled. He needn't remind her about how he felt

towards her! 'What are the hours?' she enquired as calmly as she could.

'Eight to six, every day but Sunday.'

'No, this sewing-machine is meant to change all that. Half eight to half five, and half four on Saturdays.'

Adam looked at her in astonishment. 'Have you taken leave of your senses, lass?' Didn't she understand he hadn't made his fortune yet, or turned into a philanthropist? 'Who works those kinds of hours?'

'The salesmen who came to Higginbottom's didn't work as long hours as we did. Besides, even if I'm not selling yet, once a working day is established, it doesn't get any shorter. I know that, and you know that.'

He was taken aback. He stood looking down at her. She had some spunk to stand up to him—and nerve, too, when he was doing her a favour. They were doing each other a favour, he corrected. Still, who would have thought that bedraggled slip of a girl whom he'd met from the ship two days ago would manage to look at him as she was doing now? She was different somehow even from the way he remembered Lottie Earnshaw. Surely her eyes had never been so big before, her hair so shining, her complexion so clear? And that colour frock suited her—she'd made a good choice there. She was smiling at him, confident that he'd give way. There was something provocative about that smile. Lottie provocative? It didn't fit, somehow. What had got into the girl?

'You have a grand idea of your own importance,' he told her, capitulating before that clear gaze. 'I hope it's justified.' He couldn't have said why he hadn't immediately told her that he wasn't going to stand for her conditions.

'It's agreed, then?'

'Ay, it's agreed. But we'll review it, like, if things

don't work out.' He wasn't going to look like putty in her hands.

'Can I see the machine now?'

'Tomorrow'll be soon enough.'

Lottie's face fell, and he almost relented. No, better not. If she was going to be working so closely with him, best let her see he was boss.

'You're looking hot, lass, and tired. Off and have a wash before your meal.'

'Ay, Adam,' was all she said before she left. She turned from him and walked back up the garden towards the house. Did he imagine it, or was there a dejected droop to her shoulders? He had dismissed her rather sharply. She'd have to get used to his ways.

CHAPTER FIVE

AT EIGHT-THIRTY the next morning, Lottie went to the shed in the back garden. Adam was already at work, and a big pile of material lay on the bench beside him. He looked up.

'Come here,' he instructed, and she had her first glimpse of his invention, the sewing-machine! She was secretly a little alarmed.

It stood black and strange on a wooden structure, and she could see there was some sort of thing on which Adam's feet rested.

'The treadle,' he explained. 'It's what makes the machine work. I've walked a hundred miles or more on it.'

She watched, fascinated, as the needle which formed the top part of the machine entered the cloth and left it, leaving a perfect row of stitches, each one exactly the same as the last.

'Do you never catch your fingers?' she asked, as Adam's steady hand guided the material.

'No, and you must watch that you don't,' was his quick response. 'Try it for yourself.' He got up.

Lottie sat down on the bench he had vacated. He leaned over her, his hands on hers, allowing an old piece of cotton to be taken towards the moving needle. She would have withdrawn her fingers, except that he held them fast. Then the piece of cloth was through, and they were intact. She giggled nervously.

Adam still stood behind her, his hands leaning on the work surface. Close to him like this, she felt overpowered. Of course it wasn't his nearness, she told herself, but because the machine was strange to her, and it made such a noise, too. Still, she could smell the masculine scent of him, feel his hard body behind her pressing against her back.

She bit her lip and tried to concentrate on what she was doing. She must put him out of her mind and think of something else. She could still see the expression on Dorothea's face when she had come in to the dining-room last night and caught sight of her. If Adam hadn't noticed much about her appearance, Dorothea certainly had. She'd complimented her on her hair and on her frock, and there had been a great deal of curiosity in her questions about where Lottie had had her hair done and why.

Yes, she had felt rather pleased with herself last night. Rosemary's write-up had been in the newspaper, and she'd been able to tell both girls about Adam's offer of a job to carry her over until the offer from the Mart came through. Dorothea had drawn in her breath over that.

'Keep your mind on your work!' Adam directed from behind her. 'Keep the line of sewing straight, and a nice even action on the feet.'

Lottie found it hard to keep the line straight, and couldn't help thinking that she was sewing with her feet, not her hands. She broke the thread several times by starting too quickly, and then had to rethread. Adam remained patient, and said that she would soon master the technique. He sat down at another bench, and she saw that there were, as he had said, two machines. He began working. After a while, he gave her a sleeve to do, and then another, and another.

By ten o'clock, a growing pile of sleeves rested at her elbow. Then he suggested that she tack them on to bodices, and showed her how, but he wouldn't allow her to do those on the machine.

They stopped for lunch, a quick sandwich eaten in the fresh air on the bench in the garden. Even then, the lessons went on. Adam told her the kinds of garments they were making, both in the shed and at the workroom —little girls' frocks, pantaloons, men's nightshirts and smocks—how much they cost, and what profit he expected to make. This, at least, was something Lottie had experience of, although the money was new to her and she kept trying to think of it in terms of shillings and pence.

'You must put that nonsense out of your head.' Adam was firm. 'It's dollars and cents we're talking about.'

'Yes, Adam,' she agreed meekly, and wondered if she'd ever manage to learn it all.

For the rest of the day, she alternated between tacking and sewing, and between them they cleared a good deal of work. By the time Adam called a halt, she found her back was aching and her legs glad to stop.

'We've done well today, Lottie,' he said, covering his machine with a piece of canvas. 'You're a grand worker. What do you think of the machine? It's splendid, isn't it?'

He looked and sounded so much like a little lad pleased with a new toy, that Lottie warmed to him.

'Ay,' she replied. 'How did you come to invent it?'

'It took quite a time.' He gave her a piece of sacking to use as he had done. 'People have been thinking about such a thing for years. In fact, they say a Frenchman made one fifty years ago or more, and he destroyed it.'

'Why would he do such a thing?' Lottie held the sacking in her hand.

'Tailors thought they'd lose their jobs and their livelihood. If he hadn't destroyed it, they would have.'

'But that's terrible!' she breathed. Her eyes grew larger. 'Could that happen here?'

Adam shrugged. 'I don't think so. Here in America they like to save themselves work. They admire new ideas—but just the same, the fewer folk who know about it now, the better.' A dreamy look came into his eyes. 'One of these days we'll have a proper factory making them. I'm looking for premises now, and money to back it.'

'How can you get money if you don't let people know about the machine?' Lottie asked practically.

'That's one of the difficulties,' he admitted. 'So far, the workroom has paid for the making of the machines, and the machines are paying for more machines, and maybe more workrooms. I'll be a rich man one day, Lottie, but it takes such a time! Still, that's how I felt when I couldn't get the thread to loop properly from the needle. I almost gave up, then. It was Ada's father who encouraged me to persevere. Now Ada runs my workroom for me. You'll meet her later on this week.'

'What's she like, this Ada?' Lottie's curiosity was aroused. Mary had told her about her.

'She's a small girl, a dark beauty. I don't know what I'd do without her. She's Italian, and has only Italian girls working for her. They don't speak much English, and that's good. It keeps the machines a secret.'

Lottie frowned, and tucked the covering over her machine. 'But if you told folk, they'd lend you cash for a factory.'

'Maybe, but it's not the time yet. I'll know when it is. Don't get any ideas in your head about telling Rosemary. Remember your promise.'

'Ay,' said Lottie. 'Happen you're wrong, though.' Her first thought had been of Rosemary.

'That's as may be. Are you always right about everything, Lottie?' Adam was sorting the finished garments into stacks.

'Of course not,' she retorted. For a moment she thought he meant to remind her that she had been wrong about him.

'Why did you part with that candlestick?' His tone was light and conversational.

She didn't ask what candlestick—she knew perfectly well which one he meant. Her face flushed, but couldn't tell him.

'Nay, Lottie, you shall tell me,' Adam went on. 'I knew the other day that there was more to the story than you were telling.'

Lottie sat there, opening her mouth and then closing it again without saying a word. Adam might not have noticed her new hair-do and her new frock, but he knew something about her reactions. She wouldn't have thought he'd have noticed.

'I can just see Kate giving you that candlestick,' Adam was smiling at her now, 'and saying it was her link with you.'

There it was again—Kate. Would he never stop thinking about her, mentioning her? How had he guessed just how it had been?

'What if she did?' Lottie found her tongue. 'It was mine to do as I pleased with.'

'And you gave it away? Never! What really happened?'

He waited for her to reply, but she sat mute. It was none of his business.

'You don't want to tell me.' He moved some sleeves from his bench and tied them in a bundle. 'That's answer enough. 'You certainly didn't give it to Angelina. It's Paolo who has it!'

She nodded miserably, her defences crumbled. She wouldn't lie to Adam.

He was looking at her kindly. 'I suppose he wheedled it out of you—told you some hard-luck story—and you handed it over. Well, it's not the first time a lass has been taken in by a handsome face.'

'It wasn't like that. I didn't give it to him, if you must know.' She gulped down a lump in her throat. 'He took it,' she whispered. 'At least, I think he did. He was minding my case. He's the only one who could have. He must just have slipped it out and put it in his pocket.' In a way, it was a relief to talk about it.

'When did you know it was gone? When you un-packed your case?'

'No, before that—on the boat.' She might as well admit the whole thing now. 'I opened the case again, you see, for my white gloves—I wanted to look clean when I arrived—and it was gone then.'

Adam might have made a sharp remark about white gloves being ridiculous in the circumstances of Lottie's arrival, but he passed over that as if he hadn't heard it.

'Did you tax him with it then? Ask him to return it?'

Lottie shook her head and bit her lip.

'Why not?'

'He'd been so good to me. I couldn't bring myself to accuse him. I had no proof.'

'You could have made him turn out his pockets.'

'No!' She felt as if the denial was forced out of her. 'He was my friend.'

'A friend wouldn't have done such a thing.'

That was so exactly what she felt that her eyes filled, and she rubbed them angrily. She wasn't going to cry.

'Lottie, Lottie!' Adam came over to her and put his hand on hers where it lay on top of the covered machine.

'Taken in by the first man you meet—I suppose it's only to be expected.'

She almost allowed herself to be moved by that sympathetic touch. It would be so pleasant to be comforted by Adam, but she resented looking foolish in his eyes. She pushed his hand away and tried to defend Paolo.

'He must have needed money.' She squared her shoulders. 'I would have given it to him if he'd asked.'

'Would you, indeed?' Adam stood looking down at her. 'It's worse than I thought. It's a good thing I'm here to look after your interests. You don't seem to have much sense about it yourself.'

Lottie wasn't going to be taken in charge like a wilful child! 'At least I got here with most of my property intact. I understand you were robbed of yours when you arrived,' she snapped.

Adam drew back. 'It taught me a valuable lesson— not to trust anyone. The same can't be said for you.'

They glared at each other.

Lottie's eyes dropped first. She shouldn't have taunted him. It was unfair to remind him of something he wanted to forget. She almost told him she was sorry, but his next words removed all thoughts of apology from her.

'I mean to take a brotherly interest in you, in spite of that chip on your shoulder,' he said. 'Kate would expect as much of me.'

She drew in her breath. She wished desperately she hadn't agreed to work for him for six weeks, and reminded herself that it was only a short period and she needed to earn. The sooner she cleared her debt with him, the better.

'I'm perfectly able to look after myself,' she told him, curbing her anger as best she could in the knowledge that if they quarrelled all the time, the six weeks would be

unbearable. She vowed to prove that statement to him.
She was able to look after herself.

'We'll see,' said Adam, a little more mildly. 'I'll tell
you one thing. If that Paolo fellow ever gets in touch with
you, I'll have something to say to him.'

Lottie let that pass. It seemed unlikely that she'd ever
see Paolo again, let alone hear from him. She rose from
her bench.

'Is that all?' she asked, and glanced at the fob watch
pinned to her bosom. 'It's ten past five.'

'Ay,' Adam agreed. 'I wonder he left you that!' He,
too, looked at the watch. 'I don't suppose it would fetch
much . . . Still, as you point out, we're talking in your
time. Off you go then. See you tomorrow.'

Lottie tried to make a dignified exit, her head high.

Adam packed the completed garments into a soft sack.
They'd be pressed in the workroom, and any hand-
sewing done there. He'd have to see they received them
tomorrow. He sat down to number them and check the
cost against a ledger he kept in the drawer, but as he
dipped his pen in the ink Lottie's face appeared between
him and the figures on the page.

Eh, but she'd sprung to that Paolo's defence! He had
to admire her loyalty if not her common sense. If she was
half as loyal to him, he'd not complain.

It was funny, but the shed seemed empty without her.
It wasn't that she chattered all the time. She had a soft
enough voice, and those two tiny dimples on either side
of her mouth appeared suddenly when she smiled. He'd
been watching them all the afternoon. Odd the things
you noticed about people when you worked with them.

She'd picked up the machining quick enough for
someone who wasn't in tailoring. He wondered what
Ada'd make of her. Ada was inclined to make up her

mind instantly, and it would certainly create friction if the two of them didn't get along. Still, he could handle that if he had to. Any road, it was only for six weeks.

Whistling, he began to write. Tomorrow he'd let her handle the costing, and see how she got on. He smiled to himself. It was just the thought of company in the shed, sharing the long day, that made him smile to himself. Ay, he'd test her on figures tomorrow.

For Lottie, the week sped past. By Friday, she'd mastered the intricacies of selling-price and profit on the little girls' frocks they were assembling, and had learned how many yards of material went into pantaloons and petticoats and men's nightshirts, and could make a shrewd guess about the quality of the cloth.

Adam seemed pleased enough with her progress to let her accompany him to the shops he supplied. His delivery boy, Danny O'Brien, came to the door of the shed that morning with a wooden cart on four wheels. It was loaded with completed garments tied in big bundles.

Danny was a gangling boy of fifteen or so, thin and rather ragged, but his face and hands were clean, and he wore boots. Old boots, to be sure, but Lottie soon noticed that some of the other delivery lads were barefoot, and much younger than him.

'You can put your faith in Danny,' Adam informed her as they walked along behind him. 'He's Ada's cousin, even if he has an Irish name. He's honest and he's strong. He'll see you come to no harm, and he knows all the places I deal with. He'll take you to them, when you're on your own.'

Danny fell back with them as they crossed a street. 'That's right, isn't it, Dan?' Adam asked him.

He gave Lottie a considering look. 'I ain't worked for no woman before.'

'Nonsense!' Adam was firm. 'You trot back and forth for Ada to the wholesalers all the time.'

'Ada—that's different. I'm me own boss with her.' His voice was half Irish, half the nasal twang that Adam adopted most of the time like Dorothea and Rosemary.

Adam only laughed at this answer. 'I have no doubt you'll be your own boss one of these days. In the meantime, you'll take orders from Miss Earnshaw.'

'She's your young lady, is she?' Danny manoeuvred the cart round an obstruction of boxes lying in the way. 'Well, I'll give it a try.'

Lottie was more than a little taken back by this exchange. This wasn't the way delivery boys talked to their employers back home in Rochdale, but as Adam seemed to accept it, she said nothing.

Deliveries were made to the back doors of shops down small alleys, and even though Adam had said orders had been placed the previous week, a great deal of bargaining over prices went on. The work was always inspected carefully, seams held up to the light, materials felt and pulled at. Lottie was pleased to see that nothing was rejected, and the cash passed into Adam's hands immediately.

She stood quietly, watching, while this ensued, and Danny squatted down on his hunkers in any available space, his eyes on his cart. Whether he listened or not, she didn't know. Could she fit into this world, this masculine world, as Adam had warned it would be? She supposed she would be able to do it gradually, so that her confidence would build up.

Once or twice, when the haggling appeared to be at an impasse, Adam threatened to leave and take the garments elsewhere. He was always called back and a bargain struck.

'What would you do,' Lottie wanted to know, 'if they

actually let you walk out sometime? Would you go back?'

'Never. I'd go somewhere else. It's good work—the very best stitching, well cut. No, I'd try another shop.'

'Ay.' Lottie stored this information away, thinking it was all very well for him to say he'd go somewhere else, but that might take time—valuable time, when there were girls in the workroom to pay every week.

'Never let them think that you're at their mercy,' he went on, as Danny trundled the cart to the next customer's premises. 'You've got to win. You'll find that out as you go along. That's why I've been training you to know costs. You'll be able to judge just when to give way on a price and when not to.'

She hoped she would when the time came, but it surely wouldn't come for another week or two.

All week, Lottie had been wearing her new dress, and that evening she decided she must wash it. Tomorrow she'd wear her old yellow and white sprigged one, and allow time for the new one to dry and be pressed. Adam had said they'd only be working in the shed, anyway. If she got up early, she could get it out on the line in the garden. In the morning, it was another beautiful day, and everything went according to her plan. The new dress was easy to wash, and she hung it on the line in the late May sunshine with a great deal of satisfaction.

It was unfortunate that things began to go wrong after that. Danny arrived with two messages from Ada. The first was that Adam must go there directly to meet a possible backer. The second was that there was a rush order from a shop called Calsey's, who complained they hadn't received an order of men's nightshirts. Ada had managed to get some of her girls to work very late the night before to complete it, and Danny's cart had been loaded up with the garments.

Adam was decisive. He would go to talk to the backer. Lottie must take the nightshirts.

'You have to start some time,' he told her. 'Now's as good a time as any. Danny knows the way. It should be easy enough.'

She thought longingly of her smart dress still wet and hanging in the breeze, but there was nothing for it. She must go as she was.

Danny had nothing to say. He led the way, whistling. He had no worries, she reflected bitterly, as they went through the small streets to Broadway. She had no eyes for the bustle of traffic or even for shop windows. She was busy rehearsing what she'd say.

Adam had said the price was fifty-two cents each, and there were fifty nightshirts and thirty petticoats. He hadn't told her about the petticoats at first. They had been forgotten the day before and were to go at forty-six cents each. She only hoped they would. Privately, she thought they were too plain.

Calsey's proved to be a shop they had not called at the previous day, and they went to a side door.

'You'll be all right if it's old man Calsey,' Danny told her as she hesitated outside. 'But if it's the son, you're done for. He's as mean a man as you'll find.' He opened the door for her.

The man who faced Lottie over the small counter in the dingy room she entered was young, and her heart sank.

Danny wheeled his cart in and made himself inconspicuous in a corner.

'Yes?' said young Mr Calsey. 'Was there something you wanted, miss? I think you've come in the wrong door.' He waved a hand towards her, smiling.

'Customers at the front, you know.'

'I'm not a customer. I'm a supplier—from Adam Hardcastle.'

'Employing a woman, is he? I wonder where he got that idea.' He put his head on one side. 'Cheaper, I suppose. That'll make the garments more reasonably priced—that's very welcome.'

Lottie looked Mr Calsey in the eye, which was a little difficult as he was a good foot taller than she was, and she didn't like the expression in those eyes.

'The garments are reasonably priced. I can't make them any cheaper.'

He rubbed his hands together. 'We'll have to see. They're late getting here. I should have some compensation for that.'

Lottie didn't like the way this was going, but she knew she mustn't let him see he was upsetting her with his bluster.

With a great effort of will, she smiled at him. 'Mr Hardcastle said the price had been agreed between you.'

He had the effrontery to wink at her. 'I like to see a friendly girl! Perhaps we can do business together. Let's have a look at a nightshirt, then.'

She opened up the hatch of the cart and held one up.

'Hold it against you,' he instructed. When she did so, he added, 'How much are you asking for that?'

'Fifty-two cents was the price agreed last week.'

'That was last week. Things have changed.' Mr Calsey took the nightshirt from Lottie, brushing against her as he did so.

'What's changed?'

'Hardcastle's sent a woman.'

He didn't need to remind her of that. She'd been very conscious of it when he'd touched her. Her skin had crawled at that contact.

'The nightshirt's the same,' she told him, keeping her voice even. 'That hasn't changed. Look at the workmanship and the quality of the material.'

Young Mr Calsey held the garment up to the light, staying very close to Lottie. 'I have no quarrel with the work, but Hardcastle should have come himself.'

She shot him an angry glance. 'He sent me! Do you mean to have them or not?'

Young Mr Calsey didn't give her a direct answer. 'What else do you have in the cart—my petticoats?'

Lottie pulled out a petticoat and held it up for his inspection.

He took it and held it against her body, his hands just rubbing against her breasts.

'Very plain, isn't it?'

The touch of his hands had been so light that she told herself it might have been accidental, but there was no mistaking the fact that his eyes were examining her face as he uttered the words, 'Very plain, isn't it?' She blushed, and was furious that she couldn't prevent that tell-tale colour.

'Is that the kind of petticoat you wear?' He was still holding it up in front of her.

'What I wear is no concern of yours!' She stepped to one side, and closed the hatch of the cart.

'How much are you expecting for this?' Mr Calsey felt the garment with a caressing touch. Lottie felt as though he was touching her. She knew that was the way he meant her to feel.

'Forty-seven cents.' Her voice was frosty as she raised the price above the agreed one. 'To you.'

He laughed scornfully. 'What do you take me for?'

Lottie might have retorted that she thought him detestable, a man she wanted nothing to do with, but she had to sell these garments. 'A smart businessman,' she replied, 'who knows quality when he sees it.'

Young Mr Calsey gave her an oily smile. 'Well said! You have a smooth tongue—when you choose to use it. I'm offering forty-one for the petticoats and forty-six for the nightshirts. That's my best offer—to a woman.'

That would take away the entire profit, and she gasped, 'It's not enough.'

'Well, you know your business best. That's all I'm willing to give. It's my final offer.' He threw the petticoat at her. She had to stretch to catch it.

Lottie recognised the finality in his tone. She knew he wasn't going to bargain—not with her. She let her temper go. 'That's not giving,' she stated. 'That's stealing.'

He laughed, and sauntered the few paces back to the counter, where he played with an inkwell that stood there. He shrugged, tracing the outline of the glass with a lazy finger. 'Take it or leave it. I won't go higher.'

'I'll leave it.' Lottie gathered up the two garments, and without bothering to fold them, thrust them back into the cart.

'The girls in the workroom will go short on pay,' he taunted her. 'Hardcastle won't like it. Is he a hard man to please?'

His glance was so insolent as it travelled from her feet to her face that Lottie wanted to kick him.

'Your father won't like going without stock either,' she told him coldly. 'It cuts down on profits.'

'There's no shortage of suppliers,' her tormentor sneered. 'Besides, you'll soon be back and willing to listen to reason. Hardcastle'll probably come himself.'

'Never!' Lottie signalled to Danny to take the cart out. She'd not be back here. Neither would Adam. She'd sell the things somewhere else.

As she moved past young Mr Calsey, her head high,

she wasn't quite sure afterwards how it had happened, but she stumbled. Could he have put out his foot to trip her? At any rate, she reached for the counter to steady herself, and the inkpot somehow showered its contents on to her skirt. She was mortified.

Young Mr Calsey was all attention now, scrubbing away at the inkstain with a dirty rag and spreading the damage further as he apologised profusely. 'What a tragedy! Just one clumsy step, and look what happens. Still, it'll wash out, won't it—it's not as though it's a new dress, is it?' He put his hand on her waist.

Lottie shivered. She couldn't bear his touch. What a hypocrite, when it was his foot that had tripped her, his hand that had held the ink! She was shaking with indignation and anger. She tore herself from his grasp, and as she did so she felt the material in her dress pull and tear. There was a rent in the skirt from waist to knee.

'Now look what you've done!' young Mr Calsey exclaimed. 'That's the price of impulsiveness. You must guard against that.' He took a straight pin from behind the lapel of his jacket and held it out to her. 'Perhaps this will help.'

Lottie snatched it from him. There was only one thing she wanted. That was to be out of there immediately, away from this awful man. She ran to the door and let herself out, his laughter ringing in her ears.

Danny was right behind her. 'Never you mind, miss, you were right to leave. Adam'll say so, too, but he won't like it. What's to do now, then? Sure you'll have to face Adam.'

Leaning against the wall, she breathed hard and looked down at her ruined dress. Thank heaven it was her old one, but what was she to do with the unsold merchandise? She couldn't go anywhere, looking like this. She didn't have anything to change to, except her wine wool, and that was too hot and wintery-looking and a long walk away. She felt like bursting into tears.

'Sure it's no job for a girl, this,' Danny looked anxious. 'I'll tell Adam so myself. I saw that scallywag's foot come out to meet yours. Lucky it was you didn't fall flat on your face, or I would have swung one on him!'

So she was right. He *had* tried to trip her. It was small consolation to know it for a fact. What was she going to do? Admit failure to herself and to Adam? Go back to Calsey's? Never!

Lottie tried to close the rent with the pin, but it was no use. It was too small. Best leave it alone. She threw the pin away. She didn't want anything from that man! She straightened her shoulders and spoke to Danny.

'We're not going back,' she announced. 'We're going to do what Adam would do—go somewhere else.'

Danny looked at her doubtfully. 'You can't go like that.'

'I'll have to,' Lottie replied. 'Just follow me. I'm going to try.'

He shrugged, and put his hand to the shafts of the cart. 'I dunno. Adam said I was to take orders from you. I'll give you a chance, then. I can see you're a fighter. Where are we going? I'd like to see Calsey beaten, so I would.'

'You'll see,' Lottie answered, and set off with what she hoped was a confident step.

CHAPTER SIX

ADAM RETURNED to the boarding-house early in the afternoon and was surprised to meet Rosemary sitting on the front porch.

'The very man I'm looking for!' she greeted him. 'I didn't expect to find you here at this time of day.'

'Nor I you,' he replied. 'What are you doing home?'

'I'm meeting someone here—someone who wasn't prepared to go all the way to the newspaper office. It's wonderful, really, the people who have been writing to me and the paper about coming to New York in the ships. It bears out everything Lottie said, and a good deal more besides. The conditions are really appalling. I'm doing some follow-ups. The editor's pleased with me. Lottie's been lucky for me. That's what I want to speak to you about.' She patted the wooden bench beside her. 'Can you spare me a few minutes?'

'Of course.' Adam sat down beside her. 'I can't imagine where Lottie is now. She should have been back hours ago. I don't know whether to go looking for her or not.' He frowned.

'She'll turn up,' Rosemary assured him comfortably, 'and so will my contact. Lottie's settling down very well, isn't she?'

He agreed that she was, but he would have felt a good deal easier if she'd been in the shed when he looked in. He'd been looking forward to hearing about how she'd got on.

Rosemary smiled at him. 'It's nice that you're taking an interest in her. Some men would just have left her to her own devices, but you're not like that. That's why I feel I can ask you for a favour—for Lottie.'

Adam wondered what was coming next, but reflected that it was good that this woman was taking an interest too.

'Ask away then.'

She didn't ask directly, but hedged round the subject. 'I've wondered about this Paolo she met on the boat. When she spoke of him, she seemed to hold him in some regard—did you think so?'

'Yes,' he replied with some reservations. He wasn't too sure that he wanted to have anything to do with this subject. Certainly Lottie had given him the impression that she had liked the fellow too much—too much for her own good.

'His sister, Angelina, came to see me this morning. She said Paolo had lost Lottie's address and wanted to get in touch with her. I didn't want to give her this address, but I said I'd give Lottie a message.'

Adam nodded. That seemed sensible enough. 'Tell me, what's this Angelina like?'

'A pretty little thing.' Rosemary put her hand on Adam's knee briefly. 'The office boy was quite bowled over by her! She came with a tall blonde girl who hardly spoke a word of English. She said she was part of an act with dogs.'

'I suppose she'd seen the story about Lottie,' Adam interrupted, knowing that Rosemary might go on to tell him about the dogs next.

'Yes. Anyway, Angelina and Paolo, it appears, are in the same show, and when Angelina produced two complimentary tickets for it, I thought of you.' Rosemary sat back as though everything was explained now.

Adam was taken aback. 'You want me to take you to see it?'

'No, no,' Rosemary laughed. 'I can't go on that particular night next week, but I wondered if you'd take Lottie. Wouldn't it be a lovely surprise for her? You wouldn't need to tell her who was performing. Just tell her you want to take her, and ask if she'll go with you. She'll be ever so pleased, and imagine her delight when she sees her friends on stage.' Rosemary was clearly happy about this little conspiracy. 'Angelina was very insistent that Lottie should come backstage afterwards. You could meet Paolo, and decide for yourself what you think of him.'

Adam didn't quite share her enthusiasm. He had already reached a decision about Paolo. He didn't like him. How could he approve of any man who stole a silver candlestick from an infatuated girl? But, just the same, it might be a good idea to go with Lottie. This Paolo sounded as though he'd manage to get in touch with her somehow—better to do it in his presence.

'All right,' he agreed. 'I'll take her.'

Rosemary handed over the tickets. 'If this Paolo is anything like as good-looking as his sister, I can quite understand his attraction for Lottie.'

That thought didn't please Adam. It had nothing to do with him, of course. He was just thinking of Lottie, and hoping she wasn't going to make a fool of herself over a handsome face.

He pocketed the tickets, and went off to the shed in a thoughtful mood. Yes, Rosemary was right about one thing, anyway. He would take Lottie by surprise. Then she couldn't help betraying her reaction to his chap. Yes, that was much the best way.

Lottie looked at the kingfisher blue dress in the window of the shop where she and Adam had seen it only last Sunday. She took a deep breath, and with strict instructions to Danny to wait for her, went in at the door. Without giving herself any time to pause, she went up the stairs to the dress department, and asked to try it on. Rosemary had been right when she said she needed more than one dress. Of course she did, she told herself firmly.

While the shop assistant went to the window to bring it out, Lottie experienced a feeling of considerable panic. Ten dollars and eighty-three cents, the sign had said it cost. It would be Adam's money she was spending on it—if it fitted—if she liked it. It was fortunate that she still carried that money in the belt round her waist.

She waited in an agony of indecision. She was gambling a lot on this frock, but she and Danny had visited two more small shops with the rejected nightshirts with no success. How could she hope to sell anything, with a torn and stained dress to recommend her? She suddenly remembered something Horace Higginbottom had said about a slovenly-looking salesman whom he had turned away. She had protested that his goods were satisfactory.

'Nay, all the world brings good material to Horace Higginbottom,' she'd been told. 'They know they'll sell naught any other road. But a salesman must dress to suit my importance.'

He was right, and she was acting on his advice now. When the assistant helped her into the kingfisher blue, she was certain of it. The girl who stared back at her from the full-length mirror was a different creature from the one who had been turned away by young Mr Calsey. This girl, though not beautiful, nor even pretty as Kate was, had an air about her, a quiet confidence that she looked her best and held herself proudly. The deep bluish-green brought out the soft tawny brown of her eyes and accentuated her long lashes.

'My goodness, it suits you,' murmured the shop assistant. 'Shows off your trim little waist. See how neatly it's gathered on the hips. No crinoline, of course—they may be fashionable, but to my mind they're awkward.'

'Yes.' Lottie only half heard her. She twisted this way and that to see herself to the best advantage. There was a little cape round the shoulders, and it swung most becomingly.

'Of course an added petticoat or two,' the assistant went on, 'would give a fuller silhouette. I'll just fetch one.'

Before Lottie could stop her, the girl was back with one. She couldn't resist looking at it with a professional eye. Why, it wasn't as well made as the ones she was selling!

She smiled at the girl. 'Who does your buying?'

'Mr Polonsky. Ever such a nice man,' she was informed. 'He's a partner, and he has an office on the next floor.'

Lottie stored that information away and refused any extra items of clothing, paid the assistant and thanked her for her attention. She went out of the shop with her old dress neatly parcelled and carried under her arm.

Danny whistled when he saw her. 'Come into money, have you?'

'No, but I'm going to make some!' she told him while she stowed her parcel in the cart and extracted two petticoats. 'Wait here, I'll be back.'

She went back into the shop and up the stairs to the second floor this time.

Luck was with her—as she had been sure it would be. Mr Polonsky, a long thin man with a beard, smilingly declared himself delighted to make her acquaintance. Lottie smiled at him and complimented him on her new dress. She told him how pleased she was with it and what

excellent service she had had from his staff. It was a full
five minutes before she showed him the petticoats. By
then they were friends.

He examined the garments and asked if they could be
trimmed with lace. When she agreed that they could for
an extra ten cents apiece, he told her to bring them back
in a few days and he'd take them all.

She floated down the stairs to the patient Danny.
'We've done it!' she told him. 'I've made the sale.' She
danced around him, explaining.

Danny's face split into a grin. 'I wouldn't be in your
shoes when you tell Ada about the lace! Adam won't be
laughing, either.'

'Why not?'

'More cost, more work.'

'And more profit, too, since the price is up.'

Danny shrugged. 'What if this Polonsky turns you
down when you bring them back? Like Calsey did?'

'He won't.' Just the same, she felt a chill of fear.

'Maybe. Still, that's between you and him. What
about the nightshirts, then?'

The nightshirts took a little longer to sell, but Lottie
had tasted success and wasn't prepared to give up when
the buyer in the next shop wasn't available, or in the one
after that.

Acting against Danny's advice, she tried one more, of
her own choice this time.

'We've never sold to them before,' was his comment,
'and you won't today.'

'Why not?' Lottie hesitated briefly. She liked the look
of the place.

'Quality . . . That's why not. These nightshirts are
meant for the cheaper end of the market.' He held one
up.

She refused to be dissuaded. 'I'll try, anyway.' She

went in at the front door and asked for the buyer, taking a nightshirt with her.

Mr Jones was available. He was a handsome Welsh-man who was delighted to talk to an English girl.

'Not our usual line, *cariad*,' he told her. 'Still, I'll grant you the stitching's good. How many? Fifty, did you say? It's lucky you are, then. Twenty-five I'll take.'

He got them at a penny less than Adam had wanted, but Lottie felt she was breaking new ground here and that was worth something. The remaining twenty-five went at that price, too—also to a shop Adam had never dealt with.

Danny told her she'd do, and he thought Adam would be well enough pleased. He said he'd take the petticoats back to Adam, but she herself would have to explain about them.

Lottie went straight to the shed, not quite sure how Adam would receive her news after all. She walked slower and slower. Her success had seemed very sweet—until now.

The shed door was open, and she could hear Adam machining. Taking a deep breath, she squared her shoulders.

'Where have you been?' was his greeting before she could get her mouth open. 'Did you . . .' He stopped in mid-sentence. 'That isn't what you were wearing this morning! That's the dress we saw last Sunday. Who bought it for you?' He had jumped to his feet and his hand was on her shoulder.

Lottie winced. 'I bought it. And I've sold all the things—well, half sold them.' Her explanation sounded incoherent in her own ears. Fancy Adam noticing the dress.

He took his hand from her shoulder and paced round her. 'It suits you, I'll say that for it!'

Her colour heightened. She felt Adam was really looking at her for the first time. He hadn't seemed all that impressed when she'd bought the first dress after having her hair done. Now her hair had fallen into perhaps a little softer line: the fringe so carefully put up in rags every night curled softly on her forehead; the chignon was a little more supple, as her hair had become in better condition.

'I don't know what you've done,' Adam went on, 'but you look different, somehow. Almost pretty! That colour makes your eyes look bigger.'

He looked so puzzled that Lottie smiled and then began to laugh.

'Eh, lad!' she exclaimed. 'You're a great one with the compliments. Would you say I was presentable now?'

'Ay, cleaned up gradely,' Adam smiled, and his tone was softer. 'I don't understand what happened. Best sit down and start at the beginning.'

Thankfully, Lottie sat down on the bench. Her legs had gone quite weak. It must be reaction to the shocks of the morning; certainly nothing to do with Adam saying she was almost pretty. She began to explain.

Adam banged his fist hard on her work counter when she told him about Mr Calsey and his refusal, and the way her dress had been spoiled.

'I should have known better than to send you there,' he frowned. 'I didn't think he'd be so nasty to a girl. Why didn't you come straight back and change?'

'I only have one other dress,' she was forced to the confession, 'and I'd washed it this morning. Besides, if I'd come back, I'd never have had the guts to try again. There was nothing for it. You'd given me the goods to get rid of. I had to do it.'

Adam nodded at that. 'So you bought the dress out of

your landing money . . . You won't have much left. That was meant to tide you over for a while.'

Lottie knew that: she didn't need him to point it out. A little defensively, she went on with her story.

Adam raised his eyebrows when she told him about trimming the petticoats and taking a penny less on the nightshirts. She couldn't tell from his expression how he felt, and faltered on to the end, naming the new shops she'd sold to. Then she waited for his verdict.

It was slow in coming. 'You've not done too badly, lass.'

From anyone else, that comment might have been daunting, but from Adam, she interpreted it as approval.

'Are you pleased?'

'Ay, you'll do,' he told her. 'It won't go amiss either that you've put young Calsey in his place. It'll be all over town in a few days. I shouldn't be surprised if the old man asks you to call again.'

'How will he know?'

'Danny'll tell another cart-man, I'll be bound—and he'll tell his salesman. The news will travel fast. Young Calsey isn't popular.' He smiled. 'I'd give a deal to see Calsey's face when he hears who you've sold to.'

Lottie felt as though a great weight had been lifted from her shoulders. Adam was pleased with her. He'd told her she'd do—strong words from a Lancashire man. It was strange how he often adopted his native accent when talking to her. Most of the time he spoke with an American twang.

'There's just one thing.' Adam had returned to his machine and picked up a parcel.

Lottie was apprehensive. 'Ay?'

'This parcel's for you.' He surprised her by handing it to her.

'For me? Who'd send me a parcel?' She took it from him.

Adam shruged. 'Why don't you open it and see?'

She felt the parcel cautiously. It was wrapped in paper and tied with string. It was soft to the touch. She opened it carefully.

Inside was a purple blouse, trimmed with lace at the neck. She held it in her hands, liking it instantly, judging the size, which seemed right. Beneath the blouse was a skirt, the background grey, with large purple flowers to match the top.

She stood up, holding it to her. 'It's beautiful!' she exclaimed. 'How in the world—did you . . .' She couldn't go on. She was at a complete loss for words.

Adam smiled. 'Did you think I wouldn't know you needed something to wear? I'm a tailor, after all. I know clothes are important for a salesman.'

'Oh, Adam,' Lottie's lip trembled, 'I don't know how to tell you how pleased I am. I'll be well dressed now —but you shouldn't have . . . I shouldn't take it from you.'

'Don't be daft, Lottie. You have to do credit to Hardcastle's workrooms. Think of it as your uniform.'

'A very pretty uniform.' She held it up to herself again. 'Does it suit, Adam? Will I do you credit??'

'The colour's lovely on you.'

'Did you pick it out?' she asked shyly. What did it matter if he only thought of it as a uniform?

'Ay,' he replied. 'Ada and the girls made it up. Wear it tomorrow when you go to tell her about the lace you want on the petticoats. It'll please her and the girls to see you in it—start you off on the right foot.'

Lottie's spirits fell considerably at that sobering thought. 'You'll not come with me? I haven't met Ada yet.'

'I'll come with you right enough.' He went on, 'But you'll have to break the news to Ada.'

Lottie told herself that couldn't be any worse than what she'd been through today, but she remembered very clearly Danny's reaction. Adam wasn't intending to make things easy for her—that much was evident. Well, she wouldn't let it show that she minded.

'In the shop where I sold the first lot of nightshirts,' she began, determined to place things on a businesslike level, 'they had silk nightshirts and velvet dressing-gowns. Do you think we might try something with a really high-quality material for them? Mr Jones, the buyer, was very nice.'

'Was he?' Adam looked at her. 'A large man with a moustache, is he?'

'No, clean shaven with dark curly hair—quite young —no more than thirty—handsome, too, and ever so soft spoken. The Welsh are, aren't they?'

'Wears silk nightshirts, does he? You must be careful, Lottie, about handsome men! You seem very much impressed by them.'

She drew back at that, incensed. She knew he meant Paolo. 'I can't know what kind of nightshirts Mr Jones wears,' she replied coldly. 'Or if he wears any at all.' At Adam's raised eyebrows, she went on quickly, 'It's a lovely shop. I'd like to keep dealing there.'

'Not if it means silk nightshirts,' Adam said firmly. 'I can see that a bit of success has gone to your head.'

Lottie wasn't going to be talked down. She'd been in selling all her working life. 'They wouldn't have to be silk. What about a very soft cotton—almost a lawn—in a dark colour, navy or black, with a dragon or a tiger embroidered on it in gold and red?' She felt suddenly alive with ideas. The good shops she had visited that afternoon had opened her eyes to all sorts of possibilities. She hadn't really paid much attention to their wares at the time—or thought she hadn't—but now she could close her eyes and see again some of the lovely things they had for sale.

Adam looked at her as though she'd taken leave of her senses. 'We could lose a lot of money that way.'

'Or gain a lot.'

'Learn to walk before you run.'

'Ay, Adam,' she agreed. 'But if you could have seen the stock. Our nightshirts are in striped flannelette. Very well sewn—that's why Mr Jones took them. But he took only twenty-five. There's a big market if we can come up with the right quality.'

'I'll think about it.' His answer didn't suggest he'd think very hard. 'Any other ideas? You'd best think of the practical. Put your mind on aprons and pantaloons—things like that—quick, steady sellers.'

'I have ideas about them, too,' Lottie went blithely on. 'I had a look at aprons. We can surely do better than those cheap flowered ones in Calsey's window.'

'We sold them to him,' Adam observed drily.

'All the more reason to come up with something better for a competitor!' Lottie scarcely paused with her retort.

He laughed. 'All right, you're a woman. I'm willing to admit you might know something about aprons. Draw me a picture of what you have in mind, and I'll see what can be done with it.'

'Now?'

'There's no time like the present.' Adam tore off a piece of the brown paper that had wrapped her new outfit, and produced a stub of pencil from a pocket.

She took them from him and sat down. She thought for a moment as he went back to machining, then settled to it. The outline she produced was of a full-length apron. After all, any woman wanted to protect the whole of her skirt and bodice. She sketched a frill round it, and thought to herself that eyelet embroidery would do very well for that. The neckline was heart-shaped, and she added a bow to it, then ties of the same material as the apron to hold the whole thing in place. She sat back and looked at it before handing it across to Adam.

'I'll have the pencil.' He was looking at the drawing carefully.

She rose to give it to him, and stood by his bench, to watch as he amended it. The neckline became square the frill less pronounced.

'Why? Why have you done that?'

'Cost. I don't deny that yours looks fine, but these few changes will make more profit.'

'Ye—es, but they may not catch a woman's eye in the same way. You may not sell so many.'

'We'll have to chance that.' He smiled at her.

'Are you . . . Are you really going to use it?' Lottie was pleased, in spite of the changes.

'Why not? I'm always open to new ideas. I'll take you with me when I go to the wholesaler tomorrow, and we'll pick the materials. Were you thinking of plain white?'

'No, I was not thinking of plain white.' She was taken aback at the very idea.

Adam didn't seem to resent her forthright answer. 'Stripes, perhaps? I know where we can get some cheaply.'

'Not stripes. That would look too much like a butcher apron.'

'Flowered? A dark background? Come on, tell me how you see it.' His smile was friendly. 'Here, sit beside me' —he made room for her on the bench—'and tell me.'

'How many are we going to make?' Lottie found it rather pleasant to be so close to him and to be consulted.

'Twenty is a good number. Then, if they go well, we can always make up more.'

'What about ten plain ones in a dark colour with flowered trim, and ten flowered with a dark frill or even rick-rack braid?'

'Yes, right. Take the pencil, and we'll cost it out.' Adam tore off another sheet of brown paper.

An enjoyable half-hour followed in which Lottie was measured as model and then had to write yardages and possible prices against a variety of choices.

When they had finished their calculations, Adam put his hand on her knee. A tremor of excitement shot through her as he exclaimed, 'Well done, lass! It's great to have someone to talk this kind of thing out with.'

Adam's hand rested on Lottie's knee for only a second. She told herself that it was his words that had pleased her, not the touch of his fingers. But, just the same, she felt very close to him. She didn't know how he felt, or indeed if he felt anything at all, so his next words surprised her considerably.

'You should see something of the town, Lottie. Do you ever get out with the girls?'

When she shook her head, he continued, 'I know you've made quite an impression on Rosemary. She was telling me only today that her editor is very pleased with the public's reaction to the interview she did with you. She knows everything that goes on here. She and Dorothea go to some sort of organisation for working girls. Why don't you ask if you could go along with them?'

'Yes, I will.' Lottie thought it a good idea. It was kind of Adam to mention it.

Since he seemed so approachable, she asked the question that had been in the back of her mind.

'How did your morning go? Did the man you talked to want to become a backer?'

'No, he didn't want to take any risks—particularly not with me. He wanted a sure return on his money, not to invest it in a harebrained idea. That's what he told me. But even if he hadn't, I didn't like the looks of him.'

'Why not?'

'I want an honest partner. There has to be some kind of trust—even in the business world.'

Lottie drew back at that. Poor Adam, he had looked for trust with Katie, and Katie had sent her sister. She tried not to feel guilty, but couldn't help herself.

'How much does it cost to make each machine?'

'The first one cost twenty-three dollars. That wasn't taking into account my time. The next three averaged about twenty apiece. If I could get a proper factory going, it should be less.' He frowned. 'Why?'

Lottie felt even guiltier. 'If I hadn't used the sixty dollars you sent for fare and landing money, you could have three more machines.'

'Ay, about that.' He didn't say it accusingly, but as fact.

'I'm sorry, Adam. I've made it harder for you. But when the money came and Katie didn't want it, I never thought what a sacrifice it had been for you to send it. I only thought that you could afford it—that in America, money was easy to earn.'

'Streets paved with gold,' he laughed. 'What's done is done. Eh, lass, don't look so downcast. I'll manage somehow. Get back to thy machine. The day's going, and the work's still here.'

Lottie went back to her bench, and Adam watched her go. He liked that she had thought of his feelings, however late. If she hadn't come . . . No use thinking of that.

Here she was, and doing her best to help. Ay, and spending more money! That was unfair—she'd been right plucky to go on with her dress torn and dirtied. Eh, she was a fighter.

He picked up the garment he was making. He'd been going to ask her to come to the concert with him, and at the last moment had suggested instead that she go to the Working Girls' Meeting with the others. Why had he done that? She was bound to say Yes, wasn't she? She didn't have anywhere else to go of an evening.

Rosemary had put him in a funny position—all unwittingly, of course. She didn't know how it was between Lottie and himself. But how was it between Lottie and himself? He pondered on it, as his fingers guided the material and his feet kept up their steady treadling.

She was easy to talk to, interested in everything. She had a lively mind, always had had. If he wasn't careful, she'd think she had some sort of claim to him. No, best keep their relationship on a firmer basis. She worked for him. That was all. Why had he been so disappointed when she hadn't been waiting for him on his return? He'd worried about her.

It was clear there was no need for that. She was well able to look after herself. But she was vulnerable to handsome men, and he'd warned her. She hadn't liked it, either. Thought he was interfering. Well, he intended to go on interfering. She was Kate's sister, a girl from home. He owed her that much.

He'd ask her to the concert later, nearer the time. Slip it into some conversation casually, as though it didn't matter. Of course it didn't matter.

Adam looked across at Lottie's head bent over her work. If she wanted this Paolo and he took a liking to him, no reason why she shouldn't have him. That thought unsettled him a little. He just wanted to be sure she had a secure future. Ay, he'd have to have a look at him.

Adam sighed, and dismissed the subject from his mind. She was taking up too much of his time when he had other worries. There was this business of a backer, and Lottie must talk to Ada tomorrow. That made him smile a little. Who'd come out victor there? His money was on Ada.

CHAPTER SEVEN

LOTTIE WORE her new skirt and blouse when she reported
to the shed the following morning. She liked them, and
felt they suited her very well.

Adam had breakfasted earlier, so Rosemary,
Dorothea and she ate together. Rosemary had complimented her. Dorothea gave her a very considering
look as she murmured that the colour suited her, but she
thought flowered skirts drew attention to a girl. Lottie
smiled, and asked if that wasn't what clothes were meant
to do.

Dorothea brushed that aside. 'It depends on the type
of girl, doesn't it?'

Lottie wasn't quite sure what kind of girl she referred
to, but she could make a good guess and didn't feel
flattered.

She felt further deflated when she arrived at the shed,
for Adam bestowed only a rather cursory glance on her,
and said that some sleeves must be finished before they
set out and she'd better get to work immediately. When
he began to bundle them up and declared they'd have to
carry them with them, her heart sank. The bundles were
rather large.

Lottie would have liked to have gone back to the
house for her bonnet before they set out, but Adam
wouldn't hear of it.

'Ladies wear bonnets in the streets,' she was informed. 'Not sewing-hands. Besides, you don't need
one. You don't want to look too dressed up, or the
wholesaler will raise his price.'

Gone was yesterday's easy camaraderie, and she wondered what she'd done to effect the change. She protested no more, but accepted her load, and Adam locked up the shed as they set out.

The streets they went through soon became crowded and were much less pleasant than Jones Street where they lived. The buildings were taller, dingier and closer together, and ragged children were playing, darting past them in games of tig or simple chasing. Lottie was surprised to see chickens cooped in slatted boxes right on the street. They had little room for movement. She thought chickens should have been scratching in the dirt in a field.

'They're fattening them for the pot.' Adam had noticed where her gaze was fastened. 'They live all their lives like that. The children guard them, sometimes torment them.'

Lottie brushed past one of the boxes, and a tall scrawny boy rose to his feet protectively from where he had been crouched against the wall. She shuddered and moved on quickly, as there was so much menace in his pose. Adam went straight ahead, leading the way in twisting lanes and passages. They went through an alley among the dirtier buildings until he announced that they'd reached the warehouse.

Inside the big shell of the building, materials were everywhere: in piles on benches and rickety shelves and tables. It all seemed in such disorder to Lottie's eyes that she wondered how anything could be found. But found they were. Adam appeared to know instinctively where to look, and the little fat shabby man who served them was even swifter.

In very little time, suitable lace was found for the petticoats, and the price haggled over to the satisfaction of both parties. Flowered cotton was produced as if by

magic, and gingham discarded in place of printed calico.
At a nod from Adam, Lottie made her choices among
them and the bargaining was concluded.

As a mark of favour towards a female, she supposed, a
small remnant of purple velvet was added to the pile with
a friendly smile directed towards her by the fat man.
Lottie acknowledged the gift with a murmured 'Thank
you', and noticed it was the same shade as her blouse.

Then they were out again, even more laden down.
Fortunately they had not far to go. Just down another
ginnel and up three flights of stairs to the workroom.
Lottie reached it thankfully, by now hot and breathless.

Adam opened the door on to a smallish room not
much bigger than the dining-room at Mrs O'Rourke's. It
was crowded with girls of all shapes and sizes, some at
machines, some stitching by hand. There was a great
deal of chattering, and it was hot—hotter than the
streets outside.

Suddenly, they all hushed as they looked at Adam,
and more particularly at Lottie. She felt she was being
inspected.

A small red-headed girl darted towards Adam and
threw her arms around him, bundles and all. She broke
into a torrent of Italian. Lottie knew it was Italian, and
could even pick out a few words, because Angelina had
tried to teach her some of the language. She knew from
the tone of voice that the girl was angry. She was asking
why—why—something had been done, but Lottie
didn't understand what she meant.

Adam spoke to her softly, and she swung to face
Lottie, scowling.

'Magdalena Mendoza, Charlotte Earnshaw.' Adam
put his parcels on the table.

The two girls surveyed each other, Lottie still hugging
her burden to her.

'Magdalena?' she questioned. 'Aren't you Ada?'

The other girl gave her a glance of fiery scorn from pansy-coloured eyes with long dark lashes. 'Ada is my working name, but I am Magdalena.' She patted her hair.

Lottie marvelled at that hair. It could be called red, but bright auburn would describe it more accurately, as it gleamed red and gold and copper in the sunshine from the one large window set high in the wall. Ada had it tied with a large black ribbon at the back, and it fell in one wavy swath to her waist. Around her face, short curls gave her the look, if not the expression, of a painted angel, a veritable cherub.

But this was a woman who faced Lottie—a passionate woman—she could see it in the full lips, the well-rounded bust, the small waist.

If Lottie was studying Magdalena, Magdalena was studying her. 'Not so plain, after all,' was her verdict. 'Not so plain as Adam would have me believe. Turn round then, and let me see how the back fits.' She took the parcel from Lottie and gestured with her hand.

Lottie spun round slowly while the girls and Adam looked on.

'My girls have done well,' Ada announced, as Lottie faced her again. 'They always do well. How is it that you have the audacity to bring back my petticoats? Did you and this pig Calsey decide it between you?'

Lottie denied it firmly, but quietly. It would have been very easy to raise her voice to the same pitch as Magdalena's. 'It was Mr Polonsky at Finnegan's Bazaar who suggested the lace trimming which will set them off admirably. Don't you like lace on your petticoats?'

There was a giggle from the assembled girls, a giggle which Magdalena quelled with a single glance. One of them winked at Lottie, and she knew she had struck the right note. It stood to reason that a girl as attractive and alive as Ada would want lace on her petticoat. Why, she had some round the neck of the yellow frock she wore.

'Finnegan's Bazaar,' Ada nodded. 'I didn't believe Danny when he said you had been there. There must be more to you than meets the eye. This Polonsky is no fool. Tell me, what did you say? What did he say?'

'He said he'd take them, if they were trimmed with lace.'

'Where? On the bodice? Two or three inches up from the hem? I know the very thing to make them really pretty—a tiny pink rosebud from the centre of the bodice with fine pink ribbons hanging from it—what do you say to that?' Ada smiled suddenly.

Lottie would have liked to have smiled back and agreed, but Mr Polonsky had been very definite. 'No,' she replied, 'he wants the lace round the hem. Besides, a rosebud and ribbons would add to the cost.' She was going to add that the price had been agreed, but before she could do so, Ada had interrupted her.

'Z-t-t, prices have been changed before this! We shall do it as I say, and you will see how he likes it.' Ada turned to Adam. 'Is this Carlotta to tell me what I must do? I, who have worked for you longer than she has—I, who know how things are done here?'

'You must settle it between you,' he said.

'Does that mean you listen to her, not me?' Ada demanded, with a look of disdain at Lottie.

'It comes down to cost and pleasing the customer.' Lottie kept her voice down, but she was determined to come out the victor. 'If you like, you could make a sample petticoat for me and I shall take it out to Mr Polonsky with the ones he has ordered done as he has asked for them, and we shall see if he will accept yours on a repeat order.'

For a moment it looked as though Magdalena would refuse this olive-branch, but she relented after a glance at the silent Adam. 'As you say—we shall see.'

Lottie then went on to talk about the material for the new style of aprons, and Ada was unenthusiastic until Adam produced a pattern for the cutting. She reflected that he must have spent a good part of his evening preparing it, and felt flattered that he was displaying faith in her idea. She let him and Magdalena argue it out.

While they were doing so, the girls began to work again, and Lottie was beckoned over by a tall dark-haired girl who had come forward and picked up the piece of violet velvet from the top of the materials.

'Is it yours?' she asked Lottie.

The girl took it over to her machine and sat down. She folded the velvet into a headband and held a piece of buckram behind it, and then some small very pale pink flowers and a tiny pice of net were added. She held the concoction up, and Lottie was charmed to see it was a hat.

Smiling at her, the girl demonstrated with her fingers to show that she meant to make two such articles. Lottie nodded, and the girl's clever fingers carried out a quick operation with her scissors. A little stitching completed the job, and a darling little chapeau was placed gently on her head.

The girl held up a tiny mirror, and Lottie exclaimed in admiration. With a finger to her lips, she motioned Lottie back to Ada and Adam. She put the remaining piece of velvet in her drawer.

Ada looked up. 'Where did you get that?'

Lottie didn't want to get her new friend into trouble and remained silent.

'I know where!' Ada snapped. 'From Rosa.' She broke off from English to Italian, sounding very angry.

To Lottie's surprise, the dark girl only laughed and held up her piece of velvet. 'You shall have one just the same.'

'I don't want one just the same,' Ada retorted. 'What can you do with such a girl?' she appealed to Adam.

'Rosa is her sister,' he offered by way of explanation.

'Rosa has clever fingers,' Magdalena said, 'but no head for business. She'd give anything away, if I didn't watch her.'

Lottie felt rather guilty, but wasn't going to give back her hat. It suited her too well. Fortunately, Ada didn't demand it. She dismissed them both and called her girls around her, and they heard her instructing them as they went down the stairs.

Adam didn't speak until they were half-way down. 'Will Polonsky accept the pink ribbons, do you think,' he asked Lottie, 'on the repeat order?'

She shrugged. 'That's up to him. Magdalena was very set on her own way.'

'So were you.'

Lottie thought that was unfair. 'I would have liked to have said Yes, but I want Mr Polonsky for a customer.'

'You did your best,' he said. 'Ada was trying you out. I can put up with her ways because I know she has my interests at heart. You'll get used to her.'

'I'll have to, won't I,' Lottie replied drily.

Adam looked at her with raised eyebrows as they reached the street.

'Nay, lass, walk along beside me and listen to me. You might begin to like her, or at least to understand a mite about her.'

She fell into step with him as they went through the same dingy thoroughfares. This time she didn't bother to examine them, but gave her attention to Adam.

'When I came to New York,' he began, 'I found the trip as hard as you did in different ways, but of course I was buoyed up by the sure knowledge that I was going to succeed here and send for my bride in time. I came on my own, and made friends with a Frenchman of about my own age. Pierre was his name. His English wasn't very good, but it improved a lot on the voyage. I didn't try to speak his language. In those days I thought the rest of the world must learn mine. He and I decided that when we landed, it would be cheaper and pleasanter to find a room together. We had no idea where to look or how much to pay, and ended by paying much more than we would have thought possible for a room in a tenement building.' He shuddered at the recollection.

'It was February, and bitterly cold. The room was part of a tenement flat—or apartment, as they call them here—and there were families in some of the other rooms. We shared a dingy scullery, a dark hole of a sink room, and a privy with thirty other people. We looked for work, telling each other that it would soon improve and we would move to better quarters.'

Adam guided Lottie past a crate of chickens which cackled as they passed. He continued,

'I hadn't been there more than two days when I fell ill. I burned with heat and shivered with the cold. Whether it was some disease I picked up on the trip across, jammed in that vile hold, I never knew or cared. Pierre said it was *la grippe*, and I would recover if the *Bon Dieu* willed it. He fetched water for me to drink and once or twice a bowl of greasy soup—I couldn't eat it.'

'Didn't you ask him to get a doctor?' Lottie interrupted.

Adam only shrugged. 'I was too ill to ask for anything, and I suppose Pierre didn't think of it—or if he did, dismissed it as extravagance since the *Bon Dieu* was in command.' His expression was grim.

Lottie tut-tutted sympathetically. 'You needed warmth and nursing.'

'Ay,' he agreed. 'I don't know how long I lay like that—a week, four days perhaps—at any rate I woke one morning to find myself alone, a note from Pierre with a single word on it, *"Adieu!"* My money was gone, taken from the belt round my waist, but he had left my clothes. I had the sense to pile them all upon me, and still I shivered.'

'That was treachery!' she exclaimed. 'Real betrayal! How could this Pierre have done it?'

'I suppose he'd given me up for lost,' Adam said mildly, 'and didn't want the inconvenience or expense of a dead body. At least he hadn't stripped me naked—he had enough feeling for that.' He fell silent.

Lottie put her hand on his arm. 'Who saved you then?'

Adam grinned. 'A large black cat!'

'You needn't make fun of me!' she said, withdrawing her hand.

Adam took it back under his arm. 'I'm serious! The next time I woke, there was a large black cat cuddled up to me, spreading warmth towards me. I curled myself about him and he purred mightily. It was the first comfort that I'd found in this brave new world.'

Lottie felt a lump in her throat. His words had made a vivid picture in her mind. Though he made light of it, she felt his despair and loneliness in that time. She pressed his hand in hers and raised her eyes to his face.

'I don't know how long the cat remained with me that day, but presently it stretched and stalked to the door,

mewing. I knew I had to let it out. When I did, on legs
which felt they had no bones or muscles in them, there
was a great cry from the other side of the door. A girl
with dark hair and big dark eyes screamed in Italian
at me and scooped up the cat. My legs gave way completely, and I slid down the door, trying to hang on to it
for strength. I landed at her feet, unconscious. I suppose
I fainted. I'd never done such a thing in my life!' Adam
looked away from her.

'The girl—it was Rosa—fetched others—Magdalena
and her father, and they stood over me, arguing. The
next thing I knew, I had been carried into the Mendozas'
room, which was considerably larger and more comfortable than mine, and a little fat-bellied stove was giving
out the most wonderful warmth. They put me on the
floor in front of it, on cushions, and wrapped me in
blankets. Rosa fed me with soup and wine, and
Magdalena looked on with disapproval. I began to recover. Within a few days, I was sitting up and eating
properly. That was when Magdalena had a long talk with
me.' He was still holding Lottie's hand, and released it
as though suddenly aware of it.

'What did she have to say?' asked Lottie, her curiosity
aroused. 'That she didn't like you, didn't want you
there?'

'Not exactly!' Adam laughed and increased his pace.
'I think she'd begun to get used to me and to realise that I
was no threat to her or her sister. After all, Rosa was
twelve, and Magdalena herself only fifteen, though I
thought her older. She made a bargain with me. I would
teach her and Rosa to speak English so that they could
get jobs and earn a proper living. She knew they
wouldn't get ahead here with only Italian. In return, I
could stay with them until I got a job. She would see that
my room was rented to someone else, and would keep

me in food until I began to earn, at which time I would pay for my lodging.'

'That must have been an enormous relief to you!'

'Ay, once I'd puzzled out what she was trying to say! Remember, she didn't speak much English then.'

Lottie rubbed her forehead with one hand where perspiration had begun to form. It was so hot today, and Adam was walking so fast.

He glanced at her and slowed down. 'I keep forgetting you're not used to the weather here. It'll get hotter as the summer wears on.'

'Perhaps I'll be used to it by then.' She was grateful for the less hurried pace. 'Go on with the story,' she begged. 'Did it take them long to learn?'

'Rosa was very quick. Magdalena took longer, as she was older, and thought in Italian.'

'Didn't Rosa?' Lottie frowned, not understanding quite what he meant.

'It's hard to explain. Rosa told me about it, because she knew Magdalena was cross that she was so much quicker. I can only tell you what Rosa said. It had to do with words and pictures. Rosa thought in pictures; Magdalena in words, Italian words. I didn't see what she was driving at at first, but after a while it occurred to me that it must be something like a tailor learning to sew. Some of them pick it up just from being shown; others you have to explain it to over and over, saying exactly the same things, before they cotton on.'

Lottie nodded at that. 'Don't you think it has something to do with wanting to learn?'

'No, Magdalena wanted to learn. Rosa simply fell in with her plans, but it came easy to her.'

'Is that what Rosa does—just fall in with her sister's plans?'

'Mostly,' Adam smiled. 'Rosa is a darling. She

reminds me of Kate. They both have that very soft way
about them, that way of making the other person feel
important and liked. You and Magdalena are more the
some sort, cut from the same cloth.'

Lottie did not feel flattered by this observation. She
wasn't like Magdalena at all! For a start, she kept her
temper in better check and didn't ride roughshod over
other people to get her own way. She told Adam so.

'Nay, you are like,' he insisted. 'You're both stub-
born, both ambitious to get on, and both ready to take
other people in hand. You did it with your younger
brother and sister, just as Magdalena does with Rosa.'

'I had to take care of them. There wasn't any one else
to do it,' Lottie protested, stopping dead in the street
and causing a passer-by to bump into her.

'Just what Magdalena would say!' Adam took her arm
and righted her, apologising to the woman who had
collided with her. 'Any road, you've let go of your
family. I doubt if Magdalena ever will.'

'Does that worry you?' In spite of the anger he had
roused in her, she was curious about the sisters.

'Rosa's a clever girl and draws people to her. That's a
nice little bonnet she's made you; it suits you well. Don't
you feel warm towards her?'

'Ay,' Lottie agreed, telling herself with some asperity
that she mightn't for much longer if Adam was going
to continue to sing Rosa's praises. She had thought
Magdalena was the one Adam was interested in, but
it sounded very much as though it was Rosa, whether
he realised it or not.

'How long did you stay with the Mendózas?'

'Actually living with them, only a few weeks—a
month, perhaps. By then, Mr Mendoza, who was also a
tailor, got me into the shop where he worked, and I
began to earn. I got a tiny room in the same flat, and kept

on teaching the girls in exchange for my supper. After a while they both got work in the same sewing-room, and with three of them earning they were able to move to better quarters. I never lost touch with them, though, and Rosa always teased me that I spoke nearly as good Italian as she spoke English. In a way they must have become a sort of family to me.' Adam guided Lottie across a busy road.

'Did you tell them about Kate, and sending for her when you were able?'

'They knew that from the first. Rosa thought it very romantic. Magdalena said it was too long to expect a girl to wait. It looks like she was right.' There was sadness in his voice. 'But that's past and done.'

'Do either of them have sweethearts?' Lottie asked, to get Adam away from the subject of Kate.

'Funny you should ask that! Magdalena is a very handsome girl, and many's the lad she's turned down in spite of her temper. She's always said that Rosa must marry first, and now she's found the very one for her—a young Italian of good family, with a steady job. His father has a small hotel. The boy will inherit one day. Luigi is his name.'

'You like him, do you?' Lottie thought she detected some reservation in Adam's tone.

'Well enough.'

'But?' Lottie was hesitant to ask.

'Rosa's only fifteen—sixteen next month. She's too young.'

'Just about Kate's age when you asked her to wait for you,' Lottie pointed out.

'Ay,' was all Adam said to that.

'How does Rosa feel? Does she talk about Luigi to you?'

'Rosa's always been very chatty with me, but about

Luigi she has very little to say. I can't tell how she feels. I
wish her father were still alive. He'd know.'

'You didn't say he was dead!' Lottie exclaimed. 'How
did it happen?'

'Last year—he was knocked down in the street. It was
a terrible shock to the girls; and to me, for he was my
friend. Fortunately there was a little insurance money
—enough to bury him and to provide a small dowry for
Rosa—so Magdalena said.'

Lottie drew in her breath at that. It certainly said
something for Magdalena that she had put the money
aside for Rosa's dowry. 'Nothing for herself?'

'No—that's Magdalena. She wouldn't touch that
money. She talked at first about moving to somewhere
cheaper, because without Mr Mendoza's earnings, considerably less was coming in. I helped her there by
offering her the sewing-room and both of them jobs in it.
She didn't want charity, she said. I told her it wouldn't be
that. She'd work as hard for me as anyone else, and I
needed her and Rosa. I'd had a bit of luck, you see,
about the money.'

'What sort of luck?'

For a moment, Lottie thought Adam wouldn't
answer. They were now in Jones Street and approaching
the boarding-house.

Adam shrugged. 'You might as well know. I won it,
you might say. I'd gone with a friend one evening to a
field where there was going to be horse-racing. I've
never been interested in horses, but George, my friend,
was very keen to go, so I went with him.'

They turned up the path to Mrs O'Rourke's. Past the
house they went, on to the shed.

'The first person I saw there was the very man who had
abandoned me three years before, leaving me to die. He
turned white when he recognised me and was too

surprised to move away. I clutched him by the shoulder and said the first thing that came into my head.' Adam unlocked the shed door.

'What was that?' She went in, and sat down on her bench.

He smiled grimly. 'Why, that he owed me twenty-five dollars! I don't think I expected him to repay me on the spot—or at all. But he was like a cornered rabbit, his eyes darting everywhere. He said he had only twenty, and meant to bet it on a horse. It was a sure thing, and paying off at ten to one. I couldn't prove anything against him, but I said we should each have ten and place it on the horse. That way, we'd both benefit.'

Lottie was leaning forward now. 'He was a gambler.' She said it in hushed tones, repulsed by the idea and fascinated all at once.

'Ay, and he had a silver tongue. I'd never done such a thing in my life, but I did it then—and the strange thing was, the horse won! I had a hundred dollars—enough for the workroom and to send for Kate.' Adam took the cover from his machine. 'It was more money than I had ever seen in my hand.'

'And you sent for Kate,' Lottie echoed. 'And I came. Oh, Adam!' She wasn't able to go on for the lump in her throat.

'Fortune had a twist in her tail!' Adam remarked with a grin. 'Nay, don't carry on, lass. Gamblers have to put up with fortune's ways.'

Lottie began to laugh. It was strange that Adam should speak of fortune's ways. For a moment she had the strongest impulse to tell him about the whims of fortune and that kiss that had brought her to cross an ocean and come to him, but she hesitated, and the moment was lost.

'Let's get to work,' he said, picking up a garment

waiting to be sewn. 'We must make our own fortune—
and the sooner the better.'

Lottie uncovered her machine . . .

CHAPTER EIGHT

IT WAS the following Tuesday morning that Adam produced the tickets that Rosemary had given him and
asked Lottie if she would like to accompany him to the
performance. She was thunderstruck. Adam had been
very short with her all through the accounts, which they
had done together, and she had several times nearly told
him she would be glad when she heard about her other
job. Stammering, she accepted his invitation, only
asking if he was a regular concert-goer. When he replied
that he wasn't, she was even more puzzled.

Why was he asking her, she wondered, when he could
have taken Dorothea or Magdalena or Rosa? She knew
he'd been at the Mendozas' on Saturday evening and
had taken Dorothea for a walk along the river on Sunday
afternoon. Perhaps he felt it was her turn now.

It would be very pleasant to have an evening's entertainment, she told herself firmly. Never mind why
he had asked her; she should just be grateful that he
had.

It was in some excitement that she got ready for the
jaunt. She wore the kingfisher blue dress and took extra
trouble with brushing her hair and arranging it softly
round her face. She meant to do herself credit. When she
went downstairs, Adam was waiting, and told her she
looked very well.

She had supposed they would walk or go by stage, but
Adam, very presentable in grey trousers and a long
black jacket with gold buttons, had a carriage waiting.
This was extravagance indeed, and she nearly told him

so. With a sigh of pleasure she settled back to enjoy the ride, stealing glances at the silent man.

It was only a short trip down Broadway, and when they arrived in front of the Olympic Theatre, carriages and stages were blocking the road. Lottie was astonished at the crowds in the streets, and the gas lights which were already pricking the early dusk and lighting up the scene.

Adam helped her to alight. Before them were a crowd of ragged barefoot children in clothes mostly too big or too skimpy for them, who provided an entertainment of their own. Some were standing on their heads on the pavement, some climbing the lamp-posts, some danced, or played flutes or jews-harps, or even combs with bits of paper. All of them held out their hands to beg.

Lottie's heart was touched by their evident poverty and by their bruised, knowing old eyes. Children shouldn't look as they did. She fumbled for coins.

'It's no use giving to one,' Adam said brusquely, sweeping her along to the doors. 'And you can't give to all!'

In the theatre, they were ushered into red plush seats in mid-stalls, a very good position.

Adam held out a programme to Lottie, and she took it absently, too busy looking about the well-appointed auditorium, which was filling up very quickly, to pay it much attention.

'Oh, Adam! This must be a good concert. Everybody is coming—mothers, fathers, children—look, there are two babies in their mothers' arms over there!'

'People have quite taken to these big entertainments,' he agreed. 'You'll see some very stylish clothes.'

He was right about that. Lottie looked about in pleasure. The men and women around them and in the boxes were indeed very well dressed. Of course, in the cheaper sections sat men in shirt-sleeves and women in old frocks. There were people of every nationality.

Lottie played a game with Adam, picking out Germans and Italians, French and Jews. By the time the curtain went up and Adam had presented her with a box of sweets, she was in a very happy mood. Adam was good company and had a sharp sense of humour.

The orchestra began to play, and minstrel singers were grouped on the stage. She had never seen or heard anything like them before. Their faces and hands were blacked with burnt cork and they were dressed in bright colours; the girls in reds and pinks and yellows, the men in black trousers and checked waistcoats.

They sang songs unknown to her. 'The Skeeters do Bite' was one of them, and she was puzzled about 'skeeters' until Adam whispered that they were mosquitoes, and she'd already had some experience of them.

'Negro songs,' he added, 'from the South.'

Whatever their origin, the songs were catchy and full of rhythm, and Lottie's feet longed to dance to them. The audience roared their approval.

This act was followed by performing dogs, dear little creatures who wore frills and hats and jumped through hoops and did other tricks. Two men played a sort of mandolin that Lottie had never seen before. A 'banjo', Adam called it. She found some difficulty in accustoming her ear to it and thought it jangly.

There were dancers and solo singers. One of the dancers was a girl in a short red skirt glittering with sequins and spangles, who did a rousing, spirited number first, and then a softer, more languorous, one which reminded Lottie of her own dance on the *Black Swan*. That set her thinking of Paolo and Angelina. She did so hope that they had found work.

When the interval came, Adam bought ice-cream for both of them and the programme was set aside again. He was full of talk about the costumes and how well they were made for some artists and how poorly for others. Lottie hadn't really noticed.

A comic opened the second half. Adam laughed at most of his jokes, but Lottie, too new to the American scene, wasn't very much impressed. When he had finished, the curtains parted, and Paolo and Angelina in pale blue satin ran on to the stage and began throwing a succession of balls into the air.

Lottie gasped in astonishment. 'It's Paolo!' she whispered to Adam, her face alight. 'Paolo and Angelina!' In her excitement, she took hold of his hand.

Paolo put on a black mask and a cloak, and they performed an amusing little sketch in which he drew rabbits out of a hat and finally coins out of Angelina's ears. She was very appealing, and managed to look so puzzled and astounded that the audience took her to their hearts and began to call out to her and give her advice.

The curtains closed to tumultuous applause, and Lottie realised that she was still holding Adam's hand. She dropped it. 'Weren't they good?'

'He's a better-looking chap than I expected,' he observed. 'But their outfits don't fit very well.'

There was no time for further conversation, as the minstrels were back again.

When the curtain finally came down after all the performers had appeared on stage again, Lottie was surprised that Adam was directing her away from the exit and towards the stage.

'It's the wrong way!' she protested.

'Nay, lass, we're invited back stage.'

'Who by?'

'Your friends,' Adam said. 'They're expecting you!'

'Have you met them, then? How did you know? You

Open your heart to love with 2 Best Seller Romances FREE

Can you resist the promise of wild, passionate romance...the shy glances, the stolen kisses, the laughter – and the tears? If, deep within your heart, you're a true romantic, then these are love stories for you. Stories that comprise a unique library of books from Mills & Boon – we call them Best Seller Romances. From the very first page you'll understand why these books have enthralled thousands of readers and now rank among our Best Sellers.

As your special introduction to our most popular library, we'll send you 2 Best Sellers and an exclusive Mills & Boon Tote Bag FREE when you complete and return this card.

Now, if you decide to become a subscriber, you can receive four Best Seller Romances delivered directly to your door, every two months. If this sounds tempting, read on; because you'll also enjoy a whole range of special benefits that are exclusive to Mills & Boon. For example, your own personal membership card; a free bi-monthly newsletter packed with recipes, competitions, exclusive book offers and much more – plus extra bargain offers and big cash savings.

Remember, there's absolutely no obligation or commitment – you can cancel your subscription at any time. So don't delay any longer...complete, detach and post this card today. The romance of your dreams is beckoning – don't keep it waiting!

BEST SELLER ROMANCE
The Valdez Marriage
VIOLET WINSPEAR

BEST SELLER ROMANCE
The Silken Trap
CHARLOTTE LAMB

BEST SELLER ROMANCE
Green Mountain Man
JANET DAILEY

BEST SELLER ROMANCE
Stormy Possession
HELEN BIANCHIN

FREE BOOKS CERTIFICATE

Dear Susan,

Your special Introductory Offer of 2 Free books is too good to miss. I understand they are mine to keep with the Free Tote Bag.

Please also reserve a Reader Service Subscription for me. If I decide to subscribe I shall receive 4 new books every two months for £4.40 post and packing free. If I decide not to subscribe, I shall write to you within 10 days. The free books will be mine to keep, in any case.

I understand that I may cancel my Subscription at any time simply by writing to you. I am over 18 years of age.

7A6B

Name _____
(BLOCK CAPITALS PLEASE)

Signature _____

Address _____

_____

_____ Postcode _____

Mills & Boon reserve the right to exercise discretion in granting membership. Offer expires 31st December 1986. You may be mailed with other offers as a result of this application. Valid in UK only, overseas please send for details.
Please note Readers in South Africa write to: Independent Book Services P.T.Y., Postbag X3010, Randburg, 2125 South Africa.

To Susan Welland
Mills & Boon Reader Service
FREE POST
P.O. Box 236
CROYDON
Surrey CR9 9EL

NO
STAMP
NEEDED

SEND NO MONEY NOW

might have told me . . .' Lottie found she was full of conflicting emotions. Uppermost was the thought that Paolo had wanted to see her again. Perhaps she had misjudged him.

She allowed herself to be led behind the stage, down to the dressing-rooms. Adam seemed to know where he was going, and found the right room, a poky little place. Lottie had no eyes for its limitations. All she saw as the door opened was Paolo.

His face lit up when he saw her. 'Carlotta!' he cried, and opened his arms.

Lottie went straight into them. Paolo kissed her, and then held her back a little. 'How grand you look. Your hair is different—oh, *cara*, it suits you! And your dress is lovely. Is this your fine husband?' He turned to Adam.

'No,' said Adam. 'We're not married.'

'Not married?' Paolo echoed. 'How is that? Are you not Adam Hardcastle?'

'Ay,' Adam agreed, 'and she is Lottie Earnshaw.'

'But how is this?' Paolo looked from one to the other. 'Carlotta has come all this way, and you have changed your mind.' There was censure in his voice.

'Let's say we agreed it between us,' Adam tried to make his words non-committal. He could see that Lottie looked uncomfortable, Paolo accusing. Whatever had she told him? Clearly that she had crossed the Atlantic to marry him. Would she have? Nay, the way she had gone to Paolo's arms suggested otherwise. Perhaps she had wanted to keep this fellow at arm's length. That was wise of her.

Paolo put his arms round Lottie again, and gave her a good hug. He whispered something to her, but what that something was, was lost to Adam. Well, it was no concern of his if Paolo meant to make a performance of this reunion. Why, then, was he so conscious of the pair of them behind him as he turned to Angelina and greeted her in Italian.

Angelina dimpled in delight as he complimented her on the show and her performance. He told her what a charming girl she was, and hoped that Paolo heard him.

Paolo took no notice. He was talking to Lottie.

Stung by this indifference, Adam went on to offer Angelina his services in altering the act's costumes so that they would be more flattering.

'Send your brother to me in the morning,' he told her, 'and I shall see what I can do.' He wrote the address and directions for her on a piece of paper.

Angelina was profuse with her thanks. She held Adam's hand and offered him a glass of wine.

'My brother has missed Lottie,' she confided. 'They were good friends on the boat, but of course he understood she was meant for you and never declared himself. Now, whatever it is that has made you and Lottie change your minds, Paolo must be pleased.' She gave him a sparkling glance from her dark eyes, and a smile. 'I was right to try to find her, was I not?' She indicated the other pair still immersed in each other's company.

Adam accepted the wine, and Angelina pressed a glass on her brother and on Lottie.

'Adam speaks Italian,' she said to Paolo. 'He is one of us.'

'Not quite that!' Lottie was sipping her wine. 'He has an Italian girl friend—two, in fact.'

'Well,' said Paolo, his arms still round Lottie. 'We must applaud his good taste—but wonder why he found Carlotta not to his liking.'

Adam resented that remark. Of course he liked Lottie, but he didn't want to marry her. Kate had been his choice. This Paolo took too much upon himself; even his speech was flowery. No wonder Lottie fawned on him when he told her she was beautiful; his eyes said that she was desirable. He'd turned her head with his flattery; that's what it was. What was wrong with Lottie? She knew this fellow had stolen her candlestick, and yet she'd gone straight into his arms, forgetting all about that. Women—he'd never understand them! But, just the same, he'd get some sort of explanation from him in the morning.

Paolo reached into a box under the mirror on the shelf and produced a bag which contained bread, cheese and a large sausage.

'Garlic sausage!' exclaimed Lottie. 'Like you had on the boat.'

Paolo broke off a piece of bread from the long loaf and offered it to her with the sausage and a knife.

She laughed, 'I think I'll have cheese, Paolo, if you don't mind.'

Adam tried the garlic sausage and found it very spicy, but as Paolo was eating some with evident relish he kept his opinion about it to himself.

'Do you always eat in here after the performance?' he enquired.

'No,' Paolo replied with great candour. 'It's only our first week in work, and you will understand that we are being careful.' He waved his hand at Lottie and the cheese. 'Have some more? It is good to have enough food, isn't it?' He poured more wine into her glass. 'Gin was your drink on the boat.'

Adam considered that Paolo was being altogether too familiar, but he could see that Lottie wasn't at all put out. She protested only very mildly that Arthur had said she must bring gin; she wasn't really a drinker.

'I know that,' Paolo smiled at her. 'You are too proper ever to let yourself be overcome by strong drink. Ah,

Lottie, how I have missed your way of talking and of being with us!'

Adam turned to Angelina. Paolo and Lottie seemed determined to exclude him from their conversation and to talk over old times.

'I understood you have another brother here in New York,' he said.

'He was here, but he left a letter for us. He has gone to California to search for gold. If he finds it, he will send for us. That's the way Romano is. It comes, I think, from riding so high up in the air—on his tightrope.'

Adam hadn't heard about the tightrope, and was intrigued with Angelina's description. She was an enchanting child who seemed completely unspoiled by a life which might have hardened many another. That spoke something for her personality and for the care Paolo took of her—he was fair enough to add to himself.

He couldn't help reflecting that though the existence of these entertainers would be interesting, it must have some very precarious moments. Would Lottie fit into such a life?

Angelina beamed at Lottie as they finished eating. 'Now that we have found each other, we mustn't lose touch again.'

Lottie agreed without hesitation, Adam noted. 'You must come on Sunday, and we shall walk by the river and talk and talk. You might also like to meet Adam's friends—Rosa is not much older than you, Angelina.'

Plans were soon arranged between the two girls, but nothing was said to Lottie about Adam's offer about the altering of the costumes. Well, that suited him. He would send Lottie off in the morning to do the rounds of the shops they supplied, and have his talk with Paolo in private.

When they said their goodbyes, it was with smiling

faces all round, and Adam escorted Lottie to a waiting carriage. He was pleased to see that this impressed the Italian.

Lottie settled back happily in her seat. 'Adam, it was good of you to take me, but such a surprise! Did Angelina send you the tickets, then?'

'She gave them to Rosemary, and Rosemary asked me to take you.'

'How kind,' was all Lottie said to that, but Adam could see there was a thoughtful expression on her face.

'This Paolo seems to like you.'

'And I like him,' she was quick to add. 'He was very good to me on the *Black Swan*. I don't know what I would have done without Paolo, or without the pair of them.'

Lottie rested her head against the padded wall of the carriage, a dreamy look on her face. 'Do you know, Adam, it was like coming home when I saw them—just to see a few familiar faces, people who knew me . . .' She broke off, smiling.

She was smiling to herself. Adam thought. She was infatuated with this fellow, and yet—he shook his head —somehow he felt they didn't quite match the way they should. Lottie would be throwing herself away on him. Perhaps he could make her see that.

When he helped Lottie from the carriage and paid off the driver, they walked together up the path to Mrs O'Rourke's.

It was a balmy night, the moon in its first quarter, the stars peppering the sky. From the front garden came the scent of newly-turned earth. Someone had been busy today.

As they mounted the veranda steps, Adam put his finger to his lips and took Lottie's arm. 'It's too nice to go in! Let's sit awhile and watch the stars, and talk.'

Lottie had no hesitation in agreeing. It had been a lovely evening, and she wanted to prolong it. The wine had soothed away all ordinary cares. What did it matter if tomorrow was a working day? This was almost the way she had felt on the *Black Swan* when she had danced for Paolo. She might dance for Adam. She giggled at the very idea, and sank down beside him on the wooden bench which lined the inside of the veranda wall . . . Their shoulders touched. It was very peaceful.

'Was it only because you felt Paolo was a face from home that you gave him such a welcome?' Adam asked.

'Ay, I've said so,' she answered mildly, her pulses beating a little faster because it was Adam she was sitting next to, Adam who had taken her to the concert.

'I was a face from home,' he pointed out, 'when you landed from the boat. I got no such welcome!'

'You gave me no such welcome, either,' Lottie retorted. 'What did you expect, when your first words were about Kate?' She didn't say it angrily, but it was a fact. There was no denying that.

'You must have told Paolo you were coming to marry me. What would you have done if I had said, Yes, I'll have you instead of Kate?'

Lottie stirred uneasily. What would she have done? She'd come to marry Adam, and yet . . . She didn't speak.

'Would you have thrown your arms round me as you did with Paolo tonight and kissed me?'

She giggled. Was Adam going to kiss her and release her from the bondage of that first kiss of his? Her heart pounded so loud within her breast that she wondered that he didn't hear it and comment. 'Do you want me to kiss you?' she murmured. She raised her face, bringing it closer to his, ready for his kiss.

'Why should I want that?' he countered, but she could feel his soft breath on her cheek.

'Isn't that what all men want?' She felt at ease, somehow, in command of the situation. Perhaps it was the wine that she had drunk. She wanted Adam's arms to reach out for her, his mouth to claim hers in a soft and enticing kiss—a kiss that acknowledged that he wanted her.

'You've just come from Paolo's arms.' His whisper was stern in her ears.

'What difference does that make?' Her temper was beginning to rise. What was the matter with Adam? Hadn't she just told him that Paolo was part of her family? Of course she was fond of him. She was fond of Angelina, too. Why didn't Adam just kiss her and have done with it? One way or the other, she yearned to have the whole thing finished and done with.

Lottie pressed her lips to his, her arms sliding round his neck. If he couldn't see she wanted him, she must show him.

Adam's lips fastened on hers. His arms drew her closer to him so that she felt the hard muscles of his chest, his thigh against hers. It was an angry kiss, a bruising kiss, a kiss that told her he resented her, didn't like her—and yet it was savage, demanding, arousing. There was no gentleness in it, nor was there anything of love—her shocked mind signalled that message to her. But there was everything of raw desire, of wild need. Her body recognised that, and responded to it.

He rose to his feet as though to release her, to free himself, and Lottie rose with him, her lips still yielding to his, her body pressed tight against him. She hated him that he should use her so, but she couldn't stop reacting to that elemental demand he made on her emotions, on her flesh which quivered as he touched her. With a sob that seemed to come from deep inside her body, she tried to break free. But Adam still held her, his arms hard against her back. His lips had released their hold.

'Let me go,' she begged.

'Why? You offered to kiss me! I'm just beginning to find out what I missed that first day.'

Lottie was very conscious of his body pressed so close to hers, of his masculine smell and feel. She wanted to stay there, imprisoned, but fought for her freedom. In the light cast by the thin slice of moon, she could see that he smiled at her struggles and kept her there quite easily.

'Would you have married me that first day from the boat?'

'Yes,' she whispered, the word inaudible almost, torn from her lips.

'Why?' he demanded. 'Was that after you realised that Paolo had taken your treasure, your candlestick? Was it anger and hurt that made you fix on me? Is that what it still is, Lottie?'

She shook her head. How could he be so wrong about her and know so little of her? How could she explain that she had crossed an ocean to claim his kiss again? Now that she had that kiss, he still rejected her, intimating that it was Paolo whom she wanted. Adam didn't even like her. She had thought that if he kissed her, she would know if she had been following a dream. Well, she knew that.

That first kiss, so long ago, had been a beckoning, an awakening—a tender introduction to a world of maleness. This was reality—the reality of being held in a man's arms, of acknowledging the response of her body to his. Were all men like this—so rough, so demanding?

'A minute ago you said you would have married me straight from the boat. Changed your mind, have you?

You ran from Horace Higginbottom; now you want to run from me.' Adam's voice was low.

Lottie was held so tight that she couldn't even kick against his shins, though she longed to stop his hateful words.

'Thou hast no need to fear me,' he continued, 'but others might not be so kindly with thee. When thou invite a man to kiss thee, keep that in mind.'

Numbly, she raised her face to Adam's. He didn't understand. She didn't ask other men to kiss her. She had only asked him so that she might be free of him.

'I hate you!' she exclaimed, and struggled in his embrace. She managed to free one arm and tried to push her elbow into him.

He forestalled her, and she was clasped to him even more tightly. 'I'm giving you good advice, Lottie. Don't let yourself be swept away by a handsome face. Paolo isn't the only man in the world. You'll meet others. Go slow and careful. Be sure of your feelings.'

Why was he warning her about Paolo? Lottie opened her mouth to ask that question.

The words were never uttered. Adam's lips closed on hers. It was a softer kiss, this time a kiss that turned Lottie's anger to nothing, a kiss that hinted of promise and of softness, yet Adam released her before she expected it, pushing her from him. Confused, bewildered as much by her own emotions as by his abrupt change of mood, she shivered as she stood free, hand to her mouth, on the brink of tears.

'It's late,' he said. 'Up you go to your bed.' He led her to the door, and she slipped through it and up the stairs without a backward glance.

Adam went back to the bench on the veranda. Lottie had surprised him considerably. He had surprised himself! He had meant to have a brotherly chat with her about Paolo and had ended up by kissing her; ay, wanting her. It must have been the wine—that was it—and the moonlight and the stars.

He looked up at them. Lottie had shivered by the door, but the night was still warm, sultry even. It wasn't a night for sleep, but for lying awake and talking. If Kate had come . . . there was no sense in thinking like that. Kate had not come, nor ever would. He must accept that and build his life again.

Lottie's face swam into his mind. That had been a tear he'd seen. He was sure it was. It had changed him and softened him. Women had that way of leading a man on and then retreating. For a moment there she'd been willing—more than willing, he added grimly. That had astonished him. He'd never thought of Lottie in quite that way before. If she loved a man, there would be fire and passion beneath that plain exterior. Not so plain! She had a way of smiling when he said something that amused her. One eyebrow lifted, and those two small, deep dimples at either side of her mouth sprang into view, and then were gone just as sharply when her face straightened. He'd found himself watching for it.

Paolo was not the man for her, he was sure of it. But an infatuated woman would take a deal of convincing. He was coming in the morning, with the costumes. Well, after the singular lack of success he'd had in talking with Lottie, he'd not try words again. A plan began to form in Adam's mind. Lottie had said something about Angelina meeting Rosa . . . Paolo should meet both Rosa and Magdalena. They were the same race, had the same language. They were bound to take to each other . . .

He began to smile. How to manage to make it all seem

natural? That was it . . . The answer was in his hands!

He yawned and went indoors, content with his planning. Lottie would be grateful to him yet.

CHAPTER NINE

IN THE morning, Lottie had gone to the shed in some trepidation to face Adam. What would she say to him? How should she act? She had no need to worry; he was quite matter of fact. He said Danny had arrived with the newly trimmed petticoats, and she must go with him to see Mr Polonsky. If he himself was not there when she got back to the shed, she must do the costing; and he'd left some sewing for her. Oh, and if Mr Polonsky re-ordered, it would be as well for her to bring the news to Ada right away.

Lottie had a good morning. Mr Polonsky declared himself delighted with the petticoats, and paid her, as well as agreeing to take two dozen more of Ada's design with the pink rosebuds and ribbons. When she showed him a sample of the new aprons, they, too, found favour in his eyes, and he ordered three dozen. He also admired her little purple confection of a hat and wanted to know where he could obtain some like it. After a quick calculation, Lottie mentioned a price which she hoped was realistic enough to satisfy both parties, and he agreed to it and said he'd have six for a start in pink or white. When she was safely outside the shop, she entertained Danny to a quick jig of jubilation, dancing him round on the pavement.

They called on Mr Jones as well, though they had no goods to bring him. None the less, he greeted Lottie very pleasantly and asked if she could supply him with fine lawn nightshirts. She promised to let him see a sample later in the week, and hoped she'd be able to persuade

Ada to produce one. Very pleased with herself, she rejoined Danny, to hear from him that he had had a message from one of the other delivery lads that old Mr Calsey wanted to see her.

'Not today,' Lottie decided. 'We'll make him wait!' She smiled at Danny.

He whistled. 'I like your nerve! He wants those petticoats.'

'If he wants them, he'll wait for them—or send Adam a note, not give us messages through delivery boys.'

Lottie then took Danny and his cart for a walk the length of Broadway. She noted the displays in all the windows.

Adam had said she should go to see Ada if Mr Polonsky re-ordered. She now had several things to talk over with her, and specially wanted her help on the new work. So they set off for the workroom, Danny leading the way with his cart, Lottie following a step behind him.

When Lottie went up the stairs, she could hear a man's voice, and hesitated. She didn't want to meet Adam just then; she wanted Magdalena on her own.

But that wasn't Adam's voice, and she stopped, her hand on the door. She opened it and went in.

How could she believe her eyes! Paolo was with Ada, deep in conversation, both with their backs to her, and the girls were silent, watching, listening.

For a moment no one noticed Lottie, than Rosa waved to her and Paolo spun round. So did Magdalena —a smiling, soft-eyed Magdalena. Lottie's mouth opened, but no words came out.

It was Paolo who spoke first. 'I didn't expect to see you here! Adam said you were out, selling.'

'So I was,' she told him. 'When did you see Adam?'

'Earlier this morning,' he answered with a smile.

'Didn't he tell you about the costumes? He said, as he was busy, I must come along to the workroom and introduce myself to the girls and they would do some alterations.' He held up the blue satin stage outfits.

'Have you had lunch?' Paolo went on. 'Magdalena knows a place where the spaghetti is superb. You and I and Rosa shall go there and eat. It's near by, and not too expensive.'

Lottie wondered if he meant to pay for them all. Remembering last night and the eating in the dressing-room, she quickly offered to stand treat, but he refused.

'No!' he cried. 'I have been paid today. I wish to treat my friends.' He silenced her protests. Not content with that, no sooner were they in the eating-house and their order taken than he turned to Rosa and Ada and declared that Lottie was the most generous of girls. He would tell them a story about her.

Rosa appeared quite eager to hear his story, Magdalena shot her an enquiring look, and tried to change the subject.

He was not to be deflected. 'She lent me her treasure —her silver candlestick—on landing in this country, so that I might look a man of property.'

Lottie and Magdalena both looked amazed.

'Why should that be necessary?' Magdalena asked. 'Surely you had the price of entry—the twenty-five dollars which every emigrant must bring?'

'That was just it,' Paolo smiled disarmingly. 'Twenty of my twenty-five dollars were only stage money.'

Rosa gasped. Magdalena wanted an explanation. Lottie was silent. She recognised the truth when she heard it. Besides, it sounded just like Paolo! Angelina had said he had no idea of money. She wasn't going to contradict him. He had been more than generous with her.

'When we had sold our costumes and Angelina's earrings and all the other things we owned, there was enough for our passage here from Hamburg and for my sister's landing money. It didn't bother me all across the ocean that the money I meant to show to Customs wasn't real. It was only on that last night aboard the *Black Swan*, as we drifted in the Bay, that I began to think about it. I couldn't face the idea of a voyage home in that dark hold. I was desperate, but Lottie came to my rescue.' He put his hand on hers, his eyes soft.

'A man with a silver candlestick must be a wealthy man,' Lottie said drily, and he nodded. 'Did Customs agree?'

Paolo laughed. 'He never even looked at the money properly when Angelina smiled at him.'

'Then it wasn't necessary at all, was it?' she asked gently.

'Have you given Lottie back her candlestick?' Rosa asked.

It was her to whom Paolo replied. 'Not yet. That first week here was very expensive, and then we had to buy costumes again. The candlestick is still in the pawnshop, but not for very much longer. I know Lottie will wait for it.' He beamed at all the girls, and the subject was forgotten as the waiter placed steaming plates of spaghetti before them.

Lottie decided that it would be kinder to accept his explanation and wait on developments. At least he had acknowledged that he had it, and that made her think a great deal better of him. It was useless to ask if he would have got in touch with her of his own accord.

Eating mellowed them all. Magdalena agreed to make the sample nightshirt, and Rosa to do the little hats. She even volunteered to fetch the necessary materials from the warehouse, saying she sometimes went there for the workroom, and the man knew her. That suited Lottie, and freed her to get back to Adam and the shed.

Paolo walked back with her. They went slowly in the hot sunshine, ambling through the streets like Sunday strollers, paying no attention to the people going about their ordinary tasks. He took her hand in his, and looked down at it. 'How is this that you wear no ring? Why has your Adam not married you at once?'

Lottie sighed. 'I didn't quite tell you the truth when I said I was coming here to marry him.'

'Not tell the truth? It doesn't sound like Carlotta Earnshaw to avoid the truth? What do you mean?'

Under his dark gaze, she coloured. 'I—I thought he'd marry me. He sent the money.'

Paolo frowned. 'I don't understand. Why would he send for you and then not marry you? I can see that you need someone masculine to stand up for you—to force him to make good his word. I shall be that man!'

'No, no,' begged Lottie, biting her lip. 'He never said he'd marry me. He sent for my sister, for Katie . . .'

'And you came instead!' Paolo stopped dead in the street, causing two boys who were playing tig around them to trip and fall over each other. 'That was to save the family honour—he cannot understand your feelings . . .'

'No, he doesn't,' she said wretchedly. She might have added that she didn't wholly understand them herself.

'It's very wrong of him,' Paolo declared. 'I shall certainly speak to him. I shall take upon myself the role of brother.'

'Nay!' Lottie walked away from him. 'I don't want you to speak to him. I don't want to marry him.'

'Why not?' he demanded, following her. 'He shan't get away with this shabby treatment.'

'He hasn't treated me shabbily,' she protested. Even

as she protested, she wondered what Paolo would say if she told him how Adam had kissed her last night. Well, she wasn't going to tell him. It had nothing to do with him. Just the same, she'd like to know why Adam had acted as he did. In her agitation, she walked a little faster.

Paolo took her arm, forcing her to slacken her pace. 'Has he ever made advances to you?'

'What sort of advances do you mean?'

He shook a finger at her. 'Come, come! You know perfectly well what I mean. Why are you defending him, pretending not to know what there is between a man and woman? Has he ever kissed you?' Once again, he came to a halt, and Lottie with him. He looked down at her. 'Tell me, Carlotta.'

'He—He kissed me last night,' she admitted. 'I think it meant he didn't like me.'

Paolo gave a great shout of laughter. 'There's not a man alive who kisses a girl because he doesn't like her!'

Lottie took her arm from his. 'There's no need to laugh at me. I felt he didn't like me,' she said stiffly. She looked into Paolo's eyes, and then away.

He took her arm and began to walk again. 'Carlotta, this man means something to you. What is it? What does he mean? He's made you angry, turned you down, yet it upsets you because you think he doesn't like you. What are your true feelings towards him?'

'I hate him!' She surprised herself by the strength of her reply. Yes, she did hate Adam, she told herself. He rejected her as a woman—a woman whom he found interesting, or desirable. She was less than nothing to him. Why should that hurt?

'Why did you let him kiss you, then? Did he force himself upon you?'

Lottie shook her head and blushed in shame,

remembering that it was she who had asked Adam if he wanted to kiss her. She wasn't going to tell Paolo that.

But he must have guessed at some of the conflicting emotions that shook her, for he said gently, 'Women make too much of kisses. Forget it, Carlotta. It was a moment's madness, just a tiny part of the search all men make to find a partner. He was lonely for a woman; for some kindness and softness in his life.'

'You kissed me once,' Lottie pointed out. 'Was that the way you felt?'

Paolo squeezed her hand and hesitated before he replied. 'If you have to ask a man why he kissed you, Carlotta, then you haven't understood him very well.'

'I'm trying to understand! Paolo, help me, please?'

'Oh, you English, you have to understand with your heads. A kiss is to be comprehended by the heart, not thought about, taken apart. A man kisses a woman because he wants her. Consider that as a compliment. Don't try to read too much into it.'

Far from offering her comfort, this speech plunged Lottie into despair. What a fool she was! She had come across an ocean on the memory of a kiss. She had let a kiss spoil her whole expectation of life. She felt a lump in her throat, tears at the back of her eyes. In sheer rage at her own inadequacy and idiocy she yearned to stamp her feet upon this alien soil, to spit upon it, to beat the stone wall beside her with her fists and cry out her disappointments.

Instead she answered, soberly enough, 'If I had had you for a brother, Paolo, I might be very different. There was never any talking to Jeremiah.'

'You would still be Carlotta, very sensible, very kind and very brave. I wouldn't have you changed. But if I were your brother, there is something I would tell you now.'

'What's that?' she asked, taking the turning into the series of shorter streets that led to Mrs O'Rourke's.

'I saw where you worked, this morning,' he said. 'Adam offered to do the costumes. I think that was just an excuse to see me in the light of day.'

'Why would he want to do that?' Lottie was intrigued by this idea,

'Whatever you may say about him, he seems to feel a certain responsibility for you, an interest in what company you keep . . .' He stilled Lottie's protests with a wave of the hand.

'Like most people, he thinks entertainers a strange lot—no money, no morals! You don't need to defend him because of that; it shows a certain care in him.'

Lottie smiled at that. 'Oh, Paolo, what did he decide about you, then—that you're quite respectable, even likeable?'

He shrugged. 'As to that, I don't know, but he sent me off to the workroom, and Magdalena, that sweet, beautiful girl, quickly took the costumes and made them fit. She wouldn't accept anything for doing the work. That's why I offered lunch. Such generosity is rare! Is she a special friend of your Adam?'

Lottie was taken by surprise to hear Magdalena described as sweet. Paolo seemed to like her, although everyone else was in awe of her.

'Her family helped Adam when he was new here, and he has helped them in return. They are good friends, but I think perhaps it's Rosa who is special to him,' she said slowly. 'But I don't really know.'

'No matter.' Paolo patted the parcel Magdalena had made of the stage outfits. 'It has nothing to do with the advice I was going to give you.'

'What advice?' They had reached the fence that lined the boarding-house front yard, and Lottie put her hand on the gate, turning to him.

'I don't think you should work alone in the shed with Adam Hardcastle. It's not right. It's not good for you. A girl must be careful of her reputation. Do other people not point this out to you?'

Lottie shook her head. 'He's not there half the time. Besides, I've always worked for a man. In the shop, we all worked for Mr Higginbottom. But we were careful not to be alone with him,' she added honestly.

'Exactly what I mean,' he said, opening the gate and allowing her to go first.

'But Adam isn't like him!' Lottie retorted. 'And in any case, it's only for six weeks till the shop who want to hire me have a place for me.'

'I'm glad to hear it!' he remarked. He stood inside the fence for a moment. 'The sooner you leave that shed, the better.'

Lottie had never expected such advice from Paolo. And yet, why should it surprise her? He took very good care of his sister, and didn't allow her to mix with other men. On the boat he had done this, and that was a test of any man.

With that parting thought, Paolo left her, and Lottie went back to the shed and the accounts. Adam was not there. By the time he did return, she had managed to get through a small amount of sewing.

He sat at his machine, staring into space, while she told him about the morning's triumphs . . .

'I don't believe you've heard a word I've said,' she complained as she brought her recital to a close. 'I thought you'd be pleased.'

'I am pleased,' he answered shortly. 'You're doing exactly what I hoped you'd do—taking a load off my shoulders.' He didn't move.

Lottie looked at him, frowning. He seemed to be thoroughly downcast. She had been nervous about his return. He might refer to last night; he might have talked about Paolo. But he just sat there.

'Is something bothering you?' she asked. 'Has something happened?'

He looked up at that. 'Nothing's happened. That's what's wrong.' His tone was curt.

Lottie wondered if she should carry on sewing and let him come round in his own time. She pushed a piece of material towards the needle and raised her feet to begin treadling, and found she couldn't let him sit there, idle, out of sorts.

'If you talked about it,' she said diffidently, 'it might help.'

'How would that help?'

She bit her lip. He reminded her of her younger brother when he'd had a disappointment. If she hadn't felt so sorry for him, she would have given up. She tried again.

'I thought you said you might go to the bank today.'

'I said nothing of the sort, but I have been to the bank. They thought they might just possibly have a backer for me, but it all came to naught—again.'

'I'm sorry,' said Lottie, not able to add any more.

'Ay, so am I.' Adam patted his sewing-machine absently. 'There's such a future in this machine. It'll change the world—and no one wants to hear about it.'

'It'll come, lad. I know it will.' Lottie's sympathy was aroused. 'It's a new idea. Folks have to get used to it.'

'Ay, happen they do.'

Lottie laughed out loud.

'What's so funny?' Adam's expression was truculent.

'You are! Every so often you sound so Lancashire —it's as though you've never been away. The rest of the time, you sound quite a Yankee.'

'Do I? Perhaps I do.' Adam smiled slightly. 'I think I only do it when I'm with you. I'm sorry to be so bad-tempered,' he added. 'And I'm sorry about last night. You've no need to be frightened of me. It'll not happen again.'

She felt herself blushing, and looked down at her hands. Of course she didn't want it to happen again. He'd upset her considerably. Why didn't she feel relieved by his declaration?

'I don't know what got into me, Lottie.' Adam looked at her intently. 'I only meant to tell you that this Paolo wasn't right for you.'

She bridled at that. 'That's only your opinion!'

'Ay, and it'd be wrong not to let you know about it. What kind of life would it be for you, following an entertainer about the country? Nay, lass, you'd hate it.'

Lottie blinked. Adam had got it into his head somehow that she was serious about Paolo. How could he think that after the way he'd kissed her last night—the way she'd kissed him? Men . . . She frowned, and then replied tartly that Paolo hadn't asked her. She could have added that she thought it unlikely that he would, but why should she give Adam that satisfaction? In his heart of hearts she was convinced he felt she wasn't attractive to any man.

'How about that candlestick he took from you?' Adam hadn't finished with her yet.

'He's explained that,' she said stiffly.

'When did he do that? Not last night, I'll be bound.'

'No, I met him at the workroom and went to lunch with him. Magdalena and Rosa came, too. It was because Magdalena wouldn't take anything for doing the costumes.'

'I told her not to.'

Lottie's eyebrows rose at that. 'That was kind of you.' She was touched by his generosity towards a man she was sure he didn't much like. 'You know, Adam,' she went on slowly, 'perhaps you worry too much about getting a backer. If sales continue to increase, have you thought of gradually giving all the girls machines, and even starting another workroom?'

'I've thought on it,' he admitted, 'and it may come to that. But I've set my heart on setting up a factory to manufacture my sewing-machine.'

For a moment she sat, deep in thought. 'Why not tell Rosemary all about it and get her to write it up in the newspaper? You'd soon have people interested.'

'The wrong kind of people, probably.' Adam's reply was sharp. 'Besides, I was speaking to Rosemary earlier on. She said you'd thanked her for the tickets. She put a flea in my ear about you.'

'About me?' Lottie was surprised. 'What about me?'

He answered her question with one of his own. 'How do you feel about working here in the shed with me?'

Her heart sank. Rosemary must think the same as Paolo. 'Feel? I feel all right.'

'I don't mistreat you, do I? Make you feel uncomfortable?'

'No, of course not.'

'Do you think people talk about you because you're here alone with me?'

'What people?' Lottie parried, wishing those very people wouldn't interfere in her life. Was he going to suggest that she work somewhere else? She didn't want that. It was because it was interesting working with him that she didn't want things to change, she told herself. 'Does Rosemary think that?'

'Ay, and Magdalena and Rosa as well. I don't know what they think happens here.'

Lottie coloured to the roots of her hair. 'You're often out, and so am I!' She laughed at the idea of any impropriety between them in working hours.

'Ridiculous, isn't it?'

Far from putting Lottie's mind at rest, this remark served to inflame her. Adam thought it ridiculous that she should have the kind of attraction for him that others should harbour doubts about her safety, and her reputation.

'Perhaps we can make them understand that it's a business arrangement between us—a matter of work and wages,' Adam went on. 'It was Rosa, really, more than Magdalena who mentioned it to me.'

Lottie felt a stab of pain. Rosa . . . then she was right about her. Her opinion obviously mattered to Adam. 'How—How did the subject come up between you?'

'We were talking, and I just happened to mention we might make up some of the new crinoline skirts. I wanted to know what Rosa thought of them—she has a real eye for style, has Rosa.' Adam's voice softened.

'I didn't know you were thinking of making crinoline skirts! You haven't said anything to me about it,' Lottie interrupted sharply.

'I'm saying it now. There's no need to take on! It was just an idea we had. Rosa thought if we made one for you, it would be a grand way to interest buyers if you modelled one to show it off, like.'

'Did she?' Lottie was half indignant, half intrigued. It was a good idea. She stifled a pang of jealousy. She couldn't dislike Rosa.

'It frees a woman from petticoats,' Adam continued. 'How many petticoats do you wear, Lottie?'

'Two, sometimes three,' she said without embarrassment. It wasn't really a personal question Adam was asking, she told herself.

'There you are,' he said with a smile. 'You'll find a crinoline much cooler. It will do away with all that bulk underneath.'

'It'll do away with the profit from petticoats, too,' she didn't hesitate to point out.

'We have to move with the times,' Adam retorted. 'Will you do it—wear the crinoline to show buyers?'

'Where's the crinoline coming from?'

'From the workroom, of course. You don't have to pay for it. I should think they'd make you up a little blouse to go with it, to set it off,' Adam looked pleased with himself for the first time since he'd come in. 'You will do it, won't you? Rosa thought you would.'

'Ay, I'll do it, but I'll need a sample skirt as well for the buyers to handle.' No one was going to handle her skirt while she was wearing it! She remembered young Mr Calsey's hands all too clearly.

'Right,' said Adam. 'That's settled, then.' He paused. 'There's another thing.'

Lottie waited in some trepidation. 'What's that?'

'I think it would be fair to offer you some small commission on sales, if it goes well. Say one per cent extra.'

'Three,' she replied almost automatically. 'The travellers who came to Higginbottom's got five per cent—and they didn't have to wear the merchandise.'

'How do you know about percentages?' asked Adam. 'Were you friendly with them? I suppose you've had more than one nice present from a salesman! What sort of gifts did they give you?'

'Why do you ask?' she snapped, wondering at the tight expression on his face. 'It's nothing to do with you!' She shrugged. 'Sometimes they brought chocolates or gloves.'

'No garters? Isn't that the usual present to sweeten a girl?' He gave her a considering look. 'Perhaps not your style.'

Lottie resented that. She had never had garters from a salesman, but why should Adam suppose so? She longed to tell him she'd had dozens of garters in her time, but he didn't give her the opportunity.

He went on speaking. 'Has this Polonsky offered you anything yet, or your Mr Jones?'

'Certainly not!' Her temper was rising. Just when she thought she was getting on with Adam, he began to make her feel small. Perhaps she shouldn't have asked for three per cent when he was having such a struggle to finance his machine.

'See that they don't. You're working for me, not for them. Don't forget that!'

'I'm not likely to!'

'Good. We'll agree on two per cent, then.' Adam rose to his feet. 'You'd better stand up.'

'What for?' She couldn't keep the surprise out of her voice.

'So that I can measure you, of course. The girls want your exact measurements.' He took a tape from his pocket. 'I had to do some adjustments to that other skirt they made for you. This way, they'll get it right the first time.'

Lottie got up. Fancy Adam making adjustments to her skirt! The thought made her uneasy. Better to let him measure and have done with it.

She stood in front of him and he passed the tape round her waist and then her bust.

'You're beginning to fill out a little,' he observed. 'I suppose that's to be expected after the boat.'

Lottie bit her lip. He'd noticed that.

'Do you always have lunch?' he asked. 'Make sure you do. It won't do you any good to go without.'

What a strange man he was, Lottie reflected, rubbing damp palms against each other. One minute he seemed angry, the next he was urging her to take care of herself as though he cared. How was he able to disarm her so completely? Did he know he was doing it? He seemed completely at his ease with her now.

'I'm glad you're not one of those flirty girls, always thinking a man is up to no good,' he continued, as he measured the width of her skirt.

She gulped at that, torn between a laugh and a sob. She longed suddenly to be one of those flirty girls; then he wouldn't be able calmly to measure her! He'd put his arms about her and she'd slide out of them, teasing him, tantalising him. She put that traitorous thought away. He could never see her like that. She could never be like that.

'There's no need to be overly modest with a tailor.' Adam looked up at her pleasantly from his kneeling position. 'Is there?'

This time Lottie laughed. She couldn't help herself. Adam could have absolutely no idea of her feelings at the moment—she wasn't even sure of them herself. She longed to reach out and touch his hair, to run her fingers through it and feel its texture. Just what a girl who accepted a garter from a traveller would do, she chided herself. She bit off the laugh and looked away from that smiling gaze, towards the door. With her swift intake of breath, her hand flew to her mouth.

Dorothea stood there, framed in the entrance. She said nothing, but as her eyes met Lottie's it was clear what she was thinking—and it wasn't complimentary.

Lottie flushed and felt guilty, but she couldn't have explained exactly what she was guilty of. How long had Dorothea been standing there? Had she seen Lottie's hand half reach out to Adam? Had she guessed what she was feeling?

It was Dorothea who spoke. 'You did say to come by, Adam, but if you're busy I'll come back later.' She hovered in the doorway for a moment, and then made a move to leave.

'Don't go,' Adam said, rising to his feet. 'I've finished with Lottie, and the day's work is done. She shall lock up here and I'll come with you. We can find a place to walk outside—perhaps on the veranda.'

Dorothea smiled, and Adam shut the door behind them as they went off together.

Lottie went back to her bench, automatically putting the sewing in a pile and covering the machines. What did Dorothea want with Adam? It was none of her business, of course, but just the same she had implied that Adam had invited her to come. Why should she feel so unaccountably deflated? It must be due to that strange conversation she'd had with Adam that afternoon. He seemed to have it firmly in his head that handsome men attracted her, particularly Mr Jones and Paolo. Adam thought all sorts of odd things about her—if he thought about her at all.

Best do as he said, and close up, there was no good in moping here. As she shut the door and locked it, Lottie pocketed the key, hoping she wouldn't have to pass the other two on the veranda.

They weren't there, after all, and she sighed as she let herself into the house. There'd be time for a wash and a brush up before supper. Even the thought of that plentiful meal didn't cheer her the way it would have done last week.

Lottie plodded upstairs to her room, wondering why she felt so let down.

CHAPTER TEN

THE WEEK that followed was one of achievements for Lottie. Everywhere she took the completed garments from the workrooms she met with success and further orders. Magdalena had to take on two new girls and another finished sewing-machine. And still the orders came in. All the buyers wanted the new crinoline skirt, the little velvet hats, aprons. Mr Jones approved of the sample nightshirt and asked for five dozen. He wanted to know if Lottie could make up a matching dressing-gown in a heavier material, and Rosa was delighted to try her hand at it.

Old Mr Calsey sent Adam a note asking for his representative to call. When Adam showed it to Lottie, he said it was up to her entirely if she wanted to do business with the Calseys. Having thought about it, she decided to go back. This time she was treated very courteously and came away with a large order. Young Mr Calsey wasn't there.

She was experiencing a great deal of freedom in this new life. Adam appeared to have decided that she was competent at managing, and allowed her to organise her day as she pleased. It was odd that she saw very little of him. He left messages for her in the shed and listed deliveries, even tacked patterns for pantaloons and blouses to her bench for her to bring to Magdalena. He even left her pay there on Saturday, and she was very pleased with her commission. At the rate she was earning, she'd soon be able to pay back all she owed—if only she could find Adam to give it to him!

Lottie didn't understand where he was or what he was doing, but supposed it must be to do with the machines. Now and again when she was getting ready for bed in her little attic room, she saw him going towards the shed, lantern in hand, and then the light of several candles shining through the window as he worked at his bench. The next morning, cutting directions for new garments would be waiting for her. She toyed with the thought of going and having a talk with him about the drawings she left for him for frilly blouses, nightgowns, little girls' frocks and smocks, for she was enjoying enlarging their line of work. Of course Adam modified some of them, but he did use them. She would have liked to have discussed them with him, but turned down the idea of any night-time visiting. The thought did come to her that he was avoiding her, but she pushed it aside because they were working so well together.

It was the beginning of June now, and the days were really hot. Lottie found them exhausting and was grateful for the coolness of her crinoline. In the evenings she and Rosemary often sat on the veranda, where it was pleasant after the heat of the day. Her room was like an oven. Dorothea was busy with exams at school, she said, and hardly ever joined them. After one such evening when Lottie had written a long letter to Kate, Rosemary had closed her book and gone to her room, yawning.

Lottie sat on, brushing her hair and letting it fall freely round her shoulders. For comfort, she had changed into her old yellow frock. She tucked herself on to a padded bench in the far corner of the veranda, meaning to stay for a little while, quiet in the dark and watch the stars come out. She must have fallen asleep there, for she came to suddenly to find the sky filled with stars and brilliant moonlight flooding the street.

It was a noise that had wakened her—a sound—steps

on the stairs of the long porch. Alarm prickled her spine. The footsteps were approaching her corner. Near panic enveloped her as a menacing shadow advanced, a form as grey as the night. Shrinking back on the padded bench, she tried to make herself as small as possible.

She closed her eyes and held her breath as the dark stranger lowered himself into a chair. Then she opened them, frightened out of her wits. What was she going to do? If he stayed all night, she might hide from him in the dark, but in the dawn he'd find her. She shivered. She couldn't get past him: he was blocking escape.

She studied him from her corner. Something about the shape of his head was familiar. That was Adam's head! A sigh of relief escaped her.

'What's that? Who's there?' Adam rose to his feet.

Lottie felt his hand on her shoulder, and she was pulled from her hiding-place out into a shaft of moonlight.

'What are you doing here?' he demanded.

Speechless, she was trembling with the fear that hadn't quite left her, her hair falling like a dark cloud round her.

'You should have been in your bed hours ago!' Adam's voice softened. He released his tight hold on her shoulder and his fingers tangled in her hair. 'I've never seen you with your hair down. You look like some elfin creature from the woods, and you're shaking with cold.' He put his arm about her. 'Come, sit beside me and you'll soon be warm.'

'It's not cold.' Lottie found her voice. 'I was scared.'

'So you should be!' His tone was brusque, but he guided her to the bench very gently. 'Anyone might have come on to the veranda! What would you have done if it hadn't been me?' He put his jacket round her shoulders and sat beside her. 'Do you remember my young sister

Annie? She used to sit beside me now and then on the stoop in the summer, and we'd talk and laugh in the dark. She was a funny little thing, like you. I could always talk to her.'

'I remember her,' said Lottie. 'But didn't she . . .' She stopped, not wanting to go on.

'Die?' Adam finished for her. 'Ay, she died of diphtheria when she was ten. I missed her.'

Lottie wasn't sure, but it seemed that Adam moved a little closer.

'Things happen to us all.' Adam might have been talking to himself, his voice was so soft. 'It's hard to understand why they do. Annie never harmed anyone.'

'Ay,' she said, and put her hand on Adam's. It was very comforting to lean against him and to feel the warmth of his body against hers. She felt he was a friend from home.

'It's strange, isn't it, Adam, to be on the other side of the world—away from everything and everybody we knew in Rochdale. Do you miss it, too, or does it get better as you go along?'

'He laughed softly. 'Homesick, are you? What do you miss most, young Lottie?'

'Kate and Tom and some of the girls in the shop. And sometimes I walk through these small streets round here and think I'm coming home—and home isn't there any more.'

'Ay,' he said, and put his arm about her. 'It'll get better. Why did you come, Lottie?'

She stirred. If she wasn't careful, Adam would have the reason out of her, and then he'd draw away from her. 'On an impulse,' she said lightly. 'Why did you? You could have stayed and made your way in Rochdale.'

'So I could. I'm not sure what drove me. Yes, I am. I had a row with old Davis, Gents' Furnishers. I wanted more money, a shop of my own, and he said I'd never make it on my own. I set out to show him! At least I'm working for myself. What are you working for?'

Lottie had stopped feeling cold. She was warm now, pleasantly warm. Why was there still a trembling deep inside her? She had never felt so close to anyone before.

'You.' The single word escaped. She was in a dream-like state, where she must say whatever came into her head. It was too much trouble to think about protecting herself, avoiding his questions.

'Me?' Adam was startled. She felt him tighten. 'There's no need to work so hard for me, lass. I'm not a slave-driver.' His arm was suddenly hard against her back. 'Is that how you see me?'

'I didn't mean it that way.' She tried to free herself, not wanting to explain. He was too close, too over-powering and she couldn't bear it if he drew back again. She couldn't face another rejection.

'How do you see me, Lottie?' His voice was a whisper against her unfettered hair.

'I—I don't know,' she faltered.

'Come, Lottie, you can do better than that!' He gave her a gentle shake. 'You're here, in my arms, quite happy to be here, unless I'm much mistaken. Does your heart beat faster, your breath come quicker?' He was smiling down at her.

'No.' She felt driven to deny it, though every beat of her blood acknowledged his presence in a thousand tiny ways awakening her to a kind of pleasure she knew she mustn't admit—yet she had to, at least to herself. 'Yes,' she whispered, 'there's something about this night—the dark, and a man with me . . .'

She felt Adam stiffen. 'Is that all it is—the mystery of the dark? You're more honest than most women—except about this secret that you hug to yourself. Why did you come, Lottie? Was it some man you couldn't have?'

The silence hung between them.

She sighed. 'Ay, it was some man I couldn't have.' She might as well admit it.

'Why not? Was he married?'

'Nay, he loved another.'

'You didn't stay and fight?'

'There was no use in staying.'

'Well, you know best about that. Never mind, you'll get over him.' There was kindness in his tone.

Lottie didn't want his kindness. 'So folk say—like you'll get over Kate.' She wanted to hurt him, to make him feel her pain.

Adam drew in his breath sharply. 'Why are you so prickly? You've never forgiven me for turning you down when you arrived. You're just the same with me as I was with old Davis. You're out to show me something, to prove something to me.'

'No, I'm not! Why should I care what you think of me?'

'I don't know why you do. I just know it's so. Tell me, if it had been some other man who caught you here, would you have sat with him so cosily?'

'Nay!' She was shocked at the very idea. 'I know you,' she protested.

'Do you?'

For the first time, Lottie felt a thrill of alarm. It couldn't be fear of Adam. Accustomed now to the moonlight bathing them, she searched his face. 'I think I do.'

'Am I not a man? Why do you not respond to me in the way any woman might? Softly? Willingly?

'Ay.' She longed to add that he was the only man for her, but lacked the courage. Couldn't he hear the beat of her heart, feel the longing in her for him? Was he so blind that he had to ask? Paolo's words came back to her. Surely they must apply to a man as well as to a woman. If he had to ask, she meant nothing to him. She shook her head. If only he had the same desires as other men—if only he desired her at this moment—he could blame it on the moonlight afterwards.

Her breath caught in her throat and she yearned to put her arms round his neck and pull his head towards hers, to have his lips on hers.

'Is that supposed to be yes or no?' Adam sighed and put out his hand so that he clasped a long thick, gleaming tress of her hair. It was a gentle hold, smoothing, gliding over it.

'I like the feel of a girl here with me in this silvery light, warm and waiting. But it isn't me that you want. Oh yes, you want me to kiss you. I can see that in your eyes.' He laughed softly.

Lottie's hand itched to slap him, to strike that knowledge away somehow, anyhow, but as though he sensed her feelings, he had imprisoned her hands.

'Nay, hear me out, lass. We got off on wrong foot, didn't we? You ran to me from this other chap, seeing me as some kind of chance, someone to restore your wounded pride. I was expecting Kate. Paolo says I was hard on you.'

'Paolo?' she interrupted in amazement. 'Have you been speaking to him?'

'I didn't go looking for him. I happened to run into him at the workroom this morning. The girls were doing a bit of costume work for some of the artists from the concert—paid for, this time. We walked out together and we talked. I hear he's taking you all on an outing to the beach on Sunday. He asked me to go along, but I'm not sure I can. I'll let him know later.'

'Ay,' said Lottie. 'He wanted me to ask you.'

'You didn't, though.' There was a hint of question in his voice.

'I've hardly seen you,' she protested.

'Was that the only reason?'

'I didn't know if you'd want to come.'

'You don't like No from me.' Adam still held her hands. 'It's what I was saying a minute ago. You're trying to prove something about me to yourself.'

Lottie bit her lip. She was mortified that he could read her so clearly. At least he didn't know that there was no other chap she was running from. She was trying to prove to herself that Adam meant nothing to her—that she didn't know the real man, but had crossed an ocean for the dream one.

'I've hurt your feelings, somehow,' he continued, 'wounded you as a woman. I can't undo that, any more than I could want to marry Kate one day and someone else the next. Eh, lass, it takes time to get over a disappointment like that. Thee mustn't take it personal.'

Her breath caught in her throat. Adam was telling her about himself! She recognised the truth in what he said. It came from his heart, couched in the tongue of his boyhood. She hadn't really thought about his feelings. Because Kate had found someone else, she had assumed that his feelings ran shallow, too. There she had been wrong—and perhaps in all else. She had read more into that kiss of long ago than had ever been intended.

'Oh, Adam!' she sighed, and could say no more.

'Let's start again, with no promises between us, no expectations. We can be free to be friends, to work together. If you need help, speak to me about it. We've been friends working in the shed, haven't we?'

Lottie nodded. 'I'm sorry I've been like a bull at a gate—and I'm sorry you're finding it hard to get over

Kate. Folk always love her and forgive her. I know I
do.'

'Ay.'

There was such a note of yearning in that one word,
that Lottie longed to comfort him.

'You sound just like Tom when he'd come a cropper
over summat!' she exclaimed.

Adam smiled at her. 'You were almost mother to the
lad. What did you do to help him? Fill his belly, or pat
him on the head?'

'When he were a little shaver, I'd kiss him better.'

'You could try the same cure on me,' he retorted, still
smiling.

Lottie didn't know whether he was serious or not. In
the soft moonlight she couldn't read his expression
properly, but it seemed to her that he was much like her
young brother Tom in that moment. Almost instinctively, her hand reached out to his head, and she cupped
his face in it and kissed him full on the lips.

It began as a gentle comforting kiss, a soft acknowl-
edgement of life's hardness and unfairness, a reaching
out of sympathy and friendship, even. But as his lips
responded to hers, the kiss changed. Lottie couldn't help
herself. Her lips opened under his, and such a sweet
rising yearning took possession of her inmost being that
she found both her arms had gone round his neck and
that he held her close. Time melted: it didn't exist. It was
Adam who released her. She could hear the beat of his
heart, the same beat as her own.

'That was a right healing kiss, lass!' There was a hint of
laughter in his voice. 'Did it heal thee as well?'

Lottie smiled, then giggled, then laughed outright.
She felt outrageously happy. That kiss had freed her.
Adam had acknowledged her as a woman, a desirable
woman. He had restored her pride in herself. It didn't

matter now that he had refused to marry her. It was as he had said, she had taken that refusal too personally. She was as excited as a girl at her first party. All life was before her! There were men out there waiting for her—a special man who'd want her for himself. Let Adam get on with his own life. She'd get on with hers.

As she rose, Adam's jacket fell neglected to the floor. If only there were music here, she would dance to it as she had that night on the *Black Swan*. She lifted her arms to the sky, to the stars, and softly began to beat time to that music of Paolo's flute, that music remembered in her head.

Adam watched her, smiling. 'I never thought to see thee dancing! I thought you made it up about the boat and the deck. Perhaps, after all, I don't know you quite as well as I thought. Charlotte Earnshaw isn't quite as I supposed.' He got up and held out his hand to her.

Lottie eluded that hand, dancing straight past him. 'Up the wooden hill I'm going, up to the attic. Good night, Adam! It's grand to have a friend!'

She danced along the veranda, humming, and curtsied to him by the door. With a cheerful wave of her hand towards him, she let the door swung to behind her.

Adam had followed her along the veranda, but she had been too quick for him.

Perhaps it was just as well, he told himself. He had wanted to hold her again, to kiss her again. There was something unexpected about the girl. She seemed to have cast a spell on him, so gradual that he hadn't even noticed it—until tonight. Tonight she'd been different. He'd been different with her.

He opened the screen door, and sat on the steps, as he had sat so long ago, so far away, with little Annie. There was no one to talk to now, only himself and the moonlight and the sweet smell of the earth. It wasn't a night for sleeping, but for dreaming.

If Kate had come—but it wasn't Kate he was thinking of. It was Lottie. She knew how it felt to be disappointed in love. That was it, of course. She'd shown him sympathy, and he'd responded to it. Perhaps she had kissed him better. He smiled a little at the memory of that kiss. Ay, there was a fire in Lottie. If she but found the right man, she was a fine lass with a good heart.

This Paolo wasn't for her—that he did know. He'd break her heart with his careless ways: he had no head for money, no thought for truth. Lottie couldn't have let Paolo convince her that she had lent him the candlestick. She knew right well that he'd taken it. Even Magdalena, when she'd told him about it, had been more than a little sceptical. Well, Magdalena had her head screwed on tight. She knew the world and the ways of men like Paolo. Rosa was a different story. Had he done right to introduce her to Paolo? But she'd seemed so unhappy about Luigi and the marriage Magdalena was pushing her towards.

Marriage was a fine thing with the right partner. Ay, so was business. It was time for him to make a start on that. He had talked to Rosemary about that this morning. In a way, Dorothea had forced his hand there. She'd seen the machines, and he'd had to explain the whole shebang to her anyway.

There'd be some changes soon, he was sure of it. He didn't know where his confidence had come from—but it had, quite suddenly. It would all work out. It was a pity about Sunday. He would have liked to have gone on this outing of Paolo's with the girls.

Lottie'd be right surprised when she saw the write-up Rosemary put in the paper. Perhaps he should have warned her, told her what he was doing. Why did he keep thinking of the girl and considering her feelings? He'd tell her in the morning, maybe. The piece wouldn't be in for a day or two.

As he sat there musing, he wished Lottie hadn't rushed off like that. She could have stayed a little longer. A man needed a woman to talk to, to share his plans with.

Lottie came down to breakfast at peace with herself and the world. Only Rosemary was there that Friday morning.

'They've breakfasted already,' she said. 'I stayed to show you this, Lottie.' She handed her a copy of the newspaper.

A headline caught Lottie's eye, as doubtless Rosemary had intended that it should.

'Tailor Invents Sewing Machine'—Lottie scanned the words underneath. It was about Adam, describing his invention and its possibilities. It was all there—from how he'd begun it, to the problems he'd had with it. Its actual working was described in great detail and in far more technical language than she was acquainted with.

'You've written it!' She looked up at Rosemary. 'When did he tell you about it?'

'The other day.' Rosemary looked pleased with herself. 'Didn't you know? He did say he was going to tell you.'

Lottie shook her head. 'I haven't really seen him for a day or two.' Not since the night on the veranda, she might have added. In the shed, there'd only been notes waiting for her in the morning, and she knew Mary had been keeping his meal warm for him in the evenings.

'It's strange he didn't tell you.' Rosemary buttered a slice of bread. 'He seems to think a lot of you. He said it was your idea to put it in the paper.'

Shrugging, Lottie attacked her boiled egg with a quick stroke of her knife. She couldn't help thinking that Adam might have told her.

'I just work for him.'

Rosemary's eyebrows went up. 'Is that all? I thought you had a certain tenderness for him. Is that all over, then?'

'As far as I'm concerned.' Lottie helped herself to tea. 'I was very foolish when I came first. I thought Adam was the only man in the world.'

'And now you don't?'

'Now I don't,' she agreed pleasantly, offering the other girl some jam.

Rosemary smiled, and watched Lottie eating her egg with obvious enjoyment. 'I'm glad to hear it! What brought about this change of mind, if you don't mind my asking?'

Lottie finished a mouthful of bread and answered quietly. 'We had a talk the other night—after you left me on the veranda.'

'You and Adam? I suppose he told you so?'

'No, he didn't. As a matter of fact, I kissed him.' Lottie looked at Rosemary to see how she was taking this piece of information. If she had appeared shocked, she would have stopped there.

Rosemary chuckled. 'And then?' she asked, pouring herself another cup of tea. 'I don't know why girls don't talk much about kissing. I've always thought it was an interesting subject.'

'Ay, so it is—but I don't want it in your paper.'

'Of course not.'

'I haven't been in the habit of kissing men,' she went on, forgetting to eat in her desire to explain. 'I liked it.'

'But not Adam?'

'I like Adam well enough. I think we're friends now.'

She frowned. 'But I think a friend might have told me about this being in the paper,' pointing to the article.

Rosemary began to laugh. 'I don't altogether understand you. Are you really as cool about Adam as you seem?'

'Ay, why?'

'Two reasons.'

'What are they?'

'First, I had the distinct impression that Adam has really begun to value you.'

'So he should!' Lottie went back to eating. 'I've brought in a lot of new business for him.'

'I don't mean in that way.' Rosemary set her tea cup down in the saucer.

'In what way do you mean?'

'As a person, I suppose—an eligible girl.'

'Really? I think you must be mistaken.' Lottie toyed with her spoon. 'What's the second reason?'

'It's something he said.'

'What?' She spread jam on her bread.

'Something about men looking for beauty in a woman and finding it was there all the time—inside her, not obviously just in her face or form. I thought it quite a poetic thought from Adam—and quite apt.'

Lottie considered this in silence, and washed it down with a long drink of tea. 'When did you have this interesting conversation?'

'This morning, early, I went out for a little stroll in the back garden. I often do. I like to see things growing.'

'And Adam was there. Does he share this feeling for the soil?'

Rosemary shrugged. 'He was fetching something from the shed—something for the journey, I suppose.'

'The journey? What journey?'

'Oh, I've put my foot in it! Don't you know?'

'Know what?'

'He and Dorothea have gone upstate to see her family. She invited him quite a long time ago, I think.'

'Why should she do that?' Lottie frowned. There was no need for her to feel upset. Adam had his life to lead, but wouldn't a friend have mentioned that he was going away?

'I don't think he means to offer for her—if that's what you're thinking,' Rosemary said. 'He didn't act that way towards her.'

'How Adam acts is no concern of mine,' she replied stiffly. It wasn't that she minded him going to visit another girl's family. It just seemed an odd thing to do, when he had said the other night that he wasn't over Kate. Was that a story he'd made up for her—like Paolo with the candlestick?

She felt a sense of betrayal, just as she had felt when she had discovered Paolo's theft. Were all men full of deceit? It certainly seemed so. Well, then, she must bear that in mind and not let it hurt her so.

She sighed. 'We must just wait and see. In any case, it will only be a few more weeks before I hear from the Mart about the job they have for me. I shall be better away from Adam.'

Rosemary shrugged again. 'Perhaps you will. I'm glad you can take it so calmly.' She rose from the table.

And so did Lottie.

CHAPTER ELEVEN

SUNDAY DAWNED fine. Paolo and Angelina called for Lottie early in a carriage, and they clip-clopped through the sunny morning along Broadway.

It was the first time that Lottie had seen this great street almost deserted. It was quiet and pleasant, and the willows stirred under a slight breeze. Here and there a few people walked towards small churches she had never noticed before. One or two women stood in open doorways, yawning, and stretching themselves against the day. Most folk were still sleeping. Drawn curtains showed that.

It seemed strange to Lottie that Broadway had houses and apartments where ordinary people lived, but she could see that it was so. Mixed among the shops and theatres and hotels were plain dwellings of all kinds.

They picked up Rosa and Magdalena along the way, and also a friend of Paolo from the theatre, an Irishman who worked behind the scenes, he said. Patrick Shaughnessy was a lad of seventeen or so, tall and black-haired, and with very blue eyes. He sat between Rosa and Angelina, and had them giggling with his compliments.

The carriage took them to a pier on the river, where Paolo bought tickets for them all to go on the boat that was waiting. At twelve cents each, this was a considerable outlay for him, but he wouldn't hear of any of the girls paying. They boarded the paddleboat, and found places to sit on the deck.

'Where are we going?' asked Lottie.

'To Staten Island,' Paolo replied, as he stowed baskets and bags under the seats. 'Remember how on the *Black Swan*, you thought it beautiful? Today our steamer will circle round it, through the Upper Bay and then along Kill Van Kull and into Raritan Bay.'

Lottie thought these strange names indeed, but Magdalena explained that they had been given by the first Dutch settlers here.

'I don't care about all that,' said Rosa. 'We shall find a beach when we get to wherever it is, and I shall paddle in the sea.'

The fresh breeze blew and the sun shone, and the whole of the bay opened to them as Manhattan receded from view. It was almost like being at sea again, Lottie reflected, leaning back and closing her eyes for a moment. This was a day for pleasure, for forgetting about ordinary things—and for not wondering what Adam and Dorothea were doing.

She opened her eyes and found that Paolo was telling Magdalena about the Bay of Naples and its beauty. Magdalena broke into a torrent of Italian at this, but her tone was gentle, and the liquid language sounded soft in Lottie's ears. She and Patrick smiled at each other, not understanding it.

He and Angelina and Lottie strolled round the deck, leaned over the rail and threw crumbs to the gulls that followed the boat. A party of lads waved to them from another steamer, and they waved back, laughing. Lottie felt released from all care, young and silly and heedless. By the time they reached Raritan Bay, it was mid-morning, and they had already eaten some of the fruit and nuts that they had brought with them.

They marched down the gangplank with the other emerging passengers, and set off, laden down, to the beach. It was beautiful, not crowded, with golden sands and the Atlantic waves rolling in to touch them, white-capped, blue-tipped in the blazing sun. Angelina, Rosa, Patrick and Lottie dropped the bags they were carrying and raced up and down the sand like dogs released from a leash. Magdalena and Paolo watched them, smiling, and telling them they were children.

Lottie had worn her flowered skirt, which was straight and only a little full. Rosa had a cotton print dress in blue and white. It, too, had a manageable skirt, as did Magdalena's red and white gingham. But Angelina had chosen to wear a black and white checked skirt with a crinoline hoop. With the wind blowing, she found herself bowled along, and then her crinoline began to lift like some giant shade from its base.

She tried vainly to hold it in place. Rosa and Lottie went to her help, but they were laughing so much that they weren't much use. Poor Angelina was the centre of attention that she didn't want. Her lace-edged panta-loons were exposed to everyone's view. Thoroughly mortified, she struggled back to where her brother and Magdalena sat, and dropping to the sand, struggled even to sit in the wretched garment as once again the hoop rose smartly in the air. She rose to her knees, her skirt billowing about her.

It was Magdalena who came to her rescue. 'Why do you laugh?' she scolded the others. 'The child needs help.' She took a pair of scissors from her pocket and took Angelina to one side. 'We shall take out the hoop and tuck up the skirt. It will be the work of only a few minutes to replace it tomorrow.'

Angelina hugged the older girl when the task had been completed, and in a very short time all of them sat down to lunch. They had cold meat and crusty bread, pickles and garlic sausage, cold spaghetti rings, and boiled eggs in a delicious tomato sauce. Paolo had brought red wine to wash it all down.

Angelina whispered in Lottie's ear, 'Not like we ate on the *Black Swan*, is it?'

Lottie shook her head. That terrible voyage seemed far away now, and she didn't want to think about it. She lay back on the sand with the others, and they all sighed deeply and drifted off to dreams of content and plenty.

'Shall we go and paddle in the sea?' asked Angelina, sitting up first. 'We can watch Paolo swim. I don't know why I'm not allowed to swim,' she complained.

Magdalena was shocked. She shivered. 'It's unhealthy for girls to go into the water! Everyone knows that.'

'Why is it?' Angelina persisted. 'If I had a bathing-suit like Paolo has, I should go swimming. Wouldn't you, Lottie?'

'Ay, I would and all! On a hot day like this, it would be grand to step into the waves and be cool.'

Magdalena was horrified, but Patrick declared himself in favour of the girls swimming, with proper costumes, of course.

'Covered to the ankles, I suppose,' said Angelina gloomily. 'Men have all the fun.'

Paolo and Patrick retired behind some trees to change, and then the girls trooped after them, barefoot, down to the sea. Both men were in black costumes, Paolo's with red stripes.

Patrick ran straight down the beach, but Paolo proceeded at a more leisurely pace.

'Like some oriental prince followed by his wives,' Angelina whispered to Lottie, and imitated her brother's swagger.

Lottie couldn't help herself. She laughed, and Rosa did too. Even Magdalena allowed herself to smile.

Paolo proved a powerful swimmer who breasted the

waves fearlessly while the waders applauded. Patrick was more of a ducker than a swimmer.

Lottie hid a smile when Paolo came out of the sea and was folded in a large towel by Magdalena, with strict instructions to run along the beach to get warm. It struck her then that Magdalena seemed very much interested in Paolo, but she brushed the thought aside. After all, she had seemed just as caring towards Angelina. It was a different side of her nature from the one she had revealed so far.

It was a day of magic for Lottie. She had found a family again—a family who accepted her, and liked her and wanted her. She loved the open air and being caressed by the warmth of the sun, blown a little by the bracing breeze, and well fed, too. She was enjoying herself with an ease of carefree abandon which she hadn't experienced since she'd been a young girl.

She felt alive and well. Her cheeks were pink, her hair shining, her eyes glowing. She knew that in the short time she'd been in New York, her face and figure had softened and her natural vigour had returned. Now she was alive in a way she had never been, even before that terrible voyage.

In the golden afternoon, she and Paolo walked along the sands, collecting shells, bits of wood and stone, and he told her how well she looked, and how happy.

'Today you are no older than Angelina and Rosa,' he smiled at her. 'What's happened to you?'

'For the first time in my life, I'm free—free to do as I like, to work for myself.'

'I'm happy, too,' Paolo announced. 'We're being kept on for another three weeks, anyway, and there's the possibility of more work here in New York, and maybe in Boston. Life is good, Lottie, and it's good to have friends.'

He didn't add that she'd soon have her candlestick back, but she didn't care so much about it. Even if he never returned it to her, she would never forget Kate. People were more important than possessions.

When Paolo asked where Adam was, she smiled, and raced him along the beach. As they came to a laughing halt, disputing with each other who had won, a male voice from a small group called out to Lottie.

She turned round, astonished to hear herself hailed as 'Miss Earnshaw'.

A figure came towards her in sporty white trousers and a blue blazer. It was Mr Jones from the men's shop.

He bowed over her hand. 'I wasn't sure it was you, when I saw you on the boat.'

Lottie introduced him to Paolo.

'Not Mr Jones here!' he exclaimed. 'David Jones— Dai, they call me at home.'

'Any friend of Carlotta's is a friend of mine,' Paolo declared solemnly, if not very warmly. But he soon thawed, and Dai Jones introduced them to his sister and her husband who were part of the group he was with.

They all had a pleasant chat, and afterwards Lottie and Paolo rejoined the others, who were playing ball. The rest of the food was soon finished, and they sighed that the lovely day was over. Then they gathered up their possessions and went on board.

As the light faded, and the dusk of evening descended, they drew close to each other on deck, wrapping shawls and jackets around themselves. Paolo started to sing and Patrick to play a flute, and they all joined in, gathering a little crowd, Dai Jones and his sister among them. It was very pleasant to watch the lights winking from both shores and then the brighter illuminations of Manhattan in the distance as the night darkened. Someone produced a banjo, and they listened to that. Lottie found herself with Dai Jones, and noticed that Magdalena and Paolo were sitting side by side.

'I thought at first he was your special gentleman,' Dai said, 'but I'm glad to see he's not.'

Lottie was a little surprised by this observation, but when she looked at the two Italians sitting so close together, she bit her lip. Could Dai Jones be right? She closed her mouth on a protest. It very much looked as though he might be.

'I liked you from the first day you walked into the shop,' he went on. 'But I never thought to meet you like this! Is your name really Carlotta?'

'It's Charlotte. Everyone else calls me Lottie. It's only Paolo who thinks I'm Carlotta. His sister, Angelina, started it on the boat coming over, and it's stuck as far as they're concerned.'

'Terrible, was it, the boat?' Dai asked, and they were off, discussing their Atlantic journey.

'I thought I'd never set foot on another ship,' Dai told her, 'but here I am, and glad I came!' His smile was very sweet.

He spoke well and at some length, and Lottie found she liked him. His voice was softer than hers, and the way he put things made her smile in amusement, but he was easy to be with. He wanted to know all about her and how she'd managed to find a job so quickly.

Lottie didn't mind confiding in him, but she described Adam as a friend of the family. If he chose to think of him as an older man, that was his affair. She didn't set him right.

Angelina and Rosa fell asleep beside them, arms twined round each other. Lottie and Dai talked on. Back at the pier, Patrick shook the two girls awake and Paolo piled them all into a carriage. Lottie couldn't have said how it was that Dai accompanied them.

In the heat of the June night enfolding them, she yawned. The bright gas lights along Broadway made her realise her tiredness and the lateness of the hour. They dropped Patrick, Magdalena and Rosa first, and then Angelina fell asleep again as the horses trotted their way towards Mrs O'Rourke's. When they arrived there, both Paolo and Dai handed Lottie out of the carriage. Paolo kissed her hand, and Dai followed suit.

She went up the veranda steps, waving to them. As she put out her hand to open the heavy front door, Adam's voice called to her from the shadows of the veranda.

'What time of night is this to get home?'

Lottie jumped. 'It's been a lovely day! I suppose it is a bit late. Why are you waiting for me? Is something wrong?'

'You tell me,' he suggested. 'I didn't expect to see two men kissing your hand at this time of night! What is all this hand-kissing, anyway?'

'It's just Paolo's way.' She smiled, and replied mildly. It had been such a pleasant day that she wouldn't allow herself to be upset.

'And this other fellow—is it his way, too?' Adam was frowning at her. 'Who is he—besides being tall and dark and handsome? I mistrust chaps with curly hair.'

'Dai Jones—Mr Jones who bought the nightshirts from me.' Her voice was quiet. 'You have curly hair.'

'Dai Jones! You're on first-name terms, then? I never heard he was invited on this outing. You kept that from me. And my hair waves, it doesn't curl. Curls mean trouble.'

'Don't be so soft,' Lottie snapped.

'Soft, am I?'

Adam sounded so aggrieved that she drew in her breath sharply. What was the matter with the man?

Making an effort to smile, she said sharply, 'We happened to meet him on the beach, and he came to talk to me.'

'And then brought you home, and kissed your hand.'

This was said so accusingly that Lottie was annoyed. 'I don't know what it has to do with you!'

'I have a certain responsibility for you,' Adam informed her. 'I don't intend to shirk that when I see you flirting.'

'You sound just like Jeremiah—at his most righteous! At least he was my brother.'

'Ay, I'm standing in for him.'

They stood glaring at each other.

'You have no right!' Lottie insisted, very angry now. 'I'm not going to stay and listen to any more of this.' Her hand reached out for the door again. 'I wasn't flirting.'

'No so fast,' he said, catching her hand in his. 'I want to talk to you.' He drew her away and on to the veranda proper. He thrust her down on a hard bench.

'Say it, then!' she snapped, rubbing her arm where he had gripped it. 'Whatever it is you have to say, get on with it.'

'Right, I will.' Adam stood above her, his face in the shadows. 'I wanted to see you, to tell you before anyone else does.' He paused.

Lottie willed him to go on, her lips parted. Was he going to tell her about Dorothea and himself? she wondered.

'I'm making some changes.' He sat on the bench beside her, but not close enough to touch.

'Ay?' She sensed he was ill at ease, and it puzzled her. 'Can't it wait till morning?' She wondered why he felt he had to tell her at midnight.

'It's about the work. I've hired another girl.'

For a moment, she couldn't take it in. She had been

expecting to hear that he was engaged to Dorothea. 'Another girl?' she repeated.

'She starts tomorrow. I wanted you to know before then. That's why I waited up for you. I couldn't just let you discover it at breakfast.'

'At breakfast?' Lottie wondered why she kept repeating what Adam said. She knew she must sound very slow, but she couldn't seem to help herself. 'Where's she going to work? In the workroom, I suppose.'

He shook his head. 'She came back with us, you see. I never thought she'd start so soon.'

Lottie didn't understand what he was talking about. 'Could you start at the beginning, lad, and tell me properly what you're on about?' She yawned. 'I can't seem to take it in.'

'What don't you understand?'

'Everything—nothing. What's this girl going to do?'

'Help you, of course—and me as well.'

'In what way?'

'In every way.' Adam sighed as though exasperated. 'Why are you making this so hard for me?' He rested his chin on his hand. 'We've both been working all the hours of daylight, haven't we—in spite of the hours you said you'd work? I have noticed, you know.'

She nodded. 'You've been working some of the night ones, too. I've seen you and that winking lantern going to the shed of an evening and staying there.'

He smiled. Even in the darkness of the shadows, she could see the flash of white teeth.

'It's going to be different from now on. Anna will solve all our difficulties, and there won't be any talk about you alone in the shed with me.'

'Oh!' Lottie exclaimed, feeling as though she'd been hit in the stomach. 'I suppose you minded the talk.'

'Not for myself, but for you. Anna thought of it, too.

She was very relieved to hear there was another girl to work with. You'll like her, Lottie.'

'Will I?' She wasn't too sure of that. 'How will she feel, this Anna, when I leave in two or three weeks' time?'

'Leave?' It was Adam's turn to be surprised. 'Why would you leave?'

'I started to work for you only as a stop-gap, like,' Lottie blurted out. 'You knew I had another job to go to!'

'I suppose I did. I thought you liked the work you're doing. I'm very pleased with you.'

'That's as may be,' she said coolly enough, keeping the pleasure she felt in that statement to herself. 'You never said anything to me about staying on.'

'I'm saying it now!' he protested, taking her hand in his. 'Please, Lottie, stay with me? I'll match whatever this other job offers. I don't want to lose you.'

If he had stopped there, she would have capitulated immediately. She felt flattered, and wanted.

But Adam went on. 'You'll make a gradely teacher. You'll be able to set Anna right on things, train her up to the job. She's a tailor and a cutter.'

Lottie didn't like the sound of this information. 'Happen she knows more than me!' she retorted. 'She won't want to work for me. Am I to be boss, then?'

'You'll both work for me.' Adam still held her hand. He turned it over, and traced a finger down the line that ran along her thumb. 'Eh, lass, where's the difficulty?'

'Is she to be selling too?'

'Ay, after a bit. But she'll need to learn the machine first, and the way we run things. I want you two to get along. I know you can do it, Lottie. You've managed to get along with Ada, and she's a lot more difficult than Anna.'

'I'm not sharing a tiny shed with Ada,' Lottie pointed out. 'Does Anna know what to expect—that it's only a shed?'

'We've talked about it—and talked about getting some place better against the winter cold. By that time, with the two of you at it, we'll be well able to afford it.'

She drew back at that. 'The two of you have done a lot more talking and planning than you and I have ever done.'

'Dorothea saw to that.' His voice contained so little enthusiasm that she couldn't believe he was talking about the girl whose family he had just visited.

'What's Dorothea got to do with it?'

'Anna is Dorothea's sister.'

That was too much. She snatched her hand from Adam's. She certainly wasn't going to commit herself to a binding agreement on that basis. 'No, I'll not do it. I'll not make any promises about staying on.'

'Now what's the matter?' he demanded. 'What have I said wrong?'

'It's not a question of saying it wrong! You should have told me that in the first place.'

'I thought I had,' he declared. 'I said you'd meet her at breakfast.'

'I didn't know what you were talking about then. You mean she's staying here? We'll never get away from each other.' Lottie was liking the whole thing less and less with each new revelation. 'Have you told me everything now—or is there more to come?'

'More . . . I don't know what you mean.' Adam rose and looked down at her. 'I never thought you'd turn like this on me, Lottie! But if you don't want the job, you don't have to stay on. You're free to do as you please.'

She wasn't sure that was what she wanted, either. She drew in her breath sharply. If she could have gone directly to the Mart tomorrow, she told herself, she would have had no hesitation in doing so. It would have been a pleasure to let Adam deal with Anna—and Dorothea—on his own, and serve him right, too, she added for good measure. As it was, she still owed him money, and the rent would have to be paid.

'I'll work the time I promised,' she said stiffly. 'I'll not let you down. I'll show Anna everything I've learned from you and take her round to the buyers, but I'll not do more than that. I can't promise to stay on indefinitely.'

'Very well.' Adam was as much on his dignity as she was. 'I've never forced anyone to work for me. If you don't want to, you don't want to.'

By this time Lottie wasn't sure what she wanted. There was no question but that she had liked working for Adam, but there was something very underhand in the way he'd gone about this business. He might have told her what was in his mind before he'd made all sorts of arrangements—arrangements which she was supposed to fall in with without a murmur. Well, she valued herself a bit more than that! If he wanted Dorothea and her sister for partners, she was better out of it.

'We're agreed, then,' she said coldly. 'Now, if you don't mind, I'm very tired and I need my sleep.' She got up. 'Good night Adam. Will you be here in the morning to introduce Anna, or shall I take her to the shed myself?'

'I'll be around for the first hour or so, then I have people to see. Good night, Lottie, I'll see you then.'

His 'Good night' was addressed to Lottie's retreating back. She didn't even look round at him as she opened the door, but just went off without another word.

Damnation, what was wrong with the girl that she

didn't want to stay on in the job? She liked it well enough; she had a decided flair for it.

Just as he thought he had all that nonsense about why she had come to New York cleared up with her, the wretched girl turned temperamental on him and wanted to leave! What had got into her? That hand-kissing had turned her head—given her ideas about herself. It was all due to Paolo and the fancy way he treated her.

If he himself had kissed her hand and talked to her more gently, would she have been more amenable? That wasn't his style. It was all right for the Italians—and for Dai Jones—he added. The Welsh were kin to them.

Perhaps he had been a bit hard on her there at the start. She'd looked so happy and so pleased with herself, and he'd spoiled it for her. He'd been tired after two days of haggling with the Spencers. Old man Spencer drove a hard bargain when one of the girls was concerned, and Adam had been determined to hire Anna. Lottie had to have company in the shed. Whatever she said about his feelings, it was hers he was considering. To have her turn on him and tell him she couldn't promise to stay was just too much!

He didn't want Lottie to leave. That was the long and short of it.

The knowledge hit him like a blow. It was nothing personal, of course, but he'd got used to her. That was all it was. He liked the way she looked up at him when he came back to the shed, her face lighting up as she waited to hear about what he'd been doing. It wouldn't be the same if she weren't there. He wasn't going to share his plans with this other girl.

Nay, Lottie must stay. He was an Englishman through and through, but he'd take a lesson from this Paolo chap and put on some charm. He could do it if he tried. She seemed to like this kissing and bowing. Well, she'd have some of it, then. He'd see to that.

The prospect at first intimidated him a bit. That was natural, he assured himself. He was used to being direct and straight, but he could see that wasn't the way women wanted to be treated. They all swooned at Paolo's feet. Even Magdalena had a good word to say for him, and she wasn't an easy sort of girl. Everyone knew that.

Adam smiled, and then began to laugh. Lottie didn't know what she was in for, but she'd find out shortly. He'd made up his mind she was going to stay. Let her beware. He'd show her that a Lancashire man could be as winning as any Italian!

He strode along the veranda, whistling.

CHAPTER TWELVE

BOTH ANNA and Dorothea were at breakfast the next morning.

Lottie couldn't have been more surprised when Adam introduced her. Anna was nothing like her sister. Where Dorothea was tall and fair and pretty, Anna was petite, dark and vivacious. Her features were irregular: her mouth a shade too large, her nose rather pointed. Her eyes were dark and arresting in their shrewd brightness. Dorothea's voice was high and nasal, Anna's was deep and strong and throaty.

Anna smiled at her, and Lottie was more than a little disarmed by her friendliness. If she hadn't been Dorothea's sister, she would have admitted that Anna was a girl she could take to.

Adam was as good as his word and accompanied them to the shed. Lottie was surprised to hear him telling Anna how much he depended on Lottie's skill and good temper and selling ability. It was balm to her spirit to hear herself praised. When he added for good measure that he didn't know what he'd do without her, she couldn't believe her ears.

He's just trying to get round me, she thought. Well, I'll not be won over that easily. She began work on a blouse, treadling vigorously so that Adam had to speak louder.

He showed Anna how to use the other machine and she was quick enough to learn. By the time he left, she was quite competent at it. Then, for most of the morning, there was no sound in the shed but the whirr of two sewing-machines.

Lottie had to acknowledge that Anna was a very capable and steady worker, and had been much quicker to master the machine than she had been.

When Anna had finished the first pile of aprons on her bench, she looked round for more.

'Is this all it is—just machining?' she wanted to know. 'I understood I'd be doing some cutting and some pattern-making. I wouldn't mind trying my hand at something fancier in the way of an apron. Have you thought of taffeta or velvet?'

'Yes, often,' Lottie sighed, 'but thoughts like that frighten Adam.'

Anna smiled. 'Wouldn't it be nice to show him what we could do, and keep it a secret till it's a fact? I'll make you a pattern, and then we'll talk about it.'

With a few deft strokes, she sketched a fetching little apron which immediately won Lottie's approval.

'I'm sure I could sell that to Mr Polonsky,' she said.

'Who buys the materials here?' Anna asked, her pencil behind her ear, her bright eyes shining. 'Can we get some velvet ourselves?'

'I don't see why not.' Lottie began to smile. Before she left, she was going to prove to Adam that expensive fripperies could sell, too. But why stop at velvet aprons? 'How about a frilly blouse?' she suggested. 'I saw some beautiful fine lawn, some georgette and some organdie at the wholesalers the other day.'

Anna winked at her and began to sketch again. As she watched her, Lottie kept adding to her list of ideas. 'When you see the goods in the shops here, you can't help noticing things. Little girls' dresses could be much prettier, and have more detail on them. That's where the sewing-machine should win orders for us. It's so much quicker to trim things with braid or lace or frills than it ever was by hand. Nighties and petticoats and pantaloons can be more ornate, more feminine.'

Anna produced another sketch, and another. 'I'm beginning to like this work! Can we really do it—just on our own?'

'Ay,' said Lottie, excited now by the prospect. 'You get the patterns done, and we'll cost them out and take them to Ada at the workroom. We'll start in a small way at first; get a model made up and take it round with the ordinary garments.'

Lottie had a moment of conscience when she wondered how she'd face Adam if they failed, but she dismissed it. They weren't going to fail!

She was even more convinced of the rightness of going ahead when Anna confided that she had a boyfriend in New York who worked for a wholesale grocer, and she hoped to see him soon.

'Dorothea doesn't like him,' she confided. 'She thinks the grocery trade is beneath the Spencers!'

Lottie decided that was another point in Anna's favour. She wouldn't tell her sister everything she did.

Later in the day, when she and Anna visited the workroom in the normal course of events, Lottie showed the sketches and patterns to Ada, who said that Rosa would assist them; that it was exactly the kind of thing she loved; and that she'd help them to choose materials at the wholesalers. Lottie didn't mention that Adam hadn't approved as yet, and Ada never questioned that aspect.

In two days, the samples were made up and Lottie took them round to her buyers. She was delighted and relieved when they met with instant approval—and orders. Now was the time to tell Adam, and she could tell him, too, that Dai Jones had invited her to a church social—accompanied by his sister and her husband, of course.

Her opportunity came that very afternoon as she was locking up the shed, Anna having gone ahead because she was seeing her young man that evening and wanted a wash before the evening meal.

'I've good news for you, Adam,' she began. 'You'll want to know how we've got on with orders today.'

'Ay,' he said, smiling at her. 'Sit on the bench here and tell me about it.'

Lottie sat beside him, a little puzzled. Ever since that night on the veranda, he had seemed so much more affable. She had thought he would be irritable still about her leaving, but he hadn't said a word more about it. Instead of pleasing her, that piqued somehow.

'How are you getting on with Anna?' he asked.

'Very well. She's a good worker, and is full of ideas. We've tried out some new samples on the buyers— Anna did the patterns—and they like them. They want more. Mr Polonsky wants four dozen velvet aprons, and he asked about silk ones.'

Lottie looked closely at Adam to see what his reaction would be, because he had always been nervous about expensive materials.

'Grand!' was his only comment.

'Is that all you're going to say?'

'A gentleman never says "I told you so" to a lady— but I knew fine that Anna was a goer and you'd enjoy showing her the ropes.'

Her foot itched to kick his shins—not hard, but just enough to take that self-satisfied expression from his face. She restrained herself with difficulty. 'Since when did you become a gentleman?' she contented herself with retaliating.

Adam might have lost his temper, but he only

laughed, and took her hand in his. 'I've decided that a bit of polish wouldn't go amiss. This write-up of Rosemary's in the newspaper has given me the intro to society, you might say. I've met several gentlemen in business who are seriously thinking of investing in the sewing-machine —and I've been to their houses and all. Oh, Lottie, you wouldn't believe the luxury of them! Mirrors everywhere, and gold ornaments and crystal chandeliers. That tip of Paolo's about kissing the ladies' hands does go down well.'

Lottie opened her mouth, and closed it without saying a word. This was a different Adam, one she didn't know at all.

'That's not like you! Have you nothing to say, Lottie? Perhaps you don't believe me. I'll show you, then.' He raised her hand very gently and bent his head to it, his lips just brushing its back.

That delicate caress was astonishing, and it sent a quiver of alarm through her. She was almost sure it was alarm. Or was it delight, excitement? There was something very intimate about having your hand kissed in a garden with the sun shining in the late afternoon. But she was over that nonsense about thinking Adam was the only man in the world. Although she knew she should take her hand away, she didn't.

'I'm glad to hear you may get a backer,' she managed to say. Better to bring this whole conversation back to a more ordinary level!

He grinned. 'They go out a lot, these rich folk—to concerts and theatres and restaurants, and the like. That's what I should be doing, too. I hear there's a fine piano recital to be held this Friday evening. You've always liked music, haven't you, Lottie? What do you say you come with me?'

'This Friday?' she asked with a sinking heart. She

didn't know why her heart should sink, but that was just what it was doing. Because she was so taken by surprise, she blurted out that she couldn't, that she was busy on Friday. If she'd had any warning, she could have dressed it up a little, and told him she was sorry.

As it was, 'I can't, Adam,' came out very baldly, not as she would have meant to say it.

'Oh, I see. Has Paolo the night off, then?' he enquired politely, hiding whatever feelings he had.

'It's—It's not Paolo,' she stammered wretchedly.

'Not Paolo? Who, then?' Adam released her hand.

'Dai Jones has asked me to a church social. His sister will be there.'

'He hasn't wasted any time! I can see I'll have to meet this young man.'

Lottie giggled. She couldn't help it. 'Oh, Adam, he's older than you are. He's thirty-two.'

He took this equably enough. 'I meant what I said the other night—about standing in as brother to you.'

'There's no need,' she replied stiffly. Adam might have said he was disappointed that she couldn't go, or he might have suggested another time, she reflected. Instead, he was so anxious to have her off his hands that he was proposing to meet this new friend. What did he hope to accomplish by that?

He enlightened her immediately. 'Every girl needs a family,' he assured her. 'Since you have no one else here, I shall be that family. This Dai Jones has a sister—she'll want to know what kind of stock you come from, that you're a respectable sort of girl. I can set her mind at rest.'

Lottie was forced to see the sense of his reasoning. She should be grateful to him, she supposed, but she wasn't. In Adam's mind she was already promised to Dai Jones, and she was nothing of the kind. Why was he trying to rush her into matrimony—first with Paolo and now with a man who was only escorting her to a church social? Really, it was too much. And he didn't even seem to care whether she went on working for him any more. He'd been careful not to mention that. Perversely, she would have liked him to. She was finding that working with Anna was much better than she had expected, but she wasn't going to be the first to speak of it.

'When he calls for you on Friday evening, I shall make a point of being here to greet him,' Adam said firmly.

Although she tried to persuade him otherwise, he refused to be dissuaded, and she was forced to give in.

Adam went off to the house then, and Lottie, still fuming, took a stroll round the vegetable garden to calm herself. It was there that Paolo found her a few minutes later.

'I am upset. I am devastated!' He stood before her, one hand on his heart, woebegone, scowling.

'Whatever's happened?' Lottie put her hand on his arm. 'Is Angelina all right?'

'Never better. It is not Angelina who has had a blow to the heart,' he said dramatically. 'It is I, Paolo! I have come to tell you at once.'

Lottie couldn't see any signs of a blow to his heart, no bleeding, no tear in his coat. 'Sit down,' she begged, 'and tell me what it is.'

Paolo shook off her arm. 'I cannot sit. I am too worked up. She's refused me!' He paced up and down, muttering to himself.

Suddenly he halted before her and gripped her hands. 'Lottie, tell me what I must do?'

'You must sit down and explain properly,' she insisted, pushing him down on the bench where Adam had sat. 'Begin at the beginning.'

'Magdalena has refused me. I asked her to marry me. I was sure she cared for me, as I do for her.'

Lottie considered this. 'Perhaps you asked her too soon.' She wasn't surprised that Paolo wanted Magdalena, not after Sunday's picnic.

'Did she give any reason?'

'She cannot leave Rosa.' Paolo sighed, and would have leaped to his feet again save for Lottie's restraining hand. 'I have this marvellous opportunity to travel all over America—after the booking in Boston, you understand. I had to speak immediately or lose her for ever. Carlotta, what am I to do?'

'She may not want to travel the country,' Lottie suggested. 'Perhaps she regards New York as her home.'

'No, no, it's not that.' He brushed the idea impatiently aside. 'If she loved me enough, that wouldn't matter. The tour will end in California, and my brothers will both be there by then. She would never be without a home.'

'She might change her mind.' Lottie tried to offer some comfort. 'Has she said she loves you?'

'Oh yes, she loves me,' Paolo groaned, 'but she loves Rosa more.'

'Take Rosa with you.'

'She won't come. She wants to stay in New York. She refuses to marry this Luigi she is half-promised to. Magdalena won't let her stay on her own.'

'But Rosa is quite able to take care of herself. She could move in with one of the girls in the workroom, or find a nice Italian family to live with.'

'You think that. I think that. Magdalena sees her as her baby sister.' Paolo was on his feet, pacing again. 'She says it's dangerous for Rosa,' he muttered over his shoulder.

'Dangerous?' Lottie rose and paced after him. 'In what way?'

Paolo faced her over a bed of young tomato plants. 'She wouldn't tell me at first, but after a while it all came out.'

'What came out?'

'It's to do with the machines in the workroom.'

'The machines?' Lottie was nonplussed.

'There has been lots of talk—rumours—since that piece in the newspaper. Threats about destroying the machines, cutting up the finished sewing, protecting jobs.'

'Who's made these threats?'

Paolo shrugged. 'No one knows. They're all frightened—all the girls in the workroom. Some laugh about it, but they all believe in it, I think.'

'That's awful.' Lottie shuddered. 'They haven't said anything to me. Have they told Adam?'

'He laughs at them, and calls it nonsense and says it couldn't happen in America. Carlotta, you must tell him. He'll listen to you.'

'What makes you think that? I soon won't be working for him anyway.'

'Not working for him?' It was Paolo's turn to be surprised. 'Have you quarrelled?'

'Not exactly.'

'Either you have or you haven't. What is this "not exactly"? I don't understand you, Carlotta.'

'He brought in a new girl to work in the shed.' Lottie hesitated. She didn't want to make trouble with the girls in the workroom, and Paolo might repeat what she said to Magdalena.

'Good for Adam!' Paolo responded. 'I didn't like you working here with only him for company. What's the matter—don't you like this girl?'

'I didn't think I was going to, but I do.'

'You were angry with Adam at first and said you wouldn't stay—Is that it?'

That was exactly it. Lottie nodded, grateful for Paolo's quick understanding.

'That's easy, then. You must go to him and tell him you were wrong. He'll forgive you.' He looked at her. 'Ah-ha! I see, Carlotta, you don't like to tell him that you made a mistake. Pride in a woman is a terrible thing when it is stupid pride.'

She flushed. 'Yes, Paolo,' she agreed meekly. 'Why is it that I can tell you, but when I think of telling Adam, the words stick in my throat.'

'Are you afraid of him?'

'No-o,' she replied slowly. She *wasn't* frightened of him.

'Do you want to work for him?'

'Ay, he's the best chap I ever worked for, and the work's proper interesting—always something different.'

Paolo shrugged. 'Then you must swallow your fine feelings of right and wrong and ask if you can stay.'

'Ay,' Lottie repeated. She knew Paolo was stating the obvious, but she just couldn't bring herself to speak to Adam. He should have asked her again to stay.

'And when you ask him,' Paolo went on, 'be sure you tell him of the fears of the workroom girls.'

Adam had strode off towards the house, thinking that Lottie would follow him. When there was no sign of her, he didn't stop for her. Best let her cool down a little. He meant fine what he said about meeting this chap of hers and putting him right about Lottie's family. He went straight in, and was beckoned into the front parlour by Anna.

'Could I have a word with you?' she asked.

'Of course.' Adam followed her and went to sit on one of the straight chairs just inside. 'How's the job going?'

'Just what I want to speak to you about.' She looked cheerfully at him and sat down. 'I like it very much. I've been wondering, though . . .' She paused for a moment. 'I've been wondering if you've found a backer yet for your machines.'

He wasn't sure where this was leading. 'It's looking promising,' was all he would allow himself to say. 'Was there some particular reason why you ask?'

'I'll come straight to the point. My grandmother left me some money, and it's always been my intention to invest it in a business. I like your sewing-room and shed arrangement and it would provide me with a stepping-stone into a world I want to enter. Of course it needs building up and better premises, but I feel it has possibilities for me. I'd like to buy into it. Better still, I'd like to buy outright.'

Adam was very much surprised. He hadn't really considered selling, but if he could raise money, he would be in a better position for bargaining and keeping control of the manufacture of his sewing-machines. He shook his head, undecided.

Sensing his hesitation, Anna continued, 'If we can come to some agreement, you could have a lump sum almost immediately.'

The proposition was beginning to look more attractive to Adam by the minute. 'I'll think about it,' he said cannily, not showing too much enthusiasm.

'I'll tell you what I'll do,' she suggested. 'I'll cost it out and make you an offer in writing—if that's all right?'

Adam had never been in a position of bargaining with a woman before, and was, if anything, rather impressed with Anna's directness. He had no doubt she meant what she said. A woman's money was just as good as a man's.

'Very well. I shall look forward to that. Any road, you shall have first refusal.'

'Fair enough,' Anna smiled, 'and let's keep it between us, shall we? I don't want anyone else knowing about it until it's definite.'

Anna's stipulation didn't bother him. Adam much preferred to keep things to himself until they became fact. He shook hands with her, and they parted the best of friends. Anna wasn't the only one with a costing exercise to think about. He must decide what he would accept, if he would accept at all. It meant putting everything he had into the sewing-machine venture. If it failed . . . He would much prefer to have something to fall back on. Ay, but this might be a bonny chance, the best he'd have. It needed some thinking about.

By Friday evening, Lottie was hoping that, since she'd scarcely seen Adam all week, even at meals, he would have forgotten his promise.

Dai Jones had said he would call for her at seven-thirty, and so, dressed in her copper-coloured frock, she stole down to the veranda, determined to greet him there and slip away with him unobtrusively. She smiled to herself in congratulation when she reached the front porch, as no one seemed to be there at her first quick peep.

She could have stamped her foot in vexation when Adam's voice came to her from the depths of a large wooden armchair.

'Ah, there you are! I like a woman who manages to be ready on time, even well ahead of time. You have fifteen minutes in hand.' He consulted the gold watch which hung from its accustomed chain across his chest. 'Do sit down,' he begged. 'You didn't think I'd miss this opportunity of being properly sociable, did you?'

Lottie sat on a hard bench, determined that she wouldn't allow him to spoil her evening. After all, she had only to introduce the two men. Surely she could manage to keep the conversation general: they could talk about the weather or the way sales were going. She sighed.

Adam shook his finger at her. 'Now, now, don't fret. I'm just taking a proper interest in you. Besides, while we're waiting, I have something to tell you.'

'What?' She felt none too gracious about listening. There was something about the way he was sitting there that displeased her. He looked just like a cat that had been at the cream.

'I have a backer at last. It's all settled. It's what I've been doing all week—meeting people. Now, what do you think of that?' He was smiling broadly.

'Oh, Adam,' exclaimed Lottie, her exasperation with him swept aside. 'I think it's splendid!' She rose to her feet before him and impulsively clasped his hands in hers.

To her consternation, he pulled her towards him and she tumbled into his lap, losing her balance. His blue eyes danced with merriment, and she couldn't help noticing that his hair, which was usually combed into loose waves, was tumbled and on end as though he'd run careless fingers through it.

He was laughing in pleasure and excitement. 'It's success, Lottie, beyond my wildest dreams!'

'Ay,' she said, 'I'm right pleased for you, lad.'

Lottie couldn't have said afterwards quite how it happened. She thought she struggled to get away from the undignified position on Adam's lap, but the more she tried, the tighter he held and the closer she slid towards him. One minute she was looking into his eyes and protesting, and the next his mouth had closed on her laughing mouth and he was kissing her as a hungry man might kiss her—as she had longed to be kissed.

Shivers of excitement ran from the back of her neck all down her spine. The most delicious sensations centred in that region between her breast and her stomach. She gave up all pretence of warding him off, and returned his kiss with enthusiasm and mounting desire.

And yet, one small spark of sense warned her that this was madness, that she had at last freed herself from this man, hadn't she? That was what her mind shouted at her. Her body told a different story. It wanted to remain clasped in Adam's arms, his questing mouth hard against hers. It would have welcomed his hands touching her —wherever they chose to alight.

They chose to alight on her shoulders. Her numbed brain registered that fact when he began to shake her gently.

'Lottie, Lottie, there's a carriage pulling to a halt before the garden gate,' he whispered against her hair.

She sprang away from him, half sliding, half pushed on to the broad arm of the chair, her hands trembling as they sought to tidy her somewhat disarrayed hair.

Adam rose, nearly sending her from her precarious perch to the floor. His hand steadied her.

'No harm done!' he exclaimed. 'No one can possibly have seen us from the garden gate. It's too great a distance.'

Far from comforting Lottie, that statement inflamed her. Was that all he could think about—that nobody had seen them? She drew in her breath sharply. That showed clearly enough what he thought of her—a girl to be enjoyed with no one knowing. She burned with indignation, the colour flaming in her cheeks.

Dai Jones was coming up the path, and Adam had gone to meet him. They had stopped to talk, and she could hear some mention of Dai's sister being in the carriage and Adam going to meet her while Dai came forward to the veranda.

'Your brother, is he?' Dai asked. 'I didn't know you had one. He looks uncommonly like Adam Hardcastle. Someone pointed him out to me one day.' He smiled at Lottie, and took her hand.

'He is Adam Hardcastle.' She heard her voice tremble in her ears. 'He considers himself to be duty bound to play the rôle of a brother, since I have no family here. In fact, I work for him. We come from the same town, you see.' She felt it necessary to add some explanation, so overwrought was she from the whole episode.

'A friend of the family.' Dai seemed to find nothing strange about this. 'All of us emigrants are alike—cling to people we know, folks from home, isn't it?'

Lottie smiled at him, still smoothing her hair and tugging gently at her dress where it had become a little creased. This Dai Jones was a nice man, whatever Adam might say about curly-headed chaps . . . He thought the best of a girl, not the worst. He wasn't like Adam at all. He wouldn't take advantage of a girl and then tell her that no one had seen.

She let her hand remain in Dai's as they went down the path together. She was glad, she told herself, glad she wouldn't be working for Adam much longer, glad she hadn't humbled herself and asked to stay on.

As they reached the carriage, Adam was standing on the step, laughing with Dai's sister. He bent and kissed her hand, saying, 'Good night, Myvanwy, I'm so pleased to have met you. I'm the only family Lottie has, and I'm delighted you're accompanying her. Her brother entrusted her to my care.' He still held Myvanwy's hand as he made this speech.

Lottie seethed as he stood back to allow her to get into the carriage with Dai's help, and was still fuming as they drove away, Myvanwy waving to Adam as they left and then turning to her and saying, 'What a charmer he is, such a kind man. If I weren't married already, set my cap for him, I would! Wedded, is he?'

'Not to my knowledge,' responded Lottie. 'He was engaged to my sister Kate at one time, but that's all over.'

'Pity,' said Myvanwy, 'and him so polished and friendly like; feel I've known him all my life. Why did your sister let him go, then?'

'They didn't suit,' she replied shortly. Ay, she added to herself, Kate had a lucky escape. He's a hateful man if you but knew it, Myvanwy: the kind who kisses a girl and then charms a married woman. Like a dog with a new trick, Adam is, with that kissing of hands. I don't like it . . . I don't like it at all.

Why she'd taken this sudden dislike to hand-kissing, Lottie didn't bother to explain to herself. He was just imitating Paolo—and it didn't suit him.

Dai changed the subject. 'You're looking charming this evening,' he told Lottie. 'Introduce you to my friends, I will, but mind you came with me.' He smiled so winningly that her churning feelings began to subside. It was very comforting to think that here was a man to appreciate her and soothe her.

She smiled back at him and thanked him for the compliment. Tonight, she was going to have a good time. She was determined on that. Adam was going to be put out of her mind quite firmly. He didn't merit her consideration. She wasn't going to allow a kiss to spoil her life again . . . Ah, but if he'd meant it . . . Well, he hadn't . . . It was just a way he had of exciting a girl and then forgetting her. This time, she'd be the one to do the forgetting . . . Yes, right away . . . from this moment . . .

She smiled again at Dai.

CHAPTER THIRTEEN

ON SATURDAY morning, Lottie overslept. She knew when she did wake that she should rush about and get dressed, but she lay in bed for a few more minutes, turning over in her mind the events of the night before.

She really had enjoyed herself. Dai and his sister had introduced her to all their friends, and she had danced every dance. It had been absolutely splendid.

I didn't miss Adam one bit, she insisted to herself stoutly, I was that busy enjoying myself. She wasn't quite sure why it was important for her to tell herself that. She thought again of the dancing, and the plentiful supper that had crowned the festivities of the evening. Of course Dai had sat beside her, and he had insisted that she try everything. How lovely to be escorted by a man who took such care of one. He'd said he meant to ask her out again. Adam might be surprised to hear that some men liked her and thought her attractive.

Thank heaven, Adam hadn't been waiting for her on the veranda when Dai had brought her home! Not that Dai had been too forward with her. He had kissed her on the cheek and told her how lovely she was. What girl wants an audience for that?

Lottie yawned, and stretched luxuriously. Sighing, she decided she'd better get up. She'd missed breakfast, of course, but perhaps Mary would let her have a cup of tea and a piece of bread. That would be plenty this morning.

Mary was accommodating, and wanted to hear all the

highlights of the evening. Lottie sat at the kitchen table and told her.

'Sure, I'm glad you enjoyed yourself, so I am,' Mary declared. 'Mr Hardcastle said you'd gone dancing. I thought he might have taken you himself, he's that fond of you. He was like a bear with a sore head—went off early this morning, and said he had something to talk over with that Ada.'

'Did he say when he was coming back?' Lottie was delighted, she told herself, that she didn't have to face him first thing in the morning. She hadn't quite decided whether to ignore that whole sorry business of him kissing her before Dai Jones called. That remark of Adam about not being seen had been very lowering indeed. Best pretend the whole thing had never happened.

Lottie thanked Mary and went out to the shed. Anna was there on her own. But not quite on her own, she was surprised to see. Danny came up the path, trundling his cart, which appeared to be overflowing.

'There'll be more coming,' he announced. 'Adam said the workroom must be cleared tonight of most of the materials.'

'Whatever for?' Anna looked at Lottie, and both of them took hold of Danny.

'It's just in case, like,' he said.

'In case of what?' they both demanded.

'Rosa's got hold of some story, and that Paolo's stirred them all up. He heard something in a bar about the machines being done in. Adam wasn't for believing it, but Rosa started to cry . . . She's a pretty cryer, is Rosa. First thing you know, Adam had his arm about her. Took her on his knee, he did, like some little child.' Danny paused for breath.

A picture of Rosa, pretty little Rosa, sitting on

Adam's knee with his arm about her sprang into Lottie's mind. No reason why that should disturb her. Of course it didn't. She wouldn't allow it to.

'And the upshot of it all,' Danny went on, 'is that the workroom must be cleared of all the valuable sewing, and Adam will sleep there tonight and maybe tomorrow as well. Paolo's sure that, if they do anything, it'll be tonight. Stands to reason, don't it? Saturday night's the time men get a few drinks in them. I think I might stay with Adam. Somebody'll have to run for the police.'

Both the girls gasped. Could it really be as serious as all this?

Adam. Adam might be hurt! That was Lottie's first thought. 'Will he be there all on his own?' she breathed. 'There might be a gang of them.'

'That Paolo says he'll come along after the concert, like, to keep him company.'

'That's only three—with you.' Lottie's heart sank. 'Can't he get any more?'

'That's the very thing Magdalena said, and Rosa looked as though she was going to cry again until her sister said all the girls in the workroom had boyfriends or brothers, and she'd see what could be done about getting some of them there, if they were needed.'

Lottie breathed a little more easily at that, until Danny went on again.

'Paolo was that excited, he said if they didn't win and stop such attacks, Adam could come along of him to Californya and start up there. Then Magdalena began to cry—I never saw her cry before. Adam put his arm round her and told her there was nothing to cry about. It hadn't happened yet.'

Suddenly Lottie's heart lurched at the thought of Adam going to California. Would he really consider doing such a thing?

Anna began to giggle. She couldn't stop, even when the other two turned outraged eyes on her. 'I'm sorry!' she exclaimed. 'It's not funny. It's just the thought of Adam comforting one sister and then the other. I haven't been able to decide which one he's dangling after.'

'Rosa,' said Lottie, and then bit her tongue. Why had she let that slip out?

'That's as may be,' said Danny, 'but I've got work to do. Give us a hand unloading, will you?'

The girls began to help him, and it was soon done.

'I'll be back with more,' he said, and went off with his cart.

It wasn't easy to settle to work after that, but after they'd talked about the situation and then talked about it again, Lottie began to sort through the pile of sewing that Danny had brought. A lot of it was completed work, and they decided that the wisest plan might be to deliver orders in the afternoon when Danny's cart was free. At least, then, they'd have the money in hand for them.

Anna pointed out that one of them had better stay to guard the shed, and it might even be a good idea to move some things to the house for safety. Dorothea wasn't at school today and might give her a hand. It was agreed between them that this would be the best plan, and after their lunch sandwiches, Lottie and Danny set out for the buyers.

Danny pushed his barrow ahead and Lottie trailed after him, her mind filled with thoughts of Adam. Would he really set off for California if his machines were destroyed? With their destruction, his backer might well reconsider investing. Without machines and the possibility of making more machines, Adam would be ruined. If not ruined, certainly flattened. She couldn't bear to think of it. That was looking on the dark side of things. He'd win, beat off his attackers—but he might be hurt, or crippled for life. She'd never known any good to come out of violence or men hitting each other. Why was she worrying about him, anyway? He was nothing to her—a man who didn't want to be seen kissing her.

Lottie stopped dead in the street, her hand to her mouth. The awful realisation hit her like a blow. She loved Adam! It was useless to deny it to herself any longer. With that first kiss, fortune's kiss, she'd been lost. With every succeeding kiss her fate had been further sealed. She had fooled herself into thinking he didn't matter to her, that she could escape her feeling for him. She couldn't. She couldn't!

The night before, when he had taken her in his arms on the veranda and kissed her again, her body had known his mastery. He was the most important thing in her life. She'd follow him to the ends of the earth—yes, even to California.

She bit her lip, and saw that Danny was waiting for her to follow. As she began to walk, her thoughts where bubbling. California—she might have more chance there. Rosa had said she wouldn't go to California. Magdalena wouldn't go, either. Perhaps there was hope for her yet.

Lottie followed Danny up the short streets of small shops that sold everything you could think of—bread and cakes and tobacco and meat and fruit and newspapers and shoes and boots and wool. There was a saddler's and a spice supplier and a little restaurant . . . She dawdled by the cheese palace and breathed in the smells, then again by the purveyor of teas and coffees and by the chocolate house. 'The market of the world', she called these streets. All of a sudden, the heady smell of baking bread came to her. It made her think of home, and the little bakery round the corner from Higginbottom's where she had collected fresh bread or barm cakes every day.

Home . . . That was home no longer. Home was where Adam was, if only that were true in fact. If she followed him to California, would she hanker for the sights and sounds of New York as she was longing for those of Rochdale now?

People always remembered the places where they had lived. Maybe she'd look back in California and think of the crowded tenement streets near the workroom. They were always teeming with life and movement and alive with foreign tongues and the smell of poverty—worse even than the mill town of her childhood. In New York, the smell came off the barefoot children playing in the streets just as strongly as from their ragged parents pushing for a living. Would it be the same in California? No, there was gold there—everyone said so.

Lottie shook herself. Why was her imagination playing such tricks on her? She wouldn't go anywhere . . . Adam would beat off the raiders. She'd go to her promised job in that big shop and make her own way here. She loved Adam. He didn't love her. She choked back a sob.

Adam admitted to himself that he was worried. At first he'd thought the girls and Paolo were getting worked up about nothing, but gradually they'd convinced him. It was certainly sensible to take some precautions. He wasn't going to let success slip out of his grasp—not now.

He'd insisted that the stripping of the workroom must be done quietly, making it look as ordinary as possible. He'd even sent off Rosa and one of the girls to stock up with some very cheap cotton material so that the workroom didn't look too bare. And when the girls finished working early that afternoon, he'd take off the heads of the machines and disconnect the treadles. Of course, the problem was that tonight mightn't be the night of the raid. Ay, he'd rather have it over and done with; but they, whoever they were, weren't likely to plan with his convenience in mind. Perhaps he should think of a night-watchman with a good big dog. That'd be more money to pay out—but worth it, maybe.

Nay, even if it were tonight, he wasn't too happy about it. If there were extra people about, the spoilers would be warned off. For the first part of the evening he'd be there on his own, with Danny watching from across the road, out of sight. From midnight on, Paolo'd be there with him. He wasn't sure that that hand-kissing gentleman would be much good in a hand-to-hand. Ada was doing her best to recruit some help, and he could only hope they'd be there at the right time.

It was no use going to the police. They wouldn't be interested until something actually happened. Anyway, they'd heavy-foot around for an hour or two, and just put off the inevitable. A stout stick would be his best defence—that, and the surprise of finding him there at all. There was nothing for it but to depend on himself. When all was said and done, they were his machines. He must do his best to make sure they came to no harm.

A frightening thought struck him. What if Paolo had it wrong, and it was the shed that was going to be attacked, not the workroom at all? Lottie might be just foolish enough to get hurt. She'd be on her guard. So would Anna. Was there anything he could do to give them some protection—just in case? He turned it over in his mind. He had no doubt that, if trouble came to the shed, Lottie would be in the thick of it. There were no men in the house to help—only other girls. There must be something he could do . . .

It was as they were locking up the shed, hot and tired from the exertions of the day, that the same thought struck Lottie and Anna. They looked at each other.

'What about the machines?' asked Lottie.

'We can't leave them here,' Anna agreed. 'I'm buying this business, and I mean to have them too.'

Lottie looked at her in astonishment. 'You're buying . . . but it's Adam's!'

'I didn't mean to tell you yet.' Anna stood in the doorway of the shed.

Lottie held the padlock in her hands. She needed something to grasp. Adam had done it again—swept the ground from under her feet—and she was angry. 'When was all this decided?'

'Just in the last day or two. I didn't think Adam would agree to it at first, but he has. He said you'd probably stay on for a little with me. I wanted you for longer than that, but he said he had other plans for you.'

'Other plans for me?' Lottie echoed stupidly, too stunned to take in all the implications of this move of Adam's.

'That's what he said.' Anna was trying to lift one of the machines, and finding it rather heavy. 'I suppose we could do it between us. No, I have a better idea— there's a wheelbarrow somewhere. I've seen it in the garden.'

'Ay.' Lottie sank down on a bench. 'Tell me exactly what he said.'

Anna leaned against the machine bench, frowning. 'Can't I tell you later, when we've moved these?'

'Now.'

Anna shrugged. 'There's not much to tell. I said

Harry had agreed to come in with me. Harry's my boyfriend—fiancé now . . .' She blushed rosily.

'Another secret,' was Lottie's only comment.

'It had to be. I didn't want Dorothea getting wind of it before it was all cut and dried. She's never liked him. She'd do everything she could to stop me. But it's my money. Gran left it to me.'

Lottie nodded. This secret at least was understandable.

'He'll have to give notice—a month's notice. I explained that to Adam, and he said that should fit in nicely. Those were his very words.'

'What did he say after that?'

'Just that he had something else in mind for you, so you wouldn't be available any longer than that.'

'What—What does he have in mind?'

Anna shrugged again. 'I don't know. You said earlier on that he was interested in Rosa. I suppose he meant another job. He did say you'd be taken care of. That's it!' Anna smiled. 'He means to give you a job in his machine factory, probably as a supervisor. I'm sure he means to pay you well.'

'What makes you think that?' Lottie didn't believe this conversation was really taking place.

'Just the way he said you'd be taken care of. It stands to reason he wouldn't want to lose a good, sensible girl like you, a hard worker, too.'

'Ay,' agreed Lottie dully. 'A hard worker.' She felt a lump in the back of her throat. Those words sounded the knell of any hopes she might have had of Adam turning towards her. He had said when she'd first come here that he didn't look for a good worker in a wife.

'Ay,' she repeated, overcome by the knowledge. 'Go and fetch the wheelbarrow.' She sat with the padlock gripped in her hands. What had she expected?

When they had moved the two machines to the veranda of the house, the girls sank down there.

'It's going to rain.' Anna fanned herself with a piece of buckram, and let her skirt fall back round her legs. It had been tied back to prevent her tripping. 'It's got hotter and hotter. I can feel it and smell it. That's what comes of being a country girl—you get to know the weather. It'll pour tonight, and be cooler tomorrow.'

'I hope you're right.' Lottie felt exhausted.

'Thunder and lightning are coming,' Anna went on. 'It'll be a good night for a fight. Tempers'll rip.'

Lottie looked at her. 'You're enjoying this!' she accused.

'Why not? It'll do us all good. Clear the air. Why are you looking so downcast? I've heard the story about you attacking that German man on the boat—you needn't pretend you took no satisfaction in that. Didn't you feel better afterwards?'

'That was different.'

'How?'

'It just happened. I didn't know anything about it beforehand.' Lottie felt again that solid candlestick in her hand, and the sickening thud it had made when it connected with its target. What if Adam suffered such a blow? Or Paolo? Or Danny? She wished she had that candlestick now. She'd feel safer. The raiders might come here, too.

'What happened to the candlestick?' asked Anna.

'Paolo has it.'

'Will he use it tonight?'

'I don't know. I don't want to think about it!' Lottie put her hands over her eyes. 'Oh, Anna, what if they're hurt, or killed, maybe?'

'They won't be.' Anna smiled at her. 'We'll wait for them, shall we? Bring down our blankets when it's dark, and sit here and wait for them.'

'We might tell Rosemary,' Lottie suggested. 'She'd be interested for her paper. Dorothea knows already, since she helped you earlier on. Nobody else needs to know. Mrs O'Rourke would have hysterics, and Mary would be useless, she'd be so frightened.' Lottie shivered. 'If they come here, it's only four girls.'

'We'll think of something,' said Anna. 'We'll put our heads together.' She rose and held out her hand. 'We'll go and eat now. We may need our strength.'

Lottie's throat tightened. She knew she wouldn't be able to eat, but she knew, too, that Anna wouldn't let her sit there brooding. She took her hand and they went in to supper.

Yes, they might need their strength.

Adam found the waiting hard. As dark fell, he was on edge. He couldn't even light a candle, and couldn't risk falling asleep. It was very warm in that upstairs work-room. He climbed on a chair and opened the window high up in the wall. That was a little better, but it was a sultry night, heavy with the promise of rain. There might only be an electrical storm with thunder and lightning. New York seemed to attract that kind of weather when it was as hot as this. The rain itself might not come.

He sighed, and looked out on the street. There was a single gas lamp burning just within his vision on the other side of the road. That cheered him a little. At least there weren't any mosquitoes up here. That was some-thing.

He stayed by the window for a long time, but could see no unnatural activity on the street—no activity at all. He took some comfort from the knowledge that Danny was lurking somewhere up the road in a doorway or an alley. Pray heaven he stayed awake and wary!

There was a sudden creak from within the building. On the stairs, perhaps? Just the sort of noise someone creeping up would make as the wood groaned beneath his weight.

Adam jumped noiselessly from the chair and waited, the thick stick grasped in his hands. The noise was not repeated. Just a false alarm. He relaxed a little, and sat on the chair. It was too early, anyway. Midnight was the time for raiders.

As he sat there, the thought of Lottie flashed into his mind, the feel of her as she had sat on his lap the night before on the veranda. Ay, he would have gone on kissing her and holding her if he hadn't glanced up and seen the carriage arriving. What else could he do but release her then? He wouldn't embarrass her before her friends. But what an unfortunate time to be interrupted! Lottie had been quite put out about it. He could see that, right enough. Well, he couldn't wait up and see her safely home, and this morning he'd had that message from Rosa. Ay, there'd be some sorting-out to do when this was over.

When Paolo came—if Paolo came—there'd be someone to talk to, at least. But that wouldn't be for another hour. The door was locked. Paolo would scratch gently at it three times and gain admittance. Adam yawned and sighed for patience. He rested his head against the wall, and dozed.

He couldn't have said what woke him, or what time it was. All he knew was that there was danger. A flash of lightning set his nerves on edge and revealed quite clearly that there was no one in the room—just a little mouse regarding him from the top of a table. Thunder followed, and the mouse scuttled for safety.

Adam would have given anything to do the same.

The rain came down in a sudden torrent, deluging him

beneath the window. He moved, thoroughly awake now. Before he could climb on the chair, he heard the scratching at the door. Paolo—it must be Paolo! He went towards the door.

'Who's there?' he called in a whisper.

'Tardi.'

Tardi? Adam repeated to himself. Who's Tardi? Ah, Paolo's surname. Why would he give me that answer? Something was wrong.

He gripped his stick and unlocked the door. If this was a trap, and they had Paolo, he could do nothing else. He stationed himself to one side, and as the door opened, Paolo was thrust in first. On guard as he was, Adam managed just in time not to hit his friend. Instead, the first man in after Paolo received a stunning blow to the head. He stumbled and fell, and two of his accomplices tripped over him.

In those first chaotic few minutes, Adam managed to pull Paolo back into the main part of the room with him and free his hands. They retreated behind two of the piled-up tables that usually held materials. The advantage, slight though it was, was with Adam, for he knew the geography of the room and the invaders did not. It wasn't until one of them came through the door with a lantern that they moved forward.

They began hitting tables with their cudgels, and Adam and Paolo struck out at them as they did so. In a sudden flash of lightning, Adam saw the weapon in Paolo's hand. It shone brightly as he brought it down with vigour on someone's head. Lottie's candlestick, he said to himself, and began to laugh as he brought his stick into play. A blow from a cudgel had him gasping for breath in the next instant. Fortunately, Paolo saw it coming, and thrust a table towards his opponent.

When he had immobilised the machines, Adam had

piled them in the far corner of the room and protected them as far as he was able by building a barricade of chairs and forms. Now he could hear the furniture being thrown aside, and knew it was only a matter of minutes before his precious machines would suffer. The thought galvanised him into ferocious action. He swung his stick again and again, and Paolo, candlestick abandoned in favour of a sturdy cudgel seized from somewhere, fought beside him.

But the attackers pressed inexorably on. There were four or five on the floor, and still they came. Adam and Paolo were forced back and back until they stood against the far wall upon the discarded chairs. Then Adam knew it was all up. Sheer weight of numbers must overwhelm them. Where were Danny and the police? Where were the men he had been promised by the girls?

The machines were doomed—and so were he and Paolo. Already Paolo's shirt was in tatters, and he could see blood running from a cut in his forehead. Adam, too, was hurt. One shoulder ached unbearably, and his left arm was out of action, but he fought on, with the bitter knowledge that it couldn't be long now.

When Rosemary arrived home at Mrs O'Rourke's, it was late—later than her usual coming-home time.

She inspected the piled-up veranda with interest. 'You girls have been busy!' She sat down on one of the wooden chairs. 'Yes, I've eaten, and I know all about the situation.' She stilled their explanations. 'Adam got a message through to me.'

Lottie was a little surprised by this. What did he think Rosemary could do that they hadn't done?

Rosemary answered that question before Lottie even asked it. 'I have a friend in the police, and I got in touch with him. He's promised us some help.'

'What sort of help? Is he sending someone here to keep watch?'

'Not quite as good as that,' Rosemary admitted, 'but the man on the beat will keep an eye on us, and I know approximately where he'll be at any time—if we just send a message . . .'

'A message?' Anna broke in. 'Who's going to take a message?'

'Mary will, I imagine,' said Rosemary. 'Or she'll know someone who will from all these houses around.'

'We didn't think we'd tell Mary.' Lottie spoke up. 'We've made our own preparations.'

'What sorts of preparations?' Rosemary asked. 'You can't mean to fight them off—if they come.'

'Of course they'll come,' snapped Dorothea, who had been silent up till then. 'It's what tailors have always done to protect their living.'

'Always?' Rosemary asked. 'I know they did in France, a long, long time ago. A man by the name of Barthélemy Thimonnier had a sewing-machine making army uniforms, and jealous tailors smashed it.'

'Exactly!' Dorothea's lips met in a straight line. 'Just what I said.'

'Twenty years ago'—Rosemary went on as though Dorothea hadn't spoken—'a man called Walter Hunt, an American, invented a machine, and abandoned it when his daughter told him it would put seamstresses out of work. That's more the American way.'

'Either way,' said Dorothea, 'it will put people out of work. You can't blame them for being upset. That's what I keep telling Anna—but she won't listen to me. She says the future is with the machines.'

'It will help all the women of the world,' Lottie said firmly. 'Why can't people see that?'

'It'll help the seamstresses, too, if they but knew it,'

Rosemary added. 'Have any of you ever seen seamstresses at work? The conditions are awful; the pay
pitifully small. A lot of them go blind, or die from
consumption from being huddled in dark, airless
rooms.'

'Ay,' said Lottie. 'Any as don't want to help to keep
Adam's machines safe had better back out now.' She
fixed her eyes on Dorothea.

'I'm not backing out,' said Dorothea. 'What ever gave
you that idea? I just think history is interesting. We can
all learn from it.'

'Happen we can,' agreed Lottie. 'I wouldn't be surprised if someone jealous of Adam's good fortune
wasn't whipping all this up to make a stir. We'll spike his
plans!' The light of battle was in her eyes.

Rosemary's lips twitched, and Lottie saw that she was
struggling to keep from laughing. What was there to
laugh about? Rosemary managed to compose her face.
'We shall take our orders from General Carlotta,' she
said gravely. 'Now, then, tell us what you've planned.'

Lottie sat down beside her friend and began to outline
the strategy she had mapped out.

CHAPTER FOURTEEN

IN THAT instant when Adam knew he was beaten, his left hand dangling uselessly from his hurt arm encountered a bolt of muslin resting on one of the chairs in the pile beside him. It was the muslin he had sent the girls out to buy so that the work would seem to be going on.

With a shout to Paolo, he unwound part of the bolt in one quick action with his good hand, and between them they managed to throw the material like a giant net over three or four of their opponents, trapping them in it. An exultant Paolo wound them even more securely into the net, so that they were immobile. Shouting and cursing, these particular foes could do nothing, but the three others attacking the sewing-machines hurled themselves on Adam.

He was knocked to the floor. He saw an enormous stick about to descend on his head and gave himself up for lost.

The blow never landed. Instead, he opened his eyes and found himself still in one piece. His attacker had run back to the door with the others.

'They've come!' shouted Paolo. 'They've come! They're here. The reinforcements.'

It was true. A swarm of men piled into the room, brandishing weapons, uttering the most horrible growling war-cries. Adam heard the sound of wood on bones as Paolo helped him to his feet.

Only the presence of two policemen in the rear of the vigorous relieving party stopped the mayhem. The attackers, now a sorry sight, were lined up against a bare wall, and their hands tied behind their backs with strips torn from the bolt of muslin.

Adam rested on one of the chairs. Paolo marched behind Danny, who held a lantern, along the row of prisoners. The boy held the lantern high, searching each scowling face.

'Not a decent tailor among the lot of youse,' he spat in their faces. 'Who sent you? How much did he pay you?'

The policemen motioned him away. 'That's for us to find out—down at the station. It's not for the likes of you to be upsetting the prisoners.'

There was a growl from the reinforcing party at this exchange, but Adam quietened them down.

'Just in the nick of time, lads,' he told his rescuers. 'I'll be grateful to you for ever.'

After one of the policemen had taken a short statement from Paolo and the other from Adam, they marched the prisoners off with the help of some of the rescuers. Then they were all free to go.

A protesting Adam and a laughing Paolo were hoisted to the shoulders of the remaining men and carried in triumph down the stairs, along the streets, and back to Ada and Rosa's home. Adam tried to tell them that he must get back to Lottie and the shed, but his voice made no impression on the singing men, who held him aloft in triumph.

'Eh, girls, it was a grand fight,' they told the waiting Ada. 'We won! Of course we won! The workroom's safe enough. What do a few broken chairs matter?'

Ada and Rosa and several of the other workroom girls were not satisfied with this quick statement of affairs, and begged for more details. At last, Adam was allowed down, his shoulder aching, his arm throbbing, and Rosa fussed over him and pulled him into the little house.

While she cried a little and bandaged him up, a barrel

of beer was brought out into the street for the men.

'They can't all fit into the space here,' said Rosa. 'But it was a good idea to order that barrel earlier on, Adam. That made them all the more eager for the fight.'

'Ay,' he replied, more than a little dourly. 'If they'd waited any longer in coming, they'd have carried us both laid out.'

Rosa paid little attention to this. She got one of the girls to bring him a generous helping of beer, and then insisted on putting ice on his shoulder and a sling under his arm.

Magdalena threw herself into Paolo's arms, and wept over his black eye. 'Of course I'll go to California with you,' she told him over and over. 'You've fought for me tonight. A conquering hero, that's how it should be!'

She looked so melting and so eager to please that Adam realised for the first time how it was between Ada and Paolo. How would Lottie take this?

Paolo looked inordinately pleased with himself, in spite of the beating he'd taken. He winked at Adam with his good eye.

'You'll see—it'll be just the same for you and Lottie when she hears how you've fought! When she sees you, she'll fall into your arms.'

'Do you think so? Do you really think so?' Adam was beginning to feel just a little pleased with himself. After all, he'd fought and won—and that seemed to mean a lot to women. Why, look at how the girls were going on here—not only Ada, but every girl who had a sweetheart was entwined in his arms. Even Rosa was holding hands now with the Italian boy, Luigi, and she hadn't wanted to look at him before!

Adam accepted another mug of beer and a good-sized hunk of bread spread liberally with cheese. He wasn't a beaten man . . . He was a winner!

The party went on for quite a time, spilling in and out of the tiny house into the street. And the story was told again and again, and so many embellishments were added by men who had come in only at the end that Adam began to feel he might have been in a full-scale war.

It was odd, he mused, how bravery got better in the telling. He accepted another refill with a smile. When all the girls of the workroom began kissing him and thanking him, he accepted that, too. It was as they said, and Paolo insisted, only his due. The thought of Lottie and the shed had receded into the back of his mind. No one was going to attack there—not after they'd been beaten. Besides, they were all in gaol, weren't they?

Exactly what Paolo said as the two of them walked home through the late night. The rain was long since over—it must have finished just before the rescuers broke in. That must have been what held them up—that sudden thunderstorm.

Adam was at peace with his world—at peace, and still very much elated. Everything was going to be fine. Lottie'd changed her mind about going—just the way Ada had about California.

He began to sing. Paolo joined in.

The girls had set themselves up on the veranda in their oldest clothes, corsets dispensed with by tacit agreement. They might well be a long time waiting.

Lottie wore her old white and yellow cotton frock, now washed and mended. Most of the inkstains were out; not that that would matter tonight. She'd brought down a blanket and her swansdown pillow, too. They might be able to snatch a little sleep in turns. She felt too worked up to consider resting now.

The others must have been just as excited. Anna

checked the way the machines were stationed at the far end with bolts of material on top of them and sacking on top of that in case the threatening rain came in. She kept marching up and down until Dorothea begged her to stop. Then she perched, impatient, on the edge of a bench.

Rosemary was the only one who seemed at ease. She had settled in the most comfortable of the wooden chairs, a cushion at her back, a low footstool at her feet, her knitting in her hands.

'I like to knit,' she told Lottie. 'It's so calming. I remember my father told me a story once about his mother—my grandmother. She was a grand old lady, died when I was a child. My dad said they once had an Indian attack, and she knitted all through the waiting.'

Lottie's eyes grew large, and the others came a little closer to hear about this.

'How did she know the Indians were coming?' asked Lottie. 'Surely they didn't tell the settlers ahead of time?'

'Well, they did and they didn't.' Rosemary smiled. She appeared able to knit without looking at her hands or the growing garment.

'That's silly,' said Anna, sitting back a little.

'What do you mean?' asked Dorothea. 'Did they or didn't they?'

'The Indians delighted in the surprise attack,' said Rosemary placidly, 'but sometimes the people attacked fought them off very successfully. Remember that those were the days when every man took his rifle to the fields with him and to bed at night. They weren't always caught off guard. Then the Indians might play a waiting game, showing every now and then that they were still in the vicinity, ready to pounce. They knew full well the effect of that on their victims' nerves.'

'I suppose the settlers couldn't get away?' Lottie's interest had been caught by this glimpse of the past in this strange land.

'No.' Rosemary spared one glance at her hands. 'They were pretty isolated, and had to wait it out.'

'Well, go on with the story,' Anna instructed. 'Don't stop there! Did the Indians come? Did your gran finish her knitting?'

Rosemary chuckled. 'They were frightened off by an army patrol. They never did attack.'

'Is that what you're trying to tell us?' Dorothea broke in. 'That this may be all a false alarm—and we're making too much out of it?'

'Perhaps. It is a possibility, after all.'

'Ay,' said Lottie, 'that's what they'd have us think. They'll come, all right.'

'Do you have the second sight?' asked Rosemary. 'It's an interesting thing—second sight. I've known folk with it. Generally, they look wilder than you.'

That made them all laugh, and they sat back. Very clever of Rosemary, Lottie thought gratefully. She'd made it seem the common lot of women to wait in patience. Even Anna was looking more comfortable with her head leaning against the wall. She was actually fanning herself, and sighing that it was hot and the rain must come soon.

When it did, three or four hours later, it arrived with an almighty crack of thunder and a flash of forked lightning that illuminated the whole veranda that had been all in darkness. The storm beat down, and a rising wind tugged at the girls as the rain swirled in. They were forced to move, blankets now clutched about them, to the far wall and the hard benches.

'Shall we bring down the wooden shutters?' Dorothea's voice quavered.

'No,' said Anna.

'Nay,' said Lottie in the same breath. 'We must be able to see.'

'They'll not come in this!' Dorothea protested.

But she was wrong.

The next flash showed four men creeping past the far end of the veranda towards the back garden and the shed.

'They're here,' whispered Lottie, and she picked up her stick.

Rosemary held her upraised hand. 'Give them time to reach the shed,' was her quick advice.

Lottie waited another long minute. Then her hand came down. With all her strength, she beat the drum she had borrowed from a neighbour's lad earlier in the day. 'Rat-tat . . . Rat-tat', the sound beat out above the noise of the wind and the rain.

Anna took a deep breath and began to blow a fine big horn which usually stood in Mrs O'Rourke's sitting-room, a relic of her dead husband. Dorothea had a flute, a whistling flute whose sound went through the ears. Rosemary made strange cries, half strangled screams, half throbbing chants. They were very loud. It was a frightening medley of wild noises which the four girls offered to the night.

Rat-tat, screech, wail and scream filled the darkness. The storm raged on, too.

A window flew open above their heads. 'Glory be to God!' boomed Mrs O'Rourke's strident voice. 'What's going on down there that a body can't sleep in peace? Fetch the police! Someone get the coppers!'

Windows opened all the way down the street as the lightning flashed again. Heads hung out, some with nightcaps adorning them, some with tousled hair, some with no hair at all.

'Police! Police!' They all took up the cry. And still the drum boomed out, the horn shrilled and Rosemary's war-cries echoed along the veranda.

As the rain lessened, pounding feet ran down the street to Mrs O'Rourke's premises, and two dark figures raced out past the side of the house. Straight into the arms of the law-men they cannoned, and were dragged to the veranda.

Lottie stopped banging the drum, and ran to the far end. She could just make out two figures climbing the back wall. One of the policemen gave chase at her startled scream, and caught one of the fleeing men. The other got away.

Pandemonium still reigned. True, the drum had ceased its throbbing and the horn its deep call, but Dorothea was playing a hymn of victory on the flute, and Rosemary was singing along. 'Rock of Ages' seemed to be the only words she knew, and she was repeating them over and over again in a paean of praise.

Neighbours were calling out. Mrs O'Rourke was erupting on to the veranda, her hair in rag curlers. Mary, too, was there, telling the policeman who was tying up the captives that she hadn't slept hardly a wink and it couldn't be morning.

Lottie sank on to a chair, her legs trembling beneath her. They'd done it! They'd frightened them away! The sewing-machines were safe. Too bad that one raider had got away.

Mrs O'Rourke sent Mary to make tea, much to Lottie's amazement. She was still marvelling at it when neighbours found their way to the scene of the excitement, and were treated to a hot steaming drink. She accepted a cup herself, very gratefully indeed. It was rather weak, but she was inordinately thirsty.

'Sure, have another! It won't do you any harm. Look

at herself, then,' Mary whispered. 'I haven't seen her enjoy herself so much since her old man died!' She pointed to Mrs O'Rourke, who was talking to one of the policemen. 'A lively wake it was, with food such as you've never seen, and as to drink—anything the men wanted, and lemonade and port for the ladies—and strong tea for them as had taken the pledge—not like this stuff.' She winked at Lottie and poured her another cup.

Lottie was introduced to neighbours she'd never seen before and to ones she'd barely nodded to, and all the girls were treated as heroines. She couldn't help finding it very pleasant, though she had begun to wonder why Adam didn't make an appearance. It must be very late.

Eventually all the visitors faded away, and the yawning girls were shooed into the house by Mrs O'Rourke, who locked the door with a great deal of attention.

'Off to bed with youse all! We'll talk about it in the morning. I'm not sure I like having my house turned into a fortress.' Mrs O'Rourke sounded very stern, but there was a decided twinkle in her eye.

Lottie protested that someone should wait up for Adam, but Rosemary vetoed that idea. 'There's no need. There'll be a policeman keeping an eye on that veranda all night, and it'll soon be morning. You heard the officer say that the raiders on the workroom had been taken down to the station. If I know anything about men, Adam and Paolo will be awash with beer by this time.' She gave Lottie a hug. 'Don't look so scandalised! That's the way fellows are. Adam won't be home tonight. He'll find somewhere to sleep it off.' Rosemary yawned, and led Lottie upstairs.

She went reluctantly. She supposed Rosemary was right. But Adam wasn't a drinking man—he never had been. That didn't mean he wasn't one now, she told herself. Anyway, what did she know about his habits? She went to bed, still only half convinced. She was sure she'd hear him unlock the front door when he came back. He did have his own key. That she did know.

Lottie fell asleep.

Paolo and Adam had come to the street corner, where they parted company. Each had only a few blocks to walk.

Adam would have taken a brief farewell, a muttered 'Good night', a wave of the hand, but Paolo insisted on shaking hands and making a speech about bravery and manhood. It was more than a little embarrassing to Adam. The effect of the beer had begun to wear off in the cooler night air, and he wanted nothing so much as his bed. He was aching all over, and tired as well.

Paolo's sentiments were very flowery, and at the end of them he pulled Lottie's silver candlestick out of his pocket and presented it to him.

'This is the time for truth,' he declared, 'and the truth is, dear friend, that I took it from Lottie.'

'Ay.' Adam stifled a yawn. 'I know.'

'It was wrong of me,' Paolo tried to continue piously, then stopped as Adam's words sank in. 'You knew? And you didn't say anything—and Lottie told you?'

'Ay,' Adam repeated. 'She was indebted to you—said you saved her life.'

Paolo waved that away. 'I did what I could. You would have done the same.'

'Ay,' again Adam agreed.

'Extraordinary people, the English,' Paolo remarked with a puzzled frown on his face. 'Absolutely extraordinary! To know, and say nothing.' He swayed a little on his feet. 'Just the same, you must give it back to her.' He thrust the candlestick into Adam's hands and began to walk away.

Adam ran after him. 'Thanks, Paolo! Ta very much for your help tonight. If there's ever anything you want, you've only to say.' This time Adam insisted on shaking hands, clutching the candlestick to his chest with his stiff arm.

Paolo embraced him.

If anyone else had done that, Adam would have shaken them off, but he endured it, telling himself that it was Paolo's way—the Italian way—of showing that he was moved. They called 'Good night' to each other, and parted, Paolo continuing along Broadway, Adam heading into the small streets that led home.

Adam tucked the candlestick into his pocket and strode briskly along. The darkness of the night was just beginning to be streaked with grey. Ay, Lottie'd be right pleased to have that candlestick back! He could just see her face when he gave it to her. She'd smile, that soft dimpled smile. She might even throw her arms about his neck. He wouldn't let on that Paolo had given it to him—not at first, anyway. Happen she might even be waiting up for him. Well, perhaps not . . . it was late. Still, morning would do nicely.

He turned into Jones Street. It was very quiet here, so there couldn't have been any trouble. All looked absolutely normal, from what he could make out in the gloom. He breathed a sigh of relief. It had been at the back of his mind that something might have happened. He yawned hugely and went up the path. Once through the screen door, he reached into his top pocket for his key.

It wasn't there. He tried another pocket, and another. If that didn't beat all! He stood undecided by the door. No, he couldn't wake them all at this hour. He'd just have to bed down on the veranda until Mary opened the door in the morning. That couldn't be far off, anyway. As he began to walk along the veranda, he realised that he was in some kind of luck. Someone had left a pillow and a blanket. He picked them up, plumping the pillow. It felt and looked uncommonly like Lottie's swansdown pillow that she'd brought across the Atlantic. So she had been waiting for him. That brought a smile to his lips, a feeling of contentment. He was so late that she'd given him up—very sensibly, of course. Adam wandered down the veranda in the pale light, hugging the pillow to him. If he remembered rightly, the biggest wooden chair was down at the far end, and there was a short bench that would just do as a foot-rest.

When he stumbled against a bench, he exclaimed sharply. Someone had been moving things about here. What was that down beneath the far window? He went forward to look. Bending down, he pulled sacking and material away, and was astonished to see his two sewing-machines under them. He was just straightening up, when he was grasped from behind.

'Got ya, then!' said an Irish voice. 'The last one of them dirty thieving lot. Officer Robinson was sure you'd be back.'

Adam was shoved and prodded back along the veranda.

'There's been a mistake!' he protested. 'I'm not a thief. I live here!'

'Tell that to Sweeney, not to me,' was the prompt reply. 'And you with your hands on those very machines, and a stolen pillow clutched to you.' The policeman's laugh was long and merry.

He took the pillow and the blanket from Adam's arms, and made a search of his pockets for good measure. Thus he unearthed the silver candlestick, and grasped it with an air of triumph. 'Just as I thought! Up to your tricks somewhere else. Got frightened off, I suppose, and decided to come back here.' He held Adam's arms behind his back.

Adam winced with pain. 'It's my candlestick! Well, Lottie's anyway,' he tried to explain. 'I'm Adam Hardcastle and I live here.'

'Sure,' said the policeman, 'and didn't I see you try the front door, hoping to get in that way.'

'Of course I hoped to get in that way!' Adam retorted. 'I have a key—or I had it.'

'Lost it, have you then?'

'Ay, it must have fallen out.'

'I could almost believe you,' the policeman told him sorrowfully, 'you sound that honest.' He swung Adam about to face him. 'But just look at you now. Does that look like the face of an honest man?' He regarded Adam's bruised features in the growing light. 'Been in a bit of a fight, have you? You look as though you've come off worst.'

'Look, knock at the door,' pleaded Adam. 'Ask the people who live here who I am. They'll tell you.'

The policeman shook his head. 'And while I'm doing that, you'll be off like a shot. No, I'll not be taken in that way. March.' He prodded Adam in the ribs.

Adam groaned in pain. His ribs were as sore as the rest of him. He marched. Down the steps he marched, along the path and up Jones Street again. He gave up protesting after the first few yards. Better to save his breath, the pace was so furious and unrelenting. He'd explain it all at the station.

Lottie woke for the first time around nine, and dozed off again. The house was so quiet, and she was still so tired. She rose at ten, and dressed quickly and went through the silent house towards the kitchen.

Mary made toast and tea for her and settled herself for a chat.

'Mrs O'Rourke's been up and down this street and the next, telling them all about it. Sure, she went off to early Mass just so she could! She loves a bit of excitement. Sure, don't we all?' She beamed at Lottie, and helped herself to toast and jam.

'Mr Hardcastle'll be that pleased to hear of the doings last night—when he comes home, that is.'

Lottie knew a sinking feeling in the pit of her stomach. She pushed away her plate. 'Hasn't he come home?'

Mary shook her head.

'Are you sure?'

'Certain sure. I went up to his room first thing—thinking he might have slipped in late—just peeped in, I did, not wanting to wake him if he was there—but he wasn't, and the bed not slept in at all.'

'Oh!' exclaimed Lottie, frowning. 'I suppose it's all right. He'll have stayed the night somewhere with his friends—like Rosemary said.'

She felt quite deflated, as she had been certain that Adam would find his way home somehow. He must come back and tell how things had gone with him last night! She was disappointed. A sudden disturbing thought hit her: perhaps he'd been hurt? A vision of Adam with horrific injuries swam into her mind. She tried to dismiss it. Of course he wasn't badly hurt. That policeman had told Rosemary he'd won his fight. Just the same, she hadn't heard everything he'd told Rosemary. He'd had a private sort of conversation with her that Lottie hadn't liked to interrupt. And, after that, Rosemary had sent her off to bed pretty promptly. She'd kept something from her.

'Where are the others?' she asked Mary.

'Sure, they're all still in bed, save for Miss Rosemary.

She went out early.' Mary bit into a second slice of toast liberally spread with jam. 'It's grand when the missus goes out and leaves the kitchen to me.'

'Ay,' said Lottie. 'Where'd Rosemary go?'

Mary shrugged. 'How should I know? She didn't say, I don't think. Oh, maybe she did,' Mary remembered with a frown. 'She said something about meeting the other reporter. It didn't mean much to me. She doesn't work on a Sunday.'

Lottie shook her head, trying to clear it. No, Rosemary didn't work on a Sunday, but perhaps today was different . . . Maybe they'd gone to see just how badly hurt Adam was. No, that was ridiculous. Rosemary wouldn't have taken another reporter. She would have taken her.

'Are you worried about Mr Hardcastle, then?' Mary's eyes above the layer of jam were bright and interested. 'Of course you are—I should have thought!'

At Lottie's nod, Mary went on, 'Why don't you take yourself off to church, like you do every Sunday. By the time you get back, he'll be here large as life and itching to tell you all about it. Sure, I've seen the way he likes to tell you things. I wish I had a fella like Mr Hardcastle. Thinks the world of you, he does.'

Mary's words comforted her a little. Perhaps she should just go on as she would any other Sunday. She rose from the table and went to get her hat. She might even meet Adam on the way, or he might slip in during the service.

More than a little cheered by the prospect, Lottie set out.

CHAPTER FIFTEEN

AT LUNCH-TIME, the same question was on everyone's lips. Where was Adam?

They ate roast lamb and mashed potatoes and carrots. Lottie found it was choking her, and laid down her fork.

'There can't be anything to worry about,' said Rosemary. 'He wasn't all that badly hurt, you know. I've been talking to the reporter who was with the rescue party, and he says Adam had a bruised shoulder and a stiff arm—and more than a little to drink last night.'

'Ay,' agreed Lottie, and found all three girls watching her. She picked up her fork again.

'It sounds as though he and Paolo made a very spirited defence of it,' Rosemary went on. 'They'd nearly overcome them all when the reinforcements arrived and there were ten in all. Adam threw a bolt of muslin over four of them and netted them like fish.'

Anna and Dorothea exclaimed in some awe, and begged for more details. Rosemary supplied them.

Lottie listened with half of her mind only. A nagging idea was forming in her thoughts. Adam had stayed the night with Rosa and Ada. Of course, that was it! Rosa would want to fuss over him and nurse him. Rosemary wouldn't want to suggest that obvious outcome. Sighing, she played with the good food on her plate, pushing the potatoes into the rich gravy. Why hadn't she seen it before? What a fool she'd been, mooning over him like a love-sick girl! It was Rosa he wanted and meant to have. It all fitted together. He was selling the sewing business to Anna—without even letting her know about his plans. It must have been an enormous relief to him when she had told him she was going to take up the job she had been promised. True, he had protested a little—but only a little. He had never brought up the subject again.

Lottie knew what she must do. She must write a letter to the Mart to ask them for a firm date for starting, as soon as possible.

She tried to force herself to eat. She had enough pride in herself, didn't she, not to let the others see how much it mattered to her that Adam had stayed with Rosa, had made his choice for Rosa. Just the same, her plate went back half full, but she managed to drink two cups of strong coffee.

As she was on the second, Paolo arrived. The girls made a great fuss of him, exclaiming over his eye, which was black and blue, and the size of the bandage on his arm where he had been cut.

'Where's Adam?' he demanded, when he'd had his share of praise and adulation.

They all looked at him, shaking their heads.

'Not here?' questioned Paolo. 'That's very strange.'

'What do you mean?' Lottie demanded, her thoughts in a turmoil again.

'At somewhere between four and five this morning, I parted with him on Broadway—I to go to my rooms, Adam to come here.'

There was consternation on every face round the dining-room table. Where was Adam? Mary was summoned from the kitchen, and she repeated her statement that she had peered inside Adam's room first thing that morning and he definitely wasn't there.

Lottie knew a moment's doubt. Hadn't Mary, that first night Lottie had been in this house, told her that Ada had black hair. It had been quite a shock to Lottie to discover that it was Rosa who was dark haired. Ada's hair was red. She frowned a little at the memory. But the others all accepted Mary's word.

'What could have happened between Broadway and here?' Dorothea wondered aloud.

'It's only a few short streets,' Anna pointed out.

Lottie noted that Rosemary's hand had flown to her face. 'Oh no, it couldn't be!' she began, and stopped.

'What couldn't be?' asked Lottie.

'There was a policeman guarding this house after we all went to bed,' said Rosemary. 'You don't suppose . . .' She left the thought hanging.

'He wouldn't stop Adam,' said Dorothea.

'Adam had a key,' said Lottie.

They looked at each other in mounting apprehension.

'Suppose . . .' Anna spoke slowly, 'just suppose he'd lost his key—what then?'

Again they looked at each other.

'I think we must ask the police,' Rosemary and Paolo spoke in one voice.

'Whatever's happened,' Dorothea agreed, 'we must start with the police.'

'Start what with the police?' asked a voice from the doorway, and Adam walked in.

Lottie rose to her feet and then sat down again, her legs trembling.

Questions rained on Adam.

'But where were you?' from Anna.

'What happened?' from Paolo.

'Why didn't you let us know?' from Rosemary.

'We were worried,' was all Lottie said, upset and relieved all at once.

'Not so worried,' replied Adam with a grim look round the table, 'that any of you thought to warn the man guarding the house that I might be back and want to get in!'

'You had a key!' Anna responded accusingly. 'Lottie said you had a key.'

'Ay, had it when I set out, but lost it,' he replied, and sat down at the table. 'Is there any dinner left? I'm ravenous.'

Anna ran to the kitchen, and they could hear her talking to Mary.

The others looked at Adam, apologetic, questioning. Lottie couldn't help noticing that there were dark circles under his eyes and a large discoloured bruise stretching from his cheek, down his neck and on to his collarbone, for he wore his white shirt open at the neck. His arm, Rosemary had said, was stiff. Which arm, she wondered and almost asked, but he forestalled her by reaching into his pocket and setting her silver candlestick upon the table in front of her. She was sitting directly opposite him. She gasped. The others exclaimed. Even Paolo leant forward with a smile.

'You see?' said Paolo. 'It's come home—your fighting ornament.'

Lottie smiled her thanks at Paolo, then bit her lip as she saw Adam scowling at her.

'What's to do, lad?' she asked.

'That,' said Adam pointing to it, 'was the final straw. It earned me a trip down to the station under escort in the early hours of the morning. It marked me as a thief, and worse—a housebreaker.'

Exclamations followed this statement, all round the table.

Rosemary began to laugh. 'I'm sorry, Adam, I just can't help it. What did he do—search your pockets?'

'Ay.' It was clear he couldn't see the humour of the situation. 'Happen you can laugh. I couldn't.'

'No, Adam,' said Rosemary as gravely as she could, but the twinkle was still in her eye.

Lottie couldn't help it. She saw that twinkle and was lost. She exploded into mirth. Perhaps it was just the release from the tension of the last twenty-four hours, but, once started, she couldn't stop.

Mary brought in a heaped plate for Adam and set it before him, wanting to know where he'd been hiding when she looked in.

That set Lottie off again—and the others.

Adam devoted himself to his meal. There was no talking sensibly to any of them. They were like a crowd of children, giggling at his misfortunes. He wasn't an unreasonable man, he hoped, but he couldn't see what all the merriment was about. Lottie should realise what he'd been through. It hadn't been pleasant down there at the station, treated like a common criminal.

He'd tell them so when they came to their senses. He'd never thought Lottie would go on like this. Throw herself in his arms—that was last night's rosy dream. This was reality. Women—you just couldn't tell how they'd take on! He supposed it was because they led quiet lives themselves. They just couldn't see how a man might feel.

By the time Mary brought him a second helping of apple pie with plenty of good cream on it, Adam decided he might just give them a little more information. Paolo, at least, was asking for it . . . The best of the bunch, he was. Of course, he'd been through the danger of the night, and the girls hadn't. He must make allowances for that.

'It took a lot of convincing them down at the station that I was who I said I was,' Adam declared. 'It were Rosemary's friend, that Captain Robinson, who finally listened to me, then he couldn't do enough for me. He called in the police doctor and got him to look at my arm—put some marvellous salve on it and on my shoulder; said I'd be as right as rain in a day or two.' He flexed his arm to prove it. 'They sent me home in a cab. The front door was open, and I walked straight in and up to bed. I suppose Mary looked before I'd got back—not since.'

Adam saw that Lottie's lips twitched again. Well, he couldn't help it if he hadn't put that bit about not being in bed very cleverly. He was an ordinary chap, after all.

'Ay, Adam,' said Lottie.

If it hadn't been for those twitching lips, he wouldn't have felt so put out. He was beginning to feel much more like himself. The good food had put fresh heart into him. And there was no understanding women after all. He accepted another cup of coffee from Mary.

'What's all that stuff from the shed out on the veranda for?' he demanded. 'There's no need for it—never was, I reckon. But still, it was good of you girls to take an interest.'

The girls bridled at that.

'Take an interest!' sniffed Dorothea.

'We kept it safe.' Anna was scornful.

Rosemary laughed again. 'Men!'

'Eh, lad,' scoffed Lottie, 'if it hadn't been for us, your machines would have been smashed to smithereens.'

That was too much for Adam. 'With the police here all night, what was there for you girls to do?'

'The police weren't here all night,' Rosemary said gently, 'only afterwards.'

'Afterwards?' Paolo exclaimed. 'Were you girls in danger?'

'Not in real danger,' Lottie admitted. 'We had the drum and the flute and the horn—and Rosemary with her war-cries. No, there was no danger—not to us.'

Adam couldn't believe his ears. What was all this

talk about a drum and war-cries? He demanded an explanation, and received one from Rosemary.

'It was a brilliant idea of Lottie's, all that noise,' she finished up.

'Marvellous,' Paolo enthused. 'Just what one would expect from Lottie! Why, she kept your machines safe —she, and all the others.' He beamed round the table at the girls. 'Thank them, man, for what they did. If I had friends like these amazons, I'd count myself lucky.'

Adam was astonished—astonished and tongue-tied. 'It were foolhardy,' he brought out. 'If there had been more of them, they might easily have overpowered a few girls. What then?'

Lottie glowered at him. 'Is that all you can say? Foolhardy? We did it for you.'

'Just as well we didn't do it for your thanks,' said Anna. She got up and laughed. 'Anyway, I did it partly for myself.'

Dorothea rose, too. 'Why do men never like to admit that women can be brave?' She put her arm in her sister's. 'Let's move your materials back to the shed.' They left together.

'I suppose I didn't do it solely for you.' Rosemary put her hand on Adam's shoulder. 'If I'm honest, I'll admit I did it for the story—and a good story it's going to make in tomorrow's paper.' She followed the other two out.

Paolo pushed his chair back from the table. 'A smoother tongue would suit you better, my friend. Luckily I understand you a little. See if you can make Lottie understand you.' He poked Adam's back in leaving. 'I'll give the girls a hand.'

Adam felt decidedly in the wrong. Why had they all turned against him? He'd been thinking only of their safety. What if those men had turned against them last night? They hadn't even thought of that, but his blood ran cold at the very notion.

Lottie was still glowering at him. 'I understand you all too well,' she told him. 'You keep everything to yourself. You never even told me you were selling the business to Anna. I had to find it out from her. How do you think that made me feel? I thought we were friends, at least.'

'Eh, Lottie,' Adam protested, 'I would have told you, you know that. It had all to be settled first.'

'But you are going to sell, aren't you?' Lottie wouldn't let the subject go.

He shrugged. 'Ay, if the price is right, and we're suited.' None of this was going as he'd intended. What had gone wrong? It wasn't like Lottie to be so hard on him.

'I should have known better than to trust you'—Lottie picked up the candlestick—'with your promises and your kisses.'

'I've made you no promises,' Adam interrupted savagely.

'Nor kissed me no kisses!' Lottie was on her feet, the candlestick in her hands.

For a moment Adam thought she meant to throw it at him, and he prepared to duck. My, but she was angry. Well, so was he.

'Ay, I kissed you once or twice. You made it plain you welcomed my kisses.' He was on his feet, now.

'You're horrible,' Lottie shuddered. 'I don't know what I ever saw in you—or why I crossed an ocean to come to you.'

That served to make Adam more incensed than ever. 'I never asked you to come,' he muttered through his teeth.

'Oh,' she whispered. 'You'd throw that at me, would you?' She still clutched the candlestick.

Adam eyed it apprehensively. He could see that her hand was shaking, and he was none too sure what she might say or do next. He took one quick step towards her, and snatched the candlestick.

The surprised Lottie stepped back. Had she thought he was going to hit her? He certainly felt like it.

Adam tried to explain. 'That's a strong weapon. It made me nervous to see it in your hand. It almost killed a man tonight.' He put it down on the dining-room table, well out of her reach.

She watched him by the door, one hand to her mouth. 'Afraid, that's what you are! Afraid of a woman with a candlestick in her hand—afraid of thanking a few girls —afraid of taking any chances—afraid of talking about things before you have them all sewn up! I'm glad I've seen what you are—afraid of everything!' She pulled the door open and escaped through it with one last parting shot. 'Ay, you wouldn't know how to be foolhardy!'

Adam's fists clenched into balls. He wanted to go after her and shake her into seeing reason. Hadn't he proved he wasn't afraid by protecting his machines and his workroom? Had she expected him to be here as well? Women were unreasonable. There was no question of it—unreasonable and incomprehensible—and there was no talking to them once they got an idea in their heads.

Best leave her alone for a while and let her calm down. He sat down at the table staring at the candlestick, trying to puzzle out why they had all turned on him, even Paolo. All he'd said was that they were foolhardy. And so they had been. Why couldn't they see the truth of that? It was unfair of them not to see that they had upset him. He knew they'd been brave, would have told them so—if they'd given him the chance. He couldn't help it that he'd seen in his mind's eye a picture of Lottie lying injured on the floor of the veranda, cut and bleeding, when he'd thought of the attackers turning on her.

He sighed heavily as the dining-room door opened. Ah, she'd come back to apologise. He rose to his feet.

It was Mary who entered. 'Sure, I thought everybody'd gone. Was there something more you wanted?'

Adam shook his head. There was a great deal more he wanted, but Mary wasn't likely to supply it.

He put the candlestick into his pocket, and stood undecided by his chair. 'Is Paolo still here?'

'I saw him in the garden with the girls a few minutes since.' Mary began to pile the dishes on her tray. ''Tis a lovely shiner he has, so it is. Faith, it's great to see men about the house again, I was that frighted in the night with all that banging. I'd rather have men in the house, but herself says girls are easier. I don't know how she sees that.'

'Nor I,' Adam agreed with feeling. Mary was only a simple girl, but she knew things clearly—more clearly than some.

Mary also liked to talk. She launched into her version of the previous night's doings, and he saw no way of damming the flow. He let her chatter on, not paying too much attention, as his thoughts were still turning over Lottie's puzzling attitude.

'Sure, I'm still as jumpy as a cat,' Mary finished up. 'Herself says I'm seeing shadows everywhere. But she didn't see what I saw.'

'What did you see, Mary?' he asked, because her hand, as she scraped the tablecloth with a knife, was shaking.

'There was a shadow at the scullery window,' she declared. 'I saw it clear as clear—a man's shadow. Tall he was, and looking for something—or someone. I know what a shadow at the window means.' Mary crossed herself.

'What then? What does it mean?' Adam hid a smile.

Her hand trembled more, so much that she dropped the knife and knelt on the floor to pick it up. She stayed there, her eyes on a level with the tray on the table. They were large and frightened.

'You can tell me, Mary,' Adam said kindly, because she was worked up.

'It means an attack.' She whispered the words.

For a moment she almost had Adam believing her, so great was the conviction in her hushed voice.

'Mary, Mary, that was last night,' he told her easily. 'It's all over. The men are in gaol. You're being wise after the event. Go and make yourself a cup of tea, there's a good girl, and put your feet up for a while. You're tired out and jumpy—and no wonder! I'll bet you've been up and on your feet all day. You're just worn out.'

'I am that.' Mary's answer was tremulous. 'I'm glad you're here, Mr Hardcastle. I feel better for talking to you. I'll do what you say.'

'Ay, and I'll take a look round the garden before dark just to make sure there's no bogy-men.'

Mary gave him a grateful look, and stammered her thanks as she took the tray away.

It wouldn't do any harm, Adam conceded, to have a look about, but later—a lot later. Obviously Mary was just having an attack of the vapours. He patted the candlestick in his pocket.

Lottie ran up the stairs to her room and lay on the bed, her shoulders heaving. That Adam should tell her once again that he hadn't asked her to come was the final straw. She pounded the bed with her fists. She hated him. She'd never forgive him. She didn't stop to ask herself why she was crying if the emotion she felt for him was only hatred.

He was a man with no heart at all. Why hadn't he had the grace to thank the girls? Paolo had. Another storm of weeping overcame her. He could learn a lot from Paolo—a lot that would stand him in better stead than that hand-kissing he'd picked up. He seemed to have dropped that now. Strangely, that didn't give her any satisfaction.

Well, she knew what she had to do. Sniffing, she sat up on the bed. She must finish with Adam Hardcastle, leave his employment and take up the job with the Mart. She'd write to them this very minute, that's what she'd do, to find out how soon she could start.

Her mind made up, Lottie got out pen and ink and wrote a quick note. She blotted it, and sealed it in an envelope. Perhaps Rosemary or Anna would have a stamp. She bathed her eyes and put a little rice-powder on her face, pinching some colour into her cheeks. They'd know she'd been crying, but that couldn't be helped.

Downstairs, the house was very quiet. She couldn't find any of the others, not in the sitting-room, nor on the veranda. She strolled down the steps and round the side of the house. Sometimes Anna sat in the back garden; she said the vegetables made her think of home. She wasn't there. No one was there.

Lottie sat down on a bench. She leaned her head against the side of the shed, raising her face to the sun. Idly she watched a few fluffy clouds floating against the brilliant blue of the sky. She closed her eyes. She was tired, and the garden was peaceful with the hum of bees and a sparrow hopping near her bench. She had no bread

for him today, and he flew off. The late Sunday afternoon sunshine was warming, and her head began to nod.

An arm was thrown round her shoulders, and a hand
covered her mouth. She woke with a start, the taste of
fear on her tongue, and struggled to see her captor.

With a shudder of dismay and repugnance, she
recognised young Mr Calsey.

A handkerchief was thrust into her mouth, and her
arms were wrenched behind her back and tied there with
some strips of material. A hand on her waist prevented
any escape.

Young Mr Calsey was sitting beside her on the bench.
'My luck has changed at last.'

Lottie looked at him with loathing, and he laughed in
her face.

'It's all fallen into my hands. Adam Hardcastle thinks
it's over, but it's just beginning.' His hand strayed from
her waist, ever so gently towards her bosom.

She trembled violently. She was helpless, and knew it.
She couldn't scream. She couldn't move.

'It was you on the drum last night, wasn't it?' He spoke
softly, conversationally, his hand cupping her breast,
stroking it. 'You shall pay for that.'

Lottie tried to make a lunge for freedom, kicking at
him with her feet, but he drew her closer.

'I like a girl with spirit,' he told her, his mouth at her
ear. He nipped it with his teeth, and then drew his
tongue along the lobe.

Even more tense and trembling, she was thoroughly
frightened and revolted. There was no doubt about how
he meant to use her. Why, oh why, had she thought
—had they all thought—that danger was over? No one
would even think of looking for her until it was too late.
Trussed up as she was, she wouldn't even be able to fight
him.

To her surprise, he rose to his feet, and with one easy motion before she was even aware of his intentions, he reached under the V of the low roof of the shed and pulled out the key.

'I saw them leave it here,' he told her with a chuckle, pulling her to her feet and holding her imprisoned in his arms as he unlocked the heavy padlock on the hasp of the door.

Lottie cursed the fact that the shed only had one key, which they kept handy for all of them to find. Adam had meant to have another one cut, but had never got round to doing it.

With one shove, she was thrust inside the shed to land on the floor, sprawled awkwardly with no arms to save her. She managed, with a hard struggle, to raise herself to a sitting position, but there was such a pain in her left leg that she could get no further.

Young Mr Calsey made no move towards her, but reached round the door and brought in an axe. She saw the sun gleam on it as he swung it in the air. Frightened before, she was now terrified. But she couldn't even cry out.

Young Mr Calsey stood looking down at her. 'All in good time,' he said. 'You won't have long to wait. You're the one who made them laugh at me—young Calsey to be bested by a slip of a girl—and my father still eager to do business with you—silly old fool! Well, well, you'll be smiling on the other side of your face before long—and so shall I.' He whished the axe through the air again, not caring that the door of the shed stood open.

'He's mad,' thought Lottie. 'Completely mad!' And she trembled all the more.

'First the machines,' he laughed, and stepped over her, nimbly jumping her legs.

He raised the axe, and she made one last desperate

attempt to wriggle towards the door. He swung round from his position, and dropped the axe. Then he pulled her back, and tied her to a chair by slipping a piece of tape round one of her bound arms and securing her to the chair-leg.

Again he raised the axe over Adam's machine. It came down with a sickening thud, and Lottie shuddered at the sound, closing her eyes, sobbing and praying that when her turn came, it would be equally quick.

CHAPTER SIXTEEN

As THE axe fell again and again on the machine, Lottie almost lost consciousness . . .

At first she didn't know if she was imagining it when she saw Adam's face at the window. She would have called out to him if she could. As it was, trussed up and gagged, she watched the doorway fearfully.

Her fear was even greater now. If he rushed in, that deadly axe would turn on him. Lottie couldn't bear the thought. She wanted to scream at him that he must go for help—but quickly, quickly.

By now, the first machine was lying battered on the floor, and the wooden structure which had held it was being savagely splintered. She was transfixed with horror at the strength of the blows being delivered in rapid succession.

With a shout of triumph and a roaring laugh, young Mr Calsey turned towards her.

'A man made it, a powerful man broke it! Now for the second one.' Again he turned away, and again the axe was drawn back over his head. Time was running out for Lottie.

It was then, in that last desperate moment, that Adam soundlessly entered the shed, in stockinged feet, Lottie's silver candlestick in his upraised hand.

Lottie closed her eyes. If Calsey turned . . .

But Calsey didn't turn. Adam was upon him, and the candlestick found its target. The axe dropped from his hand with a dull thud on to the machine, and Calsey fell to the ground. Adam needed no second blow; the first had done its work exceedingly well.

Picking up the axe, he strode towards Lottie. He had the gag out of her mouth, the bindings removed from her arms, and he held her close.

Sitting on the floor, he cradled her like a baby, and she sobbed out her terror. Her mouth was so dry that she couldn't utter a word.

Adam did the talking. 'Oh, Lottie, Lottie,' he murmured against her hair. 'He hasn't hurt you, has he?'

She shook her head and nestled closer to him.

'Mary shall have a reward, a big reward,' Adam went on. 'I came out to the garden only because she felt uneasy. When I saw the shed door open, I knew something was wrong. Thank heaven I had the candlestick with me. If anything had happened to you . . .' He stopped and hugged her more tightly.

Lottie said her first word then. She croaked it, mouth swollen and hard. 'Foolhardy, it were foolhardy!'

'Ay,' Adam agreed with a laugh, 'that it were.' He kissed her soundly.

'Your machine,' she managed to whisper. 'It's . . .'

'Destroyed,' Adam supplied without even looking towards the wreckage. 'But you're all right.' He kissed her again.

Lottie gave herself up to enjoying his kissing and his embrace. A feeling of such comfort swept over her that she didn't want to move away, didn't want to get to her feet. Adam valued her above his machine, had risked his life for her. That was enough. She was where she belonged. She didn't even hear the footsteps on the path, but was startled by the voices from the doorway.

'Why's the shed door open?'

'What's happened?'

It was Rosemary and Anna.

They came in, exclaiming, and Lottie was raised to her

feet and carried back to the sofa in the lounge. They wrapped her in blankets and poured brandy into her mouth until she began to stop trembling, and even slept a little.

Anna sat with her, and every time she opened her eyes, gave her the latest developments.

'Calsey is still alive,' she said, 'and taken off to hospital with a policeman beside him.' Adam was making a statement. Rosemary was writing her story. Mary had helped herself to some of the brandy and was snoring in the kitchen. Mrs O'Rourke was talking to the neighbours.

By the time Dorothea had brought in some hot soup and buttered toast, and Lottie had eaten it all, she had begun to feel almost herself again and wanted to get up. She begged them to stop treating her like an invalid, but they assured her that Adam had given strict instructions to keep her there, and they weren't prepared to go against his wishes.

Anna lit the gas lamp and turned it down very low, and Lottie must have drifted off to sleep again. When she woke, the girls had gone, and it was Adam who sat beside her.

'I didn't mean to wake you,' he said.

Lottie was suddenly shy with him . . . She sat up and looked down at her hands. 'Ay, lad, I haven't thanked thee.'

'No thanks are needed.'

'Nay, but after what I said about you being afraid,' Lottie licked her lips nervously, 'I'm right ashamed.'

'No need to be.' Adam took one of her hands in his, 'I never told thee aught. I was afraid.'

'Nay,' Lottie protested.

'Ay, I was.' Adam silenced her with a look which made her heart turn over. 'I was afraid of letting you get too close to me, of admitting how important you'd become to me. I were a fool.' As always when he was moved, his speech roughened into its origins. 'T' first day when I saw thee, all dirty and big eyed, my heart went out to thee. I couldn't comprehend myself. I'd sent for one girl—a pretty, empty doll who didn't even let me know she'd married someone else—and thee had come instead. Thee looked at me and I was lost—ay, but I fought against it! This time, I needed to make sure —certain sure.'

'Oh, Adam!' Lottie couldn't believe her ears. It hadn't been a dream, not wishful-thinking on her part. Adam cared for her.

'Why did you come?' Adam asked her.

This time she could answer, would answer, with the truth. She smiled a tremulous smile. 'I came—I came because you kissed me once under the mistletoe, and I couldn't forget that kiss. Spoilt my life, that kiss did, wouldn't let me settle for another.'

Adam gave a shout of laughter. 'Is this the truth?'

Lottie nodded.

'Eh, lass,' he exclaimed, still laughing. 'Thee art foolhardy indeed to cross an ocean for a kiss.' He captured her other hand. 'And I turned thee down. Can you forget how hard I treated you?'

Lottie put a finger to his lips, 'Ay, cruel hard—you took me home with you, fed me, sent Mary to me with a bath—and a comb—then gave me a job. Truth, lad, I love thee, have loved thee all along, crossed the ocean to come to thee! It was thee lad, from t'start.'

Adam's arms went round her, scooping her on to his knee. 'This time I'll ask thee—Wilt thou be my wife? I love thee with all my heart.'

'Ay, lad, that I will.' Lottie gave him a kiss for answer.

Mouth spoke to mouth, body to body. Lottie was lost

in a haze of pleasure. Colours swam before her eyes in the gas-lit room. Why, love was full of colour. She clung close to Adam, wanting this moment to last for ever.

This was the way she had known it could be, must be. Fortune's kiss had led her here to Adam and his love. That had been all she'd asked of life. All life was hers—hers and Adam's. The future lay before them.

In a rosy glow of pink and mauve and deep red, the future unfolded to her inner eye. Adam would take care of her, and she would sell his machines, show people how to use them—ay, he didn't know yet what a help-mate she would be. He'd find out little by little. She stirred in his arms, and smiled.

Fortune's kiss was full of magic.

The gas lamp sputtered and burned a little brighter, and the colours behind Lottie's eyes changed and deepened as Adam's lips found hers again and his arms tightened about her.

The future was the present. Adam loved her.

Family honour in Spain, ex-husband in Greece, society life in England and the sands of Arabia.

To celebrate the introduction of four new Mills & Boon authors, we are delighted to offer a unique presentation of four love stories that are guaranteed to capture your heart.

LOVE'S GOOD FORTUNE by Louise Harris
THE FINAL PRICE by Patricia Wilson
SWEET POISON by Angela Wells
PERFUMES OF ARABIA by Sara Wood

Priced £4.80, this attractively packaged set of new titles will be available from August 1986.